PRAISE FOR *GILDED*

"This richly detailed novel kept me turning the pages well into the night. Jae Hwa starts off as a strong character and ends as a noble one, using both her brains and her brawn to win the day."
—BETH REVIS, *New York Times* bestselling author of *Across the Universe*

"Farley brings South Korea's fascinating culture and mythology into vivid detail in this shining debut, and Jae is a compelling heroine. An exotic, thrilling read, *Gilded* had me utterly entranced!"
—JESSICA KHOURY, author of *Origin*

Gilded

CHRISTINA FARLEY

SKYSCAPE

SKYSCAPE

The characters and events portrayed in this book are fictitious. Any similarity to real persons, living or dead, is coincidental and not intended by the author.

Text copyright © 2014 by Christina Farley

All rights reserved.

Published by Skyscape, New York

www.apub.com

Amazon, the Amazon logo, and Skyscape are trademarks of Amazon.com, Inc., or its affiliates

ISBN 9781477847015 (hardcover)
ISBN 9781477810972 (paperback)
ISBN 9781477897010 (ebook)

Book design by Abby Kuperstock

Printed in The United States of America (R)
First edition
1 3 5 7 9 10 8 6 4 2

To Doug, for believing. Saranghae.

CHAPTER 1

Stillness fills the empty stage as I press the horn bow to my body and notch an arrow. I pull back the string. The power of it courses through me, a sizzling fire in my veins. I squint just enough so the mark crystallizes while everything around it blurs.

My dress scratches my skin, and the silk material resists as I twist my body. I shift to get comfortable, my temples pounding. I shouldn't have let the program coordinator talk me into wearing this puffy dress. How am I supposed to shoot an arrow with this thing on?

I shake my head once and breathe in deeply. I will not miss. I'll hit the mark while wearing this monstrosity. I draw back and—

"Jae Hwa!"

I flinch. My arrow shoots across the stage and veers off to the side. Its steel tip clanks against the concrete wall. Unbelievable. I haven't missed a shot since—I can't remember. I turn to face my dad.

"I've been trying to reach you," my father says. "Why didn't you answer?"

Strands have fallen forward from Dad's slicked-back hair, and sweat beads on his forehead as if he's been running. He's all dressed up in a black tux for his speech tonight. Even his shoes are polished, their sheen catching under the stage lights. None of this hides the fact that the lines across his face have grown deeper in recent years. And his brown eyes have not yet regained their spark.

My annoyance fades. I should have answered my phone, told him where I was.

Slinging my bow over my shoulder, I walk to him and tug the looped ends of his tie, straightening the bow. Mom would've done something like that, and for a moment it's as if we are all together once more.

Dad clears his throat. "Your grandfather is here. He wants to see you."

I freeze. No. Not Haraboji. As if I'm not already nervous.

"I'll find him after the show." I gather up my arrows, already planning a quick exit so I won't have to talk to my grandfather. "I need more time to practice. I can't leave until I make the shot."

"You should talk to him now." Dad checks his phone and then rubs his hand over his face. "You can't keep avoiding him like this."

"I know." I slide an arrow across my palm. Its smoothness calms me. "It'd be easier if he wasn't so awful."

"I know. Do I ever know." Dad grins. "At least he promised not to make a scene in a public place again."

I sigh. I can't ruin this night for him. "Fine. But you owe me, okay?"

"It's a deal."

But as I pack up my bow and arrows, I start to worry. Could missing this shot be an omen of tonight's performance? *No.* I resolve to hit the target tonight and make Dad proud. Despite my flamingo-colored dress and eccentric grandfather.

We leave the backstage area and head into the main lobby of the museum. The crowds jostle around me, smelling of ginseng, lavender, and—I could swear—the foul Korean alcoholic drink *soju*. I stand on tiptoe and scan the circular lobby for Grand-father.

Thick swathes of red, black, and gold material drape from the ceiling, along with rice paper lanterns larger than me. They light the room with pale yellows that make me think I've stepped back into Korea's ancient past. A wide banner with the name of the exhibit, *Illumination*, scripted across it in Hangul and English hangs against the far wall next to the weaponry and warrior displays. I can hear the deep tone of the six-string zither beneath the buzz of the crowd.

And beyond all that, past the floor-to-ceiling glass windows, lies downtown Seoul, the horizon lined with sparkling towers shooting up like bamboo stalks.

Dad points to a gray-haired man near the entrance of the traditional-housing exhibit. My grip tightens on my bow case. It's Grandfather.

I'd met my grandfather for the first time only two weeks ago. Everything I knew about him came from Dad's stories about how stubborn and traditional he was. After our formal meeting at the Shilla hotel, I learned firsthand what he had been talking about. During our short visit, Grandfather and Dad had got into such a heated fight about him bringing me to Korea that Dad and I left before they brought out the drinks.

Complete humiliation. Just remembering it makes my steps falter.

I shrug that thought away and shift my bow case to my other hand as Dad and I cut through the crowd to join Grandfather. Most of my girl friends talk about their grandfathers as being like Santa Claus, all soft and jolly. Not my *haraboji*. He stands tall before me with his shoulders pulled back, chin raised, and arms clasped behind him. He's dressed in a traditional blue tunic and pants, and his gray hair is combed neatly in place. I search for a smile. Warmth, maybe. Something other than the narrowed eyes and set mouth.

Dad clears his throat.

Right. I set down my case and lean forward to bow, but I move too quickly and almost fall over. Why can't I get anything right? I've bowed five million times in Tae Kwon Do and archery classes.

Grandfather scowls. "I see you still refuse to listen to me," he tells Dad in his thick accent. "You should not have brought her tonight."

"Abeoji," Dad says, his face going hard. "Not now."

"He's right," I say. My features are sharp and angular, and I've got a muscular frame. Definitely not the cute, sweet Korean granddaughter he really wants. "I shouldn't have come."

Grandfather's eyebrows rise. "You misunderstand me, Jae

Hwa. It is not because I do not want you here. It is for your safety." Then he shoots Dad a tight-lipped look. "You *must* take her back to America."

Safety? I resist rolling my eyes. I suppose I can't blame him since he's never seen me spar or attended any of my archery competitions.

Still, I like this idea of me going back to the States, even if he's treating me like a little kid. "He's got a point, Dad," I say. He blinks. I have to admit, I'm shocked to be agreeing with Grandfather myself. "Maybe I should go back to L.A."

The veins on Dad's face bulge. "You're staying here," Dad says. "It's what your mother would have wanted."

He shouldn't have brought Mom into this.

If only I could walk away and go back home.

Problem: home is half the world away.

Dad's company transferred him from Los Angeles to Seoul a month ago. This move was supposed to be the best thing ever. He'd climb the business ladder; I'd connect with the relatives I've never met and attend a prestigious international school.

More important, all the memories of Mom would be left behind.

He never asked what I wanted. And believe me, even though I'm obsessed with Korean archery and Tae Kwon Do, moving to the actual *country*—away from my friends—wasn't on my to-do list.

I grab my case, turn on my heels, and stalk off in the opposite direction.

"Jae!" Dad calls, but I only pick up my pace.

I can't take any more of Grandfather's looks and expectations.

I can't take Dad's insistence that I belong here. They don't get it.

It's easy for me to slip away and escape into the crowd, but this traditional dress makes it difficult to blend in since everyone else is dressed in black suits or cocktail dresses. I duck into a side room and lean against the wall, trying to collect my thoughts. A bronze object glints from across the aisle in one of the glass cases.

I move closer, set down my case, and trail my hand across the smooth glass. The plaque on the side reads:

SAMJOKO AMULET

Excavated at the Seopohang site
During the Koguryo period, the three-legged
bird was considered more powerful than
the dragon or phoenix. This amulet was
believed to be the key to the Spirit World.

The sun-patterned amulet gleams as if it's beckoning me under its spotlight. The *samjoko* meets the edge of the circle at eight points, and the crow looks alive, as if it could spring from its hold and fly away. I splay my fingertips against the cool glass, overwhelmed by a sudden need to touch the amulet.

"Quite the exhibit," a male voice says from behind me.

When I swing around, I nearly choke. It's Marc Grayson from my art class. He's standing behind me, and I can't help but notice how hot he looks in his white shirt and dark jeans. The thing about Marc is that his brown hair is always slightly disheveled, like tonight, and every time I see him I'm half tempted to reach up and run my fingers through it.

But I can't think those thoughts. Guys and I have never clicked. Maybe it's the black belt that intimidates them. Or maybe it's that I'm completely socially incompetent in the dating department. Like when Nick Casablanca tried to kiss me, and I used a pressure-point defense on his hand. It wasn't my fault he moved in before I was ready.

I find everything less awkward if I purposely avoid any boy who makes my pulse race.

And Marc definitely does.

"Hey," I say, trying to maintain an aura of calm and coolness. I peer through the crowds to make sure Dad doesn't see me talking to a non-Korean boy. He tends to freak out, as if I'm halfway down the wedding aisle. "What are you doing here?"

"Enjoying the culture, of course," Marc says with a mischievous grin that accentuates his right dimple. "Actually, I helped with the setup. I pick up hours whenever they have their big events. It's a pretty sweet gig. I get spending money; they get cheap labor. You?"

"My dad's company, Netlife, is sponsoring the exhibit. I told him I'd help with the show."

"Nice." He shoves his hands in his jeans pockets. "Free tickets."

"I'm surprised you're not at some SAT prep today, or writing a college essay," I tease.

"I'd rather see Miss Black Belt in a dress. SATs can wait."

Oh God. The Dress. I forgot I was even wearing it, with Marc standing so close, studying me with those green eyes. Or maybe it's the way he never buttons his top shirt button. Still, the last thing I need right now is for word to get around school that I wore a pink dress. I've a reputation to keep.

I decide to change tactics and move the topic off my getup. "You're one to talk. You *do* know it's black-tie tonight, right? A button-down shirt doesn't qualify."

"Yeah." He shrugs and rakes his hand through his brown hair. "Ties and I don't get along. Although that didn't go over well with my parents since they helped organize the exhibit."

"They organized it? I wonder if my dad knows them."

"Well, if he didn't before"—he jerks his head to where my dad and grandfather are standing in the lobby not far away—"he does now."

Dad is shaking hands with a couple. The woman, who I assume is Marc's mom, has sandy-blond hair twisted in a loose bun and a tight dark dress that trails to the floor. She is pure elegance. The man next to her looks the spitting image of Marc except he's heavier, with gray hair. Marc's dad leans toward Grandfather, whispers in his ear, and passes him an envelope. Grandfather nods and slips it into his suit jacket, glancing around the room. *Odd.*

I realize Marc hasn't noticed the exchange. He's still talking to me, though I haven't the faintest clue why other than the fact that we're the only teens at the event. Something about my grandfather and his parents' common interest in Korean mythology. I nod, pretending I understand exactly what he's talking about, but he loses me when he starts talking about some Namu Doreong myth.

"Well, you're here tonight, so they must be thrilled," I say.

"Actually, when I heard you were performing, I couldn't say no."

I feel a ridiculous smile start to spread across my face. Oh no, this is bad.

Very bad.

I can't get involved with a guy. It was hard enough leaving all my friends back in L.A. If my grand scheme to get Dad to send me back to the States works, I can't handle a bunch of good-byes again.

He glances at his watch. "This gig starts at eight, right?"

I nod, noticing his attention drawn to the crowds milling around us. He probably wishes he was hanging out with his buddies rather than some boring girl like me. I knew it was ridiculous to think that he'd want to have anything to do with me.

Right on cue, a gong rings through the lobby, vibrating over the clamor of voices.

Dad and two other men move to stand under a Korean gate painted in greens, browns, and reds built in front of the auditorium's doorway. The *Illumination* banner stretches above their heads in the gate's archway. Together, the three of them hold a huge pair of scissors and pose in front of the gold ribbon, symbolizing the opening of the Korean cultural exhibit.

Marc leans closer to me. He smells like soap and leather.

"Good luck tonight," he says, his breath tickling my skin. My heart skitters. "I'll be watching your show, Miss Black Belt."

Cameras flash. Polite applause erupts. My stomach churns. I've been so distracted, I nearly forgot about needing luck for my performance. And knowing he'll be watching sure doesn't help. Thanks, Marc.

"Tonight marks a momentous occasion," Dad says into a

microphone. "*Illumination* displays ninety cultural artifacts uncovered from the Old Stone and Bronze Ages. Netlife is a proud sponsor of *Illumination*, which we hope will bridge the gap between the Korea of the past and the Korea of the future. I'd encourage you . . ."

Dad continues to speak, but it's time for me to head to the stage. My stomach is like a spinning washing machine.

"Got to go," I tell Marc.

I pick up my case and take off before he gets the chance to say anything else. Halfway across the lobby, I glance back—I can't help it. He's still standing by the pillar, watching me with his hands in his pockets and a slight smirk on his face. I lift my chin higher and toss my long hair just to show him that he can laugh at my dress. I don't care.

But I do. I care far too much. Which makes me all squirmy inside.

I shortcut through the child-sized folk village to the backstage area. Once I pass through the first room, the noise dwindles to only the light twang of music from the house speakers and the swish of my skirt across the marble floor. Circular beams of light shoot down from the ceiling, illuminating different exhibits. I have the sudden weird realization that I actually know more about the American Civil War than about these displays from my own Korean culture.

A shimmer of blue catches my eye as I reach the back door. There, encased in glass at the other end of the room, is a *hanbok*. I'm not one for dresses, but I find myself padding over to the glass case. The gold plate says it is a wedding dress, supposedly worn by Princess Yuhwa. The beads on the *hanbok* wink at me under the lights, and the material, though aged, still has a sheen to it. There's something about it that's almost magical.

"There you are!" Dad huffs, his shirt untucked. "I wanted to see you before you performed. You need to stop disappearing like that. I know your grandfather can be gruff, but running off isn't the solution. I need your help, Jae. I can't do this on my own."

I shake my head to clear my thoughts. *Slosh, slosh* spins my stomach. It's as if he inserted a quarter and started up my washing machine again. "Way to calm the nerves, Dad."

He pats my shoulder. "Nervous? You've never been before. You're a pro."

The lump in my throat keeps me from arguing over the differences between a professional and high school competitor.

After I check in with the show coordinator, I peer around the curtain to catch a glimpse of the auditorium. The lights are dimming, and huge spotlights roam the audience, casting long slants of reds and yellows over the crowd. I set my case on the wood floor and unsnap it. In the erratic light, I take out my horn bow and slip off its silk *goong dae*, notch my lucky white-feathered arrow into place, and draw back the strings to test its tension. It pulls strong and steady in my grip.

Really, I could shoot an arrow in my sleep, and tonight my target will be larger than a Chuseok moon. I close my eyes and rub my hand up and down the bow as I try to block out all memory of my earlier mishap.

The thump of a drum, followed by a succession of quicker thumps, resounds through the auditorium. The audience hushes. I slide on my thumb ring, tie my *goong dae* to my waist, and tuck five arrows into its sack. Then, with my bow under my arm, I ease out to the wings to watch the show.

A pan flute cuts through the pounding.

And then silence.

A flash of crimson illuminates the stage, showing two drums and two gongs lined up as straight as arrows. At practice yesterday, one of the guys told me they were called *samulnori* instruments. They represent thunder, wind, rain, and clouds. Now, hearing them in full action, I understand why. The sound of the drums and gongs echoes through the room, alive, energetic, and creating a beat that sends my pulse racing.

It draws me in, as if I've been missing out on a piece of who I am all these years. I almost forget how nervous I am.

Two banners fall from behind the stage: one a tiger, one a dragon. They face each other, and I wonder if they're in battle or are friends. The drummers' beat calms to a steady rhythm as dancers run out, wearing vibrant *hanboks* that billow like peonies as they twirl.

The program continues as the shaman, dressed in her rags, struts onto the stage next. She dances in wild abandon to the cries of the drums as if caught in the wind and thunder. My muscles tighten and my vision sharpens. During practice yesterday, the dances and music hadn't affected me like this. Maybe it's only the added mix of lights and costumes. And the audience.

The drums' rhythm strengthens, as if calling to me. The drummers' arms swing in full motion. Their heads shake to the beat.

This is my cue.

I stride out onto the stage. The spotlight catches and follows me as I step onto the dais, my back to the audience. A massive sun lowers over the back wall of the stage. My job is to shoot my arrow into the heart of the sun. The technicians will work their magic to make it seem as if I've burst it open so streams of "sunlight" illuminate the auditorium for the grand finale.

Simple. A no-brainer.

I don't even have to hit a particular mark. All I need to do is get the arrow to cut through the thin canvas.

I lift my bow and set it against my body. The drums boom beneath me. The shaman wails. I notch the arrow in, tight and snug, and take my aim. A gust of wind kicks up around me. I frown. They hadn't created wind yesterday. What are the producers thinking? Someone needs to turn off those fans.

The drummers barrel away, oblivious of my concern. My hair whips around me. Now I wish I'd listened to the show coordinator and pulled it into a traditional topknot.

Focus!

I lift the bow slightly upward and bite the inside of my lip. The wind intensifies, and my skirts snap against my ankles. It's so strong now, I can barely stand, but there's no way I'm going to make a fool of myself and not do this.

I draw back, determined to give the special effects people a piece of my mind afterward.

And release.

The sun swirls in a rainbow before me as the arrow sinks into its center. Light scatters across the stage and spills toward the audience. But I don't move. Because inside the heart of the sun is a man. He's dressed in the traditional Korean style, with a black pointed beard and a topknot. His skin seems to blaze, or maybe that's because he's dressed in a silver *hanbok*.

He stands there, staring at me with russet-colored eyes. He's got my arrow in his hand and a crooked smile on his lips. He bows slightly to me before disappearing into the golden blaze of the sun.

Who was that man? He looked so *real*. So *alive*.

Maybe he was. Maybe the special effects people assigned him to grab my arrow and didn't tell me about it.

Behind me, I realize the audience is clapping. I squeeze my bow tight and swivel as the drummers and dancers bow below. The audience leaps to their feet, clapping vigorously in the glittery golden light. I take my bow.

Marc is to my right in the second row, clapping. I wish that smile of his didn't make my heart soar. I spot Dad in the front row, a proud look in his eyes, and Grandfather next to him. But he isn't standing. His arms are crossed, and his frown is even deeper than earlier. What a grouch.

The curtains close. My knees wobble as I take the steps back down. The drummers slap me high fives and shake my hand. One of the backstage guys I hung out with yesterday runs up to me.

"That was awesome," he says.

"Thanks, but what was up with the fans? You could have told me about them beforehand. I was lucky the arrow hit at all."

"Fans?" He stares at me like I'm crazy. "What fans?"

One of the drummers overhears us and says, "Great work on the winds, Chung So. Really cooled the stage off."

The backstage guy rubs his forehead.

I lift my hands in the air to shrug it off. "Forget about it," I say. "It worked out in the end."

I leave the crew to search for the guy who took my lucky arrow. But as I scour the backstage area, I can't find anyone even resembling him. I lightly tap my bow against my leg, trying to imagine what he'd look like without his costume.

"Where might he have gone?" I wonder out loud.

"Mine," a voice whispers from behind me.

I spin around. No one is there. The hairs on my arms prick against my silk sleeves.

Forget the stupid arrow. I can always get another.

"Mine." The whisper comes again from everywhere around me.

No question now. I'm overtired. I need sleep.

But as I zip my bow case closed, I see him—the man from inside the sun. He's perched on one of the backstage stools, holding my arrow. I march over to ask for it back.

"I knew you would come back, my princess," he says.

I stop midstride at his words. There's something about his dark-pooled eyes that causes my breath to catch and my heart to ice over.

"Just give me back my arrow," I say.

But I never get it back.

Because he vanishes in a trick of the light.

CHAPTER 2

"Jae!" Michelle calls as I make my way to the school deli. She steps in stride, her long black hair pinned away from her face and her tight jeans tucked into her boots. "How did it go last night?"

"Nightmarish." I pick up a tray and load it with *kimbap*.

Michelle Myong and I were fast friends when we both transferred to the international school here in January. She's Korean American like me and would probably fit in with Grandfather's expectation of what a perfect granddaughter should be. Not only is she a straight-A student who takes violin lessons religiously, but she has that smooth, olive complexion with a round face, small nose, and willowy figure. We're complete opposites.

At my last school I was at the top of my class and hardly had to study.

Not here.

Here I'm drowning. My IB courses, which are like the international version of my Advanced Placement courses in the States, are sending me into caffeine addiction. I never thought

I'd actually admit to missing AP classes. Going to the museum instead of doing my usual three hours of homework last night only made things worse.

"So spill about the nightmare," Michelle says.

"Nightmares," I correct her, and press my finger on the scanner to deduct money from my account. "One: I had to wear a *hanbok* that made me look like a pink flamingo. Two: my grandfather proclaimed his abhorrence for me. Well, his face did, at least. Three: Marc was there. And four: I lost my lucky arrow."

"*Abhorrence*! Great SAT word." Michelle stops to add it into her cell phone.

I roll my eyes. This is the kind of obsession I deal with every day at this school. Where it's cool to have a vocab app on your phone. Most of the students here have been attending night school, called *hagwon*, since they were in elementary school, all in preparation for the dreaded SAT. I'm convinced I've landed on a different planet.

I head to our usual table by the windows.

"Where are you going?" Michelle pokes me with her chopsticks. "Remember? NHS lunch meeting today?"

I groan. Why did she have to be so responsible? I can't believe she even roped me into National Honor Society. Not only do I so not belong there, but I don't have time for it. I can barely keep up with my studies since we moved to Seoul. Dad said it would all even out as I acclimated. Right. He isn't enrolled at an international school, where every student is Harvard-bound. Everyone except me.

Besides, eating in the Biology room always makes me feel a little queasy.

"We'd better hurry or we'll be late."

She's right. Mrs. Freeman's classroom is on the other side of the campus on the third floor.

"Fine," I say. "I'll go."

We breeze out of the deli through the automatic glass doors and into the crowded hallway. Seoul Foreign School isn't much different from my high school back in L.A. except it's four stories tall and the designers of the school must have been obsessed with glass and chrome. We're crossing one of the catwalks where either side is walled in with glass when Michelle freezes.

"Wait. Did you say Marc was there?"

I decide to skirt the topic of Marc. Just thinking of him makes my hands sweat.

"Which reminds me"—I continue walking—"I'm dropping out of NHS."

Her eyes pop out. You'd think I was about to commit a crime or something.

"Let's face it," I continue. "I'd never have qualified here. I was lucky to be nominated back in L.A. Don't flip; I'm staying in until after the ski trip."

"Give it one more month," Michelle says as we enter Mrs. Freeman's room. I nearly gag as I breathe in the shock-awful smell. "You've got to give yourself more time to get used to things here. NHS is our ticket to do something meaningful with our lives. Besides, it gets you service hours for IB."

I shift the pile of food in my hands, thinking about her words. Michelle is into believing we all have a purpose. She's already spearheaded two food drives for the tsunami victims and personally delivered a truckload of school supplies to an orphanage in the Philippines. I'm just not sure how I fit into all that. I'm not sure how I fit into anything right now.

My thoughts scatter as I spot Marc laughing with Kumar at one of the tables. With his rumpled brown hair and tight black T-shirt, Marc looks even hotter than last night. Yep. I need to quit. Too much time with this boy will only make me want to be with him more. Besides, Dad is dealing with too much to have another ulcer over me dating a non-Korean.

"What's Marc doing here?" I whisper to Michelle.

"Apparently Mrs. Freeman has been recruiting."

That explains why the room is so packed. Marc's gaze finds me. A lazy grin passes across his face, and I know, I just *know* he's remembering me in that dress. Somehow I break eye contact.

"Right." I take a deep breath and move to leave. "This sounds like the perfect day to quit."

"Please don't." Michelle latches on to me. Then, noticing Marc, she whispers, "I could arrange a private tutor for you. As in Marc. He's off-the-charts smart."

I give her my cringe look. "Don't even think about it. He's cute, but dating isn't an option for me. Speaking of which, how did your call with Charlie go this morning? You need to tell me all about it."

Her face drops, and I bite my lip, instantly regretting my words. They had promised to stay together no matter what, but since she moved to Seoul, he hasn't been good about keeping in touch.

"He must have forgotten or fallen asleep." She checks her Skype account on her phone and shrugs. "The time difference is tricky."

"Yeah." I nod, trying to be upbeat, but deep down I decide Charlie has just entered my black list. "That has to be it. Michigan is like fourteen hours difference. I bet he'll call tonight."

She presses her lips together and stares at her phone.

"Listen," I say, feeling awful for her. "I'll stay today and cheer you up."

Meanwhile, Min breezes past us, her Calvin Kleins showing off long, perfect legs—the complete opposite of mine. She slides onto the stool next to Marc and passes him a juice, batting her eyelashes at him. I think I actually hate her.

"Perfect." Michelle beams and blows me a two-finger kiss. *"Ciao!"*

She clips away to the far table next to Lily and all the gross science experiment stuff. She knows I can't stand eating near that formaldehyde smell. But once she sits, I realize there's only one stool left in the entire room. And it's directly across from Marc.

The little devil.

If I had opened a fortune cookie this morning, it would have said: "You are destined for eternal punishment." Or something awful like that.

"Jae Hwa!" Mrs. Freeman says, brightening as I edge to the table. "I was worried you wouldn't come. I had you on my list to help hand out flyers for the ski trip. Has your dad given you permission to go?"

I don't bother telling her he's too busy even to notice when

I'm home or not. "Yes."

"Great," Mrs. Freeman says, and passes me the agenda. "Then we'll start planning."

Marc tilts his stool so far back, I'm actually worried for his safety. "Hey, Fighter Girl. Good job last night. And that dress. Wow. It was very—pink."

"Pink?" Min pipes in. "I can't even imagine you in such a color. You seem more inclined to dark, drab shades."

I glare at her, thinking thoughts that would get me a first-class ticket to the principal's office.

"Actually, it wasn't that bad," Marc says. "You really nailed that performance."

Did Marc just give me a compliment? My face feels as if it's turning as red as kimchi. I can slice through a stack of boards, but when it comes to compliments, I'm useless. I duck my head and pretend I'm searching through my backpack.

"Ignoring me now?" Marc grins, showing off that adorable dimple. "Hey, did you notice anything odd going on during the performance last night?"

I think about the wind and that weird guy who called me his princess and took my arrow. But there's no way I'm going to let Marc think I'm crazy.

"No." I flip my hair over my shoulder and try to channel a composed, mature me. "Why?"

"Just wondering." It looks as if he's about to say something more but instead he rubs his chin, apparently in deep thought. I notice he's wearing a gold ring. Why is it that even a gold ring looks sexy on him?

Min of the Long Legs clears her throat and leans closer to

Marc. "So, do you want to meet for study group tonight?"

She's got this sultry voice that makes most boys gape and drool. I peer through my eyelashes to see if it works on him, too. He whispers something to her, and I look away. I wonder if I'd look cute, too, if I chopped my hair short like Min's.

No, I decide. I'd probably take on the image of something freak-worthy like a porcupine.

I focus on Mrs. Freeman's agenda for the ski trip instead. Do they really think that taking a ski trip is going to bond us as eleventh graders? I push the agenda aside and unroll the foil around my *kimbap*. The smell of dried seaweed and sesame oil fills my nostrils, and my stomach growls. The one benefit to living in Korea: the food.

But as I pop a slice of *kimbap* into my mouth, I notice how everyone is reading the agenda as if it's written in gold ink. Why does *everyone* take *everything* so seriously? What is with these people?

Fine. I'll skim the list.

Michelle and I are supposed to distribute flyers promoting the trip. Farther down, Mrs. Freeman has us making and handing out the hot chocolate on the Saturday night of the ski trip.

Michelle clears her throat. "Mrs. Freeman," she says solemnly while folding her manicured hands in front of her. "I'm sorry, but I can't hand out the hot chocolate. I'm in charge of making sure everyone's in from the slopes."

"Is that so?" Mrs. Freeman checks her list. "Yes, I see that."

"But it looks like Marc is free at that time," Michelle says with a sly grin. "He'd be a perfect candidate."

I'm going to kill Little Miss Matchmaker.

"Yes," Mrs. Freeman says. "Good point. How does that sound to you, Marc?"

He agrees and glances my way with that melt-worthy grin. I can't look at him. I can't even be near him without practically becoming a puddle on the floor. This is ridiculous.

Without being told, the whole group makes the change on the handout. Michelle has this thing about neatness, so she takes her ruler and carefully crosses out her name with a clean, straight line. You'd think we worked for some high-end ad business or something. But that's not what's got me all squirming in my seat like a slippery octopus. It's having to work with Marc.

I shoot my hand up as Mrs. Freeman reads the list out loud (the one that takes three seconds to glance over). Mrs. Freeman *finally* lifts her eyes over her reading glasses. "Yes?" she says.

"You've got me making hot chocolate," I say. "I'm not much of a cook."

"Miss Lee." You know Mrs. Freeman's annoyed with you if she uses your last name. "The *cooking* consists of mixing hot water with powder. I'm confident you can handle that."

Good point. My excuses need refining. I drum my fingers on the table as Mrs. Freeman returns to her reading, but no other options cross my mind. All I can focus on is how green his eyes felt when they slid over me.

I'm stuck. With a boy my dad would forbid, but I can't resist.

CHAPTER 3

I've been home for five minutes, barely had the chance to celebrate the fact that I've got a long weekend due to the Lunar holiday—the Korean New Year—when I get a call from Dad. It's official. We're going to Grandfather's house. Tomorrow.

"Dad," I say. "Haraboji hates me. Why can't we stay home? Think of the traffic."

"He doesn't hate you," Dad says. There's a pause as he barks something to one of his colleagues in Korean. "He's upset with me, not you. But I think we worked things out. And it is Lunar. We must go. He is still family. Despite our differences."

Guilt pulls at my chest. I've been so busy thinking about how awful my new life is that I hadn't considered how hard the move was on Dad. This new job has turned him into a complete workaholic. He isn't home much.

"Life didn't seem so complicated in L.A." I'm thinking of Mom and how it used to be with the three of us. Together. Before the cancer. Before the good-byes. And again I can't help but think that if she was still with us, we never would have moved.

"It's complicated anywhere you go. Just different complications." Dad is silent then, and I worry I've said too much. But before hanging up he says, "You might even enjoy yourself. He lives near the beach."

The thought of a beach perks me up for like two seconds. It will be freezing outside. Definitely not bikini weather. My muscles tighten. I've been home only ten minutes and already I'm stressing. Maybe it's the fact that we live in a cramped, two-bedroom apartment. Back in L.A. we had a four-bedroom house and even a sunroom. And that home was full of *her*. Mom's favorite chair where she drank her tea. The stain on the carpet where I knocked over the paints from her latest project. Her bookshelf, stuffed with volumes passed down from her own mother.

This apartment never knew Mom. And it feels as if I've lost her for good.

I sit on the floor and stare at my phone. Michelle's going to be ticked when I tell her I can't come to the concert at the Coffee Bean this weekend.

I text her. **Can't come Sat. Have to visit fam.**

Bummer! I already invited Marc!

Tell me u r joking.

She doesn't reply. I roll my eyes, groaning.

Any news from Charlie? I ask.

Not yet. Will keep you posted.

I'm getting ready to wallow in misery when I realize I'm going to be late for Tae Kwon Do class. I rummage through my dresser for my *dobok*, stuff the uniform into my duffle bag, and hurry out of the apartment. Once in the hallway, I skip the elevator. We live on the ninth floor, and often I take the stairs just to hear the pounding of my sneakers echo through the stairwell. When I reach the last landing, I leap over the remaining stairs down to the main level, staggering and nearly colliding with the wall. The thrill of not knowing whether I'll land or fall invigorates me. I've never fallen.

I steal across the building lobby, nod at the security guard, and push the glass doors open into the cold early evening. The air bites the back of my throat as I stroll down the uneven sidewalk.

There's an odd assortment of shops along our busy road. The herbal store with the big jars of fermenting ginseng roots. I've always thought those roots look like cut-off fingers floating in vinegar.

There are the *hagwons*, or as Michelle calls them, "cram-schools," with their advertisements promising all their students will go to Harvard. Yeah, right.

But my favorite is the doggie boutique where you can watch miniature dogs run around inside a glassed-in room, dolled up in polka-dot and striped outfits with bows.

Usually the dogs cheer me up if I'm feeling off; but, at the corner, I have this odd sense that someone is following me. I glance over my shoulder, but all I can see is the seafood restaurant's tank packed full of squid.

I shake my head to clear my wild imagination and cross the street to where the vendors set up their carts. The fruit-and-veggie guy has plastic containers filled with strawberries stacked in the back of his weathered pickup. I'd stop for my usual steamed sweet potato fix from the wrinkled *ajumma* at her cart, but today there's no time. Pale orange streaks the sky as the sun sets over the jagged mountains that ring Seoul. I clip it the rest of the way to my *dojang* and take the stairs, running up the three stories to get my heart pumping. As I pass the dental office on the second floor, I can already hear the class counting in Korean: *hana, tul, set, net.* . . .

Crap. I'm late.

In the entryway, I slip off my sneakers and socks and try to open the door without being noticed. Of course, that's practically impossible since two of the four walls are lined with mirrors. When I open the door, the smell of sweat and old rubber mats washes over me; and there, reflected in every mirror, is me strolling in late.

Master Park frowns. I slink into the back row and join in with the jumping jacks, wondering how many push-ups he'll make me do this time.

"You have no respect for Tae Kwon Do," Sung-joo tells me in Korean. "Not only do you speak like a *waygookin*, but you act like one, too."

There are about twenty of us in this class, with a mix of belt colors. The only person even close to being as good as me is Sung-joo, a college student at Yonsei University. He's got a thick torso and is about five foot eight, and he's the only one who sends my blood pressure through the roof.

I shoot him a withering glare. I know I have an accent, but him calling me a foreigner kind of stung. "You're just intimidated because I'm a younger girl who can whip your butt," I whisper back in Korean. "Just like I'm going to do today."

Master Park rarely pairs us up, though. He says I have to learn to control my power. I suppose he's right. Sung-joo tends to bring out my aggression.

Sometimes I do like being paired with the new belts. There's something fun about teaching them the *poomsae* and breaking down each move until it's perfect. But today is different. I'm thinking about my annoyance with Dad, seeing Marc with Min, remembering how Grandfather wanted to ship me off, and wishing Mom was here right now; and I need to let those emotions out.

Now.

So when Master Park divides us up to spar, I point my helmet at spike-headed Sung-joo, saying, "We're on!"

Sung-joo scowls as he wiggles into his protective gear. I don't blame him. I'm sure he doesn't want to be disgraced when I beat the crap out of him in front of everyone. Serves him right for messing with the wrong girl on the wrong day.

"*Charyot*," Master Park calls. "*Kyung ye.*"

Hearing the command, Sung-joo and I bow to Master Park and then to each other. When the master says "*Chunbee*," I spring into a ready stance, bouncing lightly on my toes. I always attack first, rushing in close and fast, so the moment the master says "*seijak*!" I fake a right jab and then land a straight punch to his chest. He bounces backward as I expected he would. Next, I push-kick, which backs him up farther. Now he's right where I want him. That's when I unload a back kick that sends him stumbling.

Recovering, he attacks me with an ax kick. But I'm expecting his counterattack and block him as I sidestep away. Then I throw a mean kick to his chest. He grunts, which doesn't surprise me. I have a fast, powerful kick.

Sung-joo moves to grab my leg, but I'm quicker. Seeing he's open, I break out a back-leg roundhouse and strike at his head. He staggers sideways. Taking advantage of his confusion, I hit a spinning roundhouse, almost flying now. He tries a push-kick to stop me, but I step to the side and knock him to the ground with a front kick.

Master calls the match over. My pulse drums in my head and disappointment fills me. I was just getting started. With the adrenaline pumping through my veins, it takes everything in me to lower my fists and stop moving. Sung-joo groans from the floor. I try not to gloat.

Master Park starts yelling at me, his Korean so fast I can only catch snippets of phrases, like, "Too aggressive! Must control yourself!"

And "Leave and come back when you are able to master your emotions."

The elation of winning sinks into the pit of my stomach. What did I do? I didn't mean to actually hurt Sung-joo. So maybe I did get too caught up in the moment. I glance around the room. Everyone is staring at me. Finally, Sung-joo stands with help from two other classmates, but his breathing is short and his eyes look dazed.

It hits me then that he really is hurt. How is that possible? I'm not that strong, am I?

My chest tightens. I should've been easier on him.

Somehow I manage to bow to Sung-joo and then to Master Park. Everyone moves out of my way, creating a path to the door. My face burns as I slip on my socks and shoes, and rush back down the stairway and out into the street. Usually I don't want to leave the gym, but now I don't even feel as if I belong there anymore.

The last time I felt like this was when I stared into Mom's open casket and touched her cold skin. That feeling of cold aloneness races through my veins.

I jaywalk through the traffic-clogged street, barely missing a weaving scooter loaded with car parts. The streetlights flicker on, and restaurant signs flash neon as I take the first alley on the right as a shortcut home.

It's darker here, and the smell of trash overtake my senses. A gust of wintry wind cuts through the alley, stealing my breath away. I lower my head and draw my scarf over my face.

A growl rumbles. I look up and freeze. A massive, lionlike creature, eyes glowing yellow, stands in my path.

I scream, staggering backward, falling against a crate of rotting cabbage leaves. I snatch up a handful and toss them at the creature's face. The thing is so close I could touch its scales. The face reminds me more of a dragon than a cat. A horn rests in the center of its head, and fangs jut out from its frothing mouth.

The thing roars with the strength of a dragon. I jerk out of my stupor and snap out a kick at the dragon-lion's nose. That kick should've stunned or knocked it back. Instead my own leg throbs as if I'd kicked a stone statue. Maybe I did. Maybe this is all a figment of my imagination.

A chill prickles my toes as if I've stepped into freezing water. Golden tendrils of smoke curl around my feet, then wind their way around my knees. I try to move. I can't. It's as if I'm a block of ice.

The creature before me rears on its hind legs. The eyes blaze.

A snarl curls its lips, showing off those sharp fangs. Cold fear streaks through me until I realize it's not looking at me but at something behind me.

I twist my body to see what the dragon-lion creature is looking at.

It's the shadow I saw behind the sweet potato lady earlier.

Emerging from the murkiness, the shadow solidifies into a glittery figure of a man.

The glittery man blocks my escape. Golden ooze drips from his fingers as if he's clawing for me. The ooze trails up my body until not only my legs are frozen, but my stomach, my chest, my arms.

It circles me, faster and faster, as if I'm captured in the center of a typhoon. The ooze forms shimmering walls that trap me inside. I squirm, trying to free myself from these transparent barriers. But then my body goes rigid as the wall appears to fade away. Instead of the grungy alleyway, emerald-green meadows roll before me while waves crash against pearly white beaches. I blink rapidly and try to make sense of what I'm seeing.

The dragon-lion leaps over my head and dives into the glittery man, sending them both tumbling into a trash heap. The golden typhoon dissipates, as does the strange mirage. I can feel my body parts again, tingling as if they were asleep.

I don't wait.

I scramble on top of the Dumpster and jump over their wrestling bodies, roll across the slimy alley, and take off in a sprint, splashing through muddy puddles and skirting broken beer bottles. *What were those creatures back there?*

I run to the main street. Where it's safe. Hot breath blows

on my back. I'm being pursued. The creature chases at my heels, teasing, taunting me.

I careen out onto the main road, amazed I am still alive. Silence rules the street. The cars have disappeared. The vendors have vanished as if they never existed. A piece of newspaper drifts across the empty street, spiraling in the wind. I stumble to a halt.

Chills ricochet down my body.

Clenching my fists, I spin to challenge the creature. His face tells me I'm his captive. I take the fighting stance. It's not over yet.

It pounces. I tumble backward, crushed against the cold rough sidewalk. Its weight and the fall knock the air out of me. Then it's off me, as if I'm some cat toy to be tossed around for fun before finally being eaten. I gasp and push my body up. I'm on my hands and knees when the creature appears again, looming over me, smelling of wild animal and ginseng. I tense, prepping for its next attack.

"Beware," it says in a voice that rumbles like thunder.

I scramble to stand and gaze up. It must be three times the size of a lion.

"He wants you."

The creature talks. This is not happening. I close and open my eyes. Still there.

"Who—who are you?" I finally ask.

"I am the Guardian of Seoul. Some call me Haechi. I have been sent by Palk to warn you and offer my protection."

"But—but you attacked me," I sputter. "And how do you know English?"

A rumble emits from its mouth. "An impetuous one, you are."

"I don't need protecting. I was doing just fine before you pounced on me."

"You have been sought out by a dangerous immortal. He nearly took you moments ago."

I shake my head. "Who?"

"Time is fading. You must flee," he says, and, in a breath, he disappears.

It's as if a switch has been flicked. Honking cars, the pound of construction, the roar of the buses replace the creature's breathing. I swivel in a circle. Everything is back in place as if nothing happened. I press my cold hands to my cheeks.

Blood trickles from a cut on my palm. Probably from when I fell. That was all. I fell, hit my head, and had some crazy dream. How long was I out?

The sweet potato lady eyes me from under the green scarf wrapped around her head. She wobbles over in her bulky trousers and stuffs a dirty towel on my bleeding hand. I'll probably get an infection from it, I think dully.

She rattles off something in Korean, but I'm too dazed to listen. I do notice she's holding a piece of my coat. I peer over my shoulder and realize the back of my coat is shredded as if some wild animal with giant claws has ripped through it.

Impossible.

"*Flee!*" the wind whispers into my ear.

I run the rest of the way home.

CHAPTER 4

We leave Seoul hours before sunrise the next morning. Dad hopes to avoid the Han River traffic. Still, five a.m. seems a little extreme, especially since I hardly slept last night thanks to that horrible Haechi creature attacking me. Or as it seemed to believe, "protecting" me. Some protection.

I'm still not sure what to think about last night. Was it real? It felt real.

But none of it could possibly have happened. That stuff belongs in movies and fairy tales. I rub the egg-sized bump on the back of my head. I'm guessing I hit my head and then dreamed up an insane story.

I stare out my window as the first rays of sunlight sparkle across the skyscrapers on the other side of the Han River while, on my right, concrete buildings line the edge of the road like a massive wall.

Haechi. Glittery Guy. Palk. Why had I imagined those creatures?

Last night, mind racing, I'd dug through my unpacked

boxes until I found the book of Korean folktales Mom read to me every night as a kid.

"These are your stories, Jae," she'd say. "They are a part of who you are."

Never once had I imagined those stories would come to life and attack me.

I cross my legs in the backseat of the car and rest Mom's thick hardcover in my lap. The pages are soft and worn under my fingers. I flip through them until I find the illustration of Haechi. Underneath it is the definition:

> **Haechi—A legendary creature resembling a lion; a fire-eating beast; guardian against disaster and prejudice.**

It looks exactly like the creature I hallucinated last night. I flip to the index and search for Palk. He's listed as one of the two great immortals and the counterpart of Kud, the immortal of darkness.

> **Palk—The sun god and founder of the realm of light. He is the personification of all that is light, good, and beneficial.**

I press my palms against my eyelids as if to push away last night's memory. For a year after Mom died, I saw a psychologist to help me cope with my nightmares. Maybe moving to Seoul reawakened those nightmares, but at a whole new level this time. Because last night in the street facing those creatures felt real.

Too real.

I tuck the book to my chest. I can almost hear Mom's voice reading to me like she would when I was little. When she was sick, really sick, I'd lie next to her, watching the shadows creep across the walls like the hands of a clock.

"Read to me," she'd say.

So during her last days, I was the one who would read until my throat would ache and my voice would rasp.

It hadn't always been that way. Before Mom got sick, we were busy. She with her paintings and I with my archery tournaments. If she was here now, would I have talked to her about last night? If she hadn't gotten sick, would we have ever gotten that close?

My heart balloons up until I can't take the pain of it anymore. I throw the book across the car.

"Jae!" Dad says, jerking me back to reality. "What is wrong?"

What is there to tell him? That I'm losing my mind?

"School," I finally say. "Too much studying."

We merge into the three-lane Gangbyeon Expressway as Dad nods solemnly. "Well then, it will be good for you to take a break for this holiday."

Cars clog the highway, reminding me of L.A. at rush hour. Dad maneuvers through the traffic, hands gripping the steering wheel. Even when he drives he's got that intensity and determination. People used to say I looked just like Mom, but I have got my dad's personality. Maybe that's why we don't sit down and just chat. Sitting and introspection aren't exactly our strengths.

Soon we ease out of the city, and rolling hills and greenhouses replace skyscrapers and concrete. The hills, packed with evergreens, feel alive compared to the desert-like landscape of

California. We pass a dormant rice field, brown stalks chopped off like a bad haircut. An airplane soars above us—we're quite close now to Incheon Airport—and a pang runs through my chest. I wish I was on one of those planes, whisking over the Pacific to L.A. If only I could convince Dad to move back home.

I'm in the middle of a daydream in which I've secretly stowed myself on a plane when I realize we're already driving off the ferry onto a tiny, two-lane road on Muui Island, where Grandfather lives. Metal-framed shacks line the curb with vendors selling crab and tangerines, an odd combination. We curve inland and climb a hill, passing an old man spreading his peppers out on blankets to redden them in the sun.

It turns out that Grandfather's house isn't on the beach but above the coast, built on the edge of a cliff. It's a traditional Korean home, with the fluted roof line and cross-beamed walls. I wonder how old this place is. It's absolutely stunning. As I scoot out of the car, the scent of pine and that icy smell of winter wash over me.

A servant answers the door with a bow and whisks away our bags. I slip off my boots, as is customary in all Korean homes, and follow Dad through the entryway into the main room. The house has an airy feel even in its old age due to its sparseness and the geometric screened windows overlooking the ocean. A near life-size stone statue of a winged horse rests on a wooden platform by the far wall. A gold plaque labels it Chollima. On the other side of the room is a uniform fitted on a manikin. I move closer to study it.

"Do you know anything about this?" I ask Dad, but he's busy studying the mural of a tiger on the far wall. It's painted in traditional Asian style, with the tiger stretched out as if running. Its jaws gape wide, revealing sharp, jagged teeth.

"Annyeong hashimnikka," Grandfather greets us as he enters the room. He's wearing loose black pants and a silken gray tunic that buttons down the center. We bow as is expected.

"That is a reproduction of General Yu-Shin Kim's uniform," Grandfather says, nodding toward the manikin.

I don't know what to say and apparently neither does Dad. The silence that follows is painfully awkward. I find myself thinking of my friends back in L.A. who would rush into their grandparent's arms with hugs, and my chest aches for that kind of openness. But they didn't have thousands of years of tradition and ancestors hanging over them.

I tap my fingers against the sides of my thighs, waiting for his eyes to turn to mine and frown. When his attention does slide to me, his eyelashes squeeze tight and he nods once. I squirm and lower my eyes, not expecting that response.

"So she stays," Grandfather says.

"Abeoji," Dad says, "We've just arrived. Please try to keep the peace."

"Peace?" Grandfather scoffs, settling onto a pillow at the traditional square table in the room's center. "Peace is what I live for. What our ancestors lived for."

"Good," Dad says, now smiling. His shoulders relax and he, too, sits.

"Sit, sit." Grandfather waves to me, his gold ring flashing as he does so.

We sit cross-legged on silk cushions on the oak floor as a servant sets out tea and *tteok* for us. I choose a pink-colored one and pop it into my mouth. Sesame and brown sugar have been tucked inside. These are the best rice cakes I've ever tasted.

"How do you like Korea?" Grandfather asks me.

"It's okay, I guess," I say, studying the tea leaves in my cup. "But I miss my friends back home."

"I am sure you miss your American education," he says.

My head jerks up, and I search his face. He looks dead serious.

"She attends an international school," Dad says. "They have the same American education as any top school in the States."

Grandfather nods while crossing his arms. "Do you not think boarding school in America would be more appropriate for Jae Hwa? Many families send their children to boarding schools. Taking her away from her homeland must be difficult."

I nearly drop my teacup. "There are boarding schools in L.A."

"Is that so?" Grandfather asks.

Boarding school! Why hadn't I thought of that? Maybe Grandfather's antagonism might work for my good.

"It's out of the question." Dad's scowl is firmly back in place. "Jae needs more time to adjust. Besides, she's far too young to be off by herself."

"Jae seems quite mature," Grandfather says. "I would be pleased to contribute any funds needed for such an enterprise."

"No," Dad says flatly.

"It is merely a thought. I do not see why you keep resisting my generosity." Grandfather's eyes are tight with anger. Or is it worry?

"I love your painting of that tiger," I say, deciding to switch the topic. "It almost looks alive."

"Ah yes, the Tiger of Shinshi," Grandfather says. "You remember the legends, yes?"

I reach for another *tteok*. "Something about him protecting the Korean people throughout time?"

"Excellent memory!" Grandfather beams. "It is he who watches over the Golden Thread that binds our people as one."

"Speaking of time, when are the others supposed to arrive?" Dad's still on edge.

"I commissioned an esteemed Korean-American painter to create the mural," Grandfather says, ignoring Dad's comment. I can't blame Dad, though. It's strange no one else from our family has arrived yet. "It serves as a continual reminder of my duties here on Earth."

Yep. He's completely *michutda*.

"Jae Hwa, would you care to take a stroll with me on the beach?" Grandfather asks.

My hand freezes while I'm reaching for my teacup. He wants to take *me* for a walk? The granddaughter he's so ashamed of that he's thinking of ways to get me out of the country? Or have I somehow exaggerated how he feels about me? Mom had always said I go overboard sometimes. Still, this could turn into an opportunity—like boarding school.

The servant hurries over and hands me my coat, scarf, and boots. As we step out the back door, Dad calls to Grandfather, his forehead bunching up like it does when he's worried.

"Just a walk, Abeoji," he says. "None of your stories, remember? She doesn't need nightmares."

Nightmares? Two days ago I would've glared at Dad for treating me like a five-year-old. But today I start to wonder if Dad isn't right.

CHAPTER 5

Once outside, I draw in a breath of salt air and gaze down into the dark-indigo ocean, the afternoon sun scattering rays across its surface.

Mom would've wanted to paint this place.

Crops of rounded hills rise up out of the water. Sluggish waves lap against the black sand like fingers touching a keyboard. It's such a contrast to the ten-foot waves that crash against the Malibu beaches where my friends and I hung out.

"These are the tidal flats." Grandfather swings open a waist-high gate and starts down a set of wooden stairs that lead to the beach. "Soon, very soon, all the water will be gone, leaving only mud."

I can't imagine how that much water could disappear. I hurry after him. The sound of wind and rushing water grows once I hit the dark sand, hard and icy. I scramble to catch up as he strides out to stand at the muddy water's edge, his hands clasped behind his back, his eyes tuned to the skyline.

"They said it was impossible to land an army here in

Incheon." Grandfather's wrinkles appear deeper in the daylight. "That is why General MacArthur surprised the North Koreans and won the war. He took the impossible and made it possible."

Now I know where Dad gets all his sayings. Dad is big on motivational stuff like "The best way to predict your future is to create it," which he has hanging over his desk.

"So you think it's possible for me to go to boarding school?" I ask.

"Of course. I must first convince your father."

"That might be more difficult than you think."

He chuckles, his chin coming up as he does. "Jae Hwa, your father and I have disagreements. But my greatest concern is for your safety."

My stomach rolls, wondering how he could know about my hallucination. But he couldn't know. He's probably thinking about boys. I smile. "I don't think you need to worry about me, Haraboji."

If he only knew. Like when the third-grade class bully, Jacob Cantor, strutted up to me, pulled my long braid, and called me a worthless immi (short for *immigrant*). If he'd been smart, he would've picked on some other immi. But unlucky Jacob picked me. I stood and knocked him a blow that sent him tumbling into the trash can. Where he probably felt right at home.

I say, "I have a black belt in Tae Kwon Do. Besides, Seoul is way safer than L.A."

Except for what happened last night, I think. I rub the back of my head, pushing away that thought.

"Not for you," he says.

I press my lips together and resist rolling my eyes. Here comes the whole girls-need-to-be-protected lecture.

I'm about to explain to him how I can take care of myself when he motions to a set of smooth rocks to our left and sits on one. I follow, dragging my boots so they make a snakelike trail in the sand behind me. Great. I've let myself get lured out here with my lunatic grandfather.

"In ancient times there was a daughter of the spirit of the river."

I'd rather discuss potential boarding school options. "I thought Dad didn't want you telling me stories," I say, trying to steer the conversation back on course.

"Her name was Princess Yuhwa," he continues, ignoring my comment. "In fact, she was about your age. She had such beauty, anyone who laid eyes on her fell in love with her. One hot day, she and her sisters were bathing in a pond. This was the very day Haemosu, a demigod, decided to pay a visit to the people of the earth and set his mark on the land."

Demigod? I press my chin to my tucked-in knees and stare out at the rounded island just beyond our beach.

"He saw her and fell instantly in love," Grandfather says. "Haemosu decided he must have Princess Yuhwa as his wife. But she refused. He gave her a beautiful bracelet gilded of heavenly gold and promised he would change her mind. Four more times he returned, entreating her to come with him to his beautiful land. Yet still the princess refused. This infuriated him, and he decided to marry her against her will."

"Why don't princesses ever *do* something in all these old stories?" I interrupt. "Like try to escape or get someone to help them?"

"She did tell her father, the water god, Habaek. When he

discovered that Haemosu did not follow the proper marriage ceremony, he fought with Haemosu. Habaek lost. Helpless, the princess was taken away in Haemosu's chariot, Oryonggeo, driven by five dragons to the Spirit World."

I dig the toe of my boot into the sand. "That's a great story. But if you're worried about me getting whisked away, you don't need to. I can take care of myself." Although a chariot driven by five dragons does sound pretty cool.

His eyebrows knit as he frowns. "I have not finished."

"Oh. Right. Sorry." It's then that I notice the tide has pulled back about twenty feet, leaving behind a bank of mud. I sit up. When did that happen?

"What Haemosu underestimated was Princess Yuhwa. She secretly withdrew a golden pin from her hair, cut her way through the bottom of the chariot, and fell back to her people."

I'd always thought princesses were more of the fainting type. Good for Yuhwa. "I guess Haemosu wasn't too thrilled about that," I say.

"He was furious," Grandfather says, fingering the ring on his finger. "The legend says he searched everywhere for her, but she remained hidden in her father's palace. Secretly, she bore Haemosu's son, Chumong, who later became the founder of the Koguryo kingdom in ancient Korea."

Is this some warped idea of happily ever after? "So it all worked out. Good for her."

Grandfather rises, smoothing out the wrinkles in his tunic. "But it didn't."

I'm not sure if it's from the tone of his voice or the oddness of the story, but a heaviness presses on me like a storm cloud.

"What the legend does not mention is that the princess fled to China, where Haemosu had no power." Grandfather focuses on me. "Even today Haemosu still seeks her."

Chills slither up my spine as I think about this twisted fairy tale. I nearly jump when one of the servants rushes up to us. "Sir," he says in Korean. "Your brother's family has arrived."

"Well then." Grandfather stands and pats me on the shoulder. "I must greet them. I had hoped for us to have more time together. Perhaps tomorrow?" When I don't answer, he says, "Do you wish to join me? You have yet to meet the rest of the family."

"Maybe later," I say with a shrug. Meeting another set of strangers sounds even more painful than listening to Grandfather's psycho stories.

"As you wish." He starts off, but stops and glances over his shoulder. "Do not go to the outer island without me. It would not be wise."

He turns and heads back to the house, his stride sure and quick, even with the wintry breeze whipping at his tunic.

I stare out at the island, wondering what Grandfather meant. A sound of rushing water catches my attention, and I notice how the water level is rapidly decreasing. A makeshift bridge of stepping stones from Grandfather's beach to the tiny island not forty feet away appears. The stones must have been hidden under the water, and now that the tide has pulled back, their surfaces poke out of the mud, slick and shiny in the winter sun.

I slide off the rock and rub my hands together. Curiosity tugs at me like the tide, and I can't stop myself. I cross the stepping-stone bridge, careful not to slip on its mud-slathered surface.

Once on the island, I follow an overgrown trail across a

meadow, which leaves me at a series of volcanic-like boulders that spike up, jagged and taller than a two-story house. Looking around, I can't figure out what's so dangerous about this place that Grandfather had to warn me explicitly about it.

I start climbing the rocks for fun, trying to remember the moves I learned at summer camp two years ago in Montana. I'm halfway up a rock side when I spot a narrow passageway between two boulders that twists its way from the beach to the rocks. I drop to the ground.

The passageway is so narrow I have to shimmy sideways. Above, the sky looks like a zigzag streak of paint between the uneven rock walls. At the end rests a wooden door, typhoon weathered. *Why in the world is there a door here?* I wonder. I turn the handle, and, with a click, it opens.

Is this place Haraboji's? Sure, he's my grandfather, but what do I really know about him? I peek inside. It's dark as pitch. On a stone ledge just inside the door sits a metal box from which I extract a lighter. I ignite the torch lying against the wall, and instantly the long, rock-walled corridor is illuminated.

This is absolutely the most fascinating place I've ever seen. I know I shouldn't be here. I could head back to Haraboji's house to meet the distant relatives and attempt smiles, all the while tortured with curiosity over what lies at the other end of this corridor.

Or I could explore.

I glance over my shoulder, licking the salt from my lips. I'll just go to the end of the hallway, I promise myself. Grandfather will never know.

Musty air saturates the corridor as I follow the torch-lit path, trailing my hand over the smooth walls that must have been carved out by ancient waves. A sharp breeze howls through the tunnel and slams the door shut behind me. I jump and nearly trip over myself.

Now free of the wind, the passageway is damp and cold. The torchlight flickers ghostly shadows over the walls, and the air is silent. I shudder and eye the door, debating whether to go back or explore. Ultimately the lure of the unknown draws me deeper.

At the end of the corridor I discover a space about fifteen feet in diameter. I stare. It's like some ancient tomb we'd study in school. But it isn't a tomb. It's something else entirely.

Sconces hang from each of the walls and, wanting to see the room clearer, I light them. Two of the walls show a mural of a princess riding in a chariot drawn by five golden dragons. Though the colors have faded to pale yellows and light blues, I know she must be Princess Yuhwa. I move closer, studying her. She looks just like me. *Creepy.*

I back away to check out the rest of the room. Along the far wall is a wooden shelf packed with scrolls and leather-bound books. Hundreds maybe.

I rub my sweaty hands down my jeans. Okay, so I'm definitely not supposed to be here. I should go. Dad's probably wondering about me, too.

But my attention is pulled, almost by force, to the fourth wall, which is covered with bows, quivers, and arrows hanging on pegs. I eye the smooth wood of one horn bow, so old it should be in a museum. The image of the Blue Dragon, one of the four immortal guardians of Korea, is painted on it. The horn bow is unique to Korea, known for its ability to shoot arrows farther than any other bow. My fingers itch to take it off the wall, string it, and draw back on it to feel its pull.

Without thinking, I grasp it. An electric shock runs through me, and I nearly drop the bow. The bamboo is as smooth as pearl against my hands. My fingers set into the notches on the bow, and a buzz of nerves courses through me because the bow fits my hand perfectly. I drag my fingers along the string, wondering if that hum I'm hearing is my imagination.

I replace the bow and move to the low teak table in the center of the room. On top lies an aged scroll, unrolled and revealing ancient Chinese symbols. I clamp my sweaty hands in my lap and lean forward. Seeing an ancient scroll that isn't behind glass is beyond cool. The rice paper appears faded, but the swirled texture is still intact.

I slide my finger gingerly over the scroll's rough surface. I expect grime to gather along my fingertips, but instead my fingers are caked with gold. The particles rise from my hand in a glittery spiral above the scroll and stream toward the mural.

The gold dust fuses into the outline of Princess Yuhwa riding in the dragon-led chariot. Beams of light shoot from the walls. The princess turns to me and stretches out her hand, saying, "Help me!" in Korean.

My head pounds, almost as if the drums from the museum ceremony are beating again.

This can't be happening. This can't be real.

My hand shakes, and before I realize what I'm doing, I reach out and grab hold of her hand.

CHAPTER 6

Gravity chains my feet to the floor, resisting the princess's pull. My bones can't take much more pressure. But then I fall head-first through the mural into blinding light. I clamp my eyes shut and fight against the instinct to curl into a ball. I hit a hard, cold surface, and my body smashes against a wall.

When I open my eyes, I expect to see a chariot or perhaps the princess. They're nowhere in sight. Instead, a heavy mist drifts over toothed rocks at my feet. I manage to lean against the small pagoda behind me, my arm still aching from being pulled to wherever I am.

What is this place? What just happened to me?

I take a deep breath and slowly release it. That's what Master Park from Tae Kwon Do class tells us to do in overwhelming situations. I can totally handle this. I must have fallen or something. That's it. Just like I did next to the sweet potato lady. I need to find my way back to wherever I was.

The wind rails against my cheeks, whipping my long hair across my eyes. I cling to the vertical wooden beams running alongside the pagoda to keep myself balanced against the gusts. I'm about to take my first step when the wind shifts, pulling away the mist.

My foot hovers over nothingness.

I scream. My heart plunges to the pit of my stomach. I claw for the pagoda, all the while eying the vertical drop of maybe a freaking thousand feet.

Oh God.

My heart struggles to regain a steady beat. I press my body against the pagoda, fighting the storm that's desperate to toss me off this pinnacle. Fighting the need to throw up.

I will not *panic,* I tell myself over and over. But my hands won't stop shaking, and my legs buckle underneath me.

The wooden walls I'm clinging to, with their Chinese characters engraved on them, become my entire focus. I hardly know any Chinese, but I recognize some of these. I try to focus on them, hoping the sight of something familiar will help me pull myself together. Because I'm totally losing it.

Soo Jin
Young Mi
Hana
Min Sung

Wait. These are names. The entire pagoda's surface is carved with them. But why? I shuffle along the edge of the pagoda, reading the names I can decipher and hoping to find the door leading inside. If there is one.

As I move, I realize the pagoda is more like a small shrine, with a diameter of about ten feet. It's built on top of a rock pinnacle, with a small, maybe-two-foot ledge circling it. I have yet to see a ladder, stairwell, door—anything to show how this place was even built.

Farther along, I come to a section where the ledge is so narrow that one misstep will send me flying. My winter coat lashes at my legs. I grip the ledge until my knuckles are white, paralyzed even to attempt this section.

Characters. I just need to focus on them, and that will distract me. That's when I read something very strange. My vision blurs, and I nearly lose my grip.

The names are all too familiar. My great-aunt's, *Lee Yang Hee,* along with another name, *Lee Sun,* is carved there.

And then.

On top and blazing in gold.

My name.

Lee Jae Hwa.

My pulse throbs against my temples. From the corner of my eye, I spot something on the horizon, moving through the air like a bird. I wait as it grows closer, hoping it's a rescue of some kind, but soon I realize it's a dragon-led chariot. Except Princess Yuhwa isn't driving it. It looks like a man.

I suddenly remember Grandfather's story and scoot back along the shrine's edge. The chariot draws closer. I can see the gold-plated scales on the dragons and the gleam of their red eyes.

Then I hear a voice calling my name.

"Jae Hwa!"

I search the area for who is calling me, but I can't find anyone. "Help!" I yell.

The rock floor is wider in this section, and for a moment I'm relieved until I realize this is where I started. Which means there isn't a door into the shrine. There's no escape.

"Over here, Jae Hwa!" The voice sounds like Grandfather's. With my back pressed against the pagoda, I stare out over the edge where I hear his voice; and there, through a shimmery mirage, I can just make out Grandfather, reaching for me through the clouds.

"Jump, Jae Hwa!" he shouts. "Jump before he finds you!"

He wants me to jump off a pinnacle that's forever high. Right. That makes a lot of sense. But then, what about this place makes sense?

"You cannot run from me, my princess," another voice, rich and deep, calls out. "You are mine. We are destined to be together for eternity."

Careening around the corner, the dragons emerge. Snorting. Their scales reflecting the beams of the sun.

Deep breath.

I leap off the pinnacle, stretching my body toward Grandfather's outstretched arms. For a heartbeat I'm suspended over nothingness, falling through the mist.

And I wonder if I've just leaped to my death.

CHAPTER 7

But I haven't. My hands meet Grandfather's, warm and strong. He drags me through the blinding light until I'm tumbling across the cave's sand-scattered rock floor. He quickly unfurls a huge black tarp, then digs through a chest and procures a roll of duct tape. I gawk at his calm and efficient movements as he starts duct-taping the tarp over the mural.

"Haraboji," I finally manage, breathless. "That mural—it took me to this place."

He doesn't even glance my way. "Help me. This will block off all light from the cave. He will not be able to enter."

I jump up and grab the other end of the tarp, holding it tight against the wild wind, and together we secure it against the wall. As we do, the wind vanishes.

I stand still, expecting the dragons to come bursting through our makeshift barrier, but nothing happens.

"You need to tell me right now what's going on," I say.

"Haemosu still seeks his princess, his bride who escaped

him." Grandfather wipes sweat from his brow. "You did not listen to me. I told you this island was dangerous."

"You could have emphasized the danger more." I cross my arms. "So what is with this Haemosu guy? Wasn't it like a thousand years ago that Princess Yuhwa left him?"

"Indeed. But to a demigod a thousand years is nothing. He hunts and kidnaps the oldest unwed female of each generation of Habaek's family."

"That is—" I want to say "freaking impossible." But how can I deny what I just experienced?

"Princess Yuhwa's bloodline pumps through your heart. You are the oldest female in this generation," Grandfather explains, snuffing out one of the sconces. "But you already know this."

I think about my name glowing in gold. "So that was him back there. Coming to kidnap and whisk me away in his chariot."

"Yes." Grandfather frowns. "This is why I told your father not to bring you to Korea. We should leave this place. It is no longer safe."

This is all too much to process. But then the words *no longer safe* rise out of the muddle in my brain. I swallow. "You were able to save some of the girls, right?"

As if to avoid my question, he turns toward the weapons lining the far wall. Swords gleaming in the firelight. Bows waiting to be plucked off the wall and strung.

"My great-great-grandfather had hoped to kill Haemosu. He collected ancient—and what he believed—magical weapons. He failed. So similar to Habaek, when he tried to stop Haemosu from taking away Princess Yuhwa."

"You act like I'm already dead."

He hesitates before snuffing out another sconce. "The only survivors were those who married before they turned fifteen, or those who left the country. Haemosu must relinquish his power to the immortals of other lands.

"Your father deemed all this nonsense even after I showed him these scrolls. But the proof is here." Grandfather gently picks up the scroll on the table.

That does sound like Dad. He only believes in what he can see and touch. It was always Mom who believed in the spiritual. My heart squeezes.

A gust of wind tears through the room and extinguishes the third sconce. A crash vibrates down the tunnel, followed by footsteps. Only the last torch on the wall keeps us from total darkness. Someone is coming. *Haemosu?*

But it's only Dad, storming into the room like a tsunami.

"What have you done?" he bellows at Grandfather. "You promised never to take her here."

"I was saving her." Grandfather lifts his chin and straightens his back. "I told her not to come. She would not listen."

"You've filled her mind with nonsense, haven't you?" Dad says. "I told you, I begged you to keep the peace!" Dad focuses on me. "Don't believe any of it," he tells me, his eyes pleading. "Don't listen to his lies."

"But what if he's right, Dad?" I ask, not really sure I believe it all myself, yet unable to explain being sucked into a mural and chased by a dragon-led chariot.

Dad stares for a second. Then: "Look what you've done!"

He points a shaking finger at Grandfather, windblown hair hanging over wild eyes. "This must stop!"

I've never seen Dad lose his cool like this. He may have lived in America all his life, but he always held to the Korean traditions of respect and honor to one's elders. I press my back against the clammy wall.

"I am trying everything I can to save her." Grandfather clenches the scroll in his hand so tight, I'm worried it might crumble.

"Like you did with Sun and Eun. You drove them insane with all your stories and incantations. I won't allow you to infect my daughter."

Sun. I think back to the pagoda on the pinnacle. Wasn't that the name directly under mine?

"Who are Sun and Eun?" I ask.

A strong wind sweeps down the corridor, swirling around the three of us. A tip of the tarp tears free from the stone wall. Light shoots from the corner of the tarp, and a wind gushes into the cave. I watch in horror as the celadon incense burner crashes to the floor, breaking and scattering like green sand. The tarp erupts into an inferno, and I dive for the scrolls and books, bundling them in my arms, expecting to see the dragons raging through the blaze at any moment.

"No!" Grandfather leaps toward the flames, yanks off his coat, and starts beating out the fire with it. It's useless. The fire only grows, as if some magical force is at work.

"Haemosu!" Grandfather yells. He glares at Dad. "You left the door open and allowed the light in!"

"It's a fire, Abeoji." Dad shrugs off his coat and joins in

Grandfather's attempts at beating out the fire. "This isn't about mythological creatures!"

I've no idea how the light has anything to do with this, but it's too late for accusations. The flames lick the scrolls like hungry serpents. Heat burns my skin, and smoke chokes my lungs. I start coughing. Through the gray haze, I see Dad trying to pull Grandfather away from the firestorm, yelling in Korean for him to get out.

Then Dad focuses on me, and there's pure panic in his face. I suddenly understand that losing me would probably kill him. He pushes me out of the room. We all rush down the tunnel, doubled over from coughing, and burst out of the cave onto the beach. I suck in fresh sea air and clutch the few scrolls I rescued tight to my chest.

Black smoke now puffs from the mouth of the tunnel and spirals up in the air.

"I could not save any of it," Grandfather says, his face sooty and his once-crisp clothes burned and ragged. "Everything— gone."

"Not everything," Dad says. "The two of you are safe. That's what matters." Then he holds my face between his hands, staring at me with such intensity. "I couldn't bear losing you, too."

I'm not the hugging type—at all—but those words send my emotions out of whack, and the reality of what just happened overwhelms me. Tears stream down my cheeks, and I can't stop them. I drop the scrolls and throw my arms around Dad. He stumbles back as if surprised, but he doesn't pull away. He holds me tighter and stares vacantly at the smoke, as if lost in another time. "Perhaps it's for the best," he mutters. Then he seems to come out of his stupor, letting out a long breath, his jaw set. "We should leave."

"Now?" I dry my face with my sleeve. "What about meeting the rest of the relatives?" I'm grasping onto every excuse to spend more time with Grandfather.

"Yes, now," Dad says, insistent, as if he too is running away from something. "We should never have come."

"You cannot leave now," Grandfather says. "Not after what has just happened. Haemosu knows she is here. Nothing will stop him until she is his!"

"You lied to me." Dad scowls at Grandfather. "You promised you'd take medication for your delusions. You promised there would be no more drama. And here we are. Barely alive. You nearly got her killed with your ridiculous torches and caves and weapons. Jae will have no part in your life from now on."

"I won't go." I cross my arms. "What if Haraboji is right? I need to figure this all out."

"There is nothing to figure out," Dad says, wrapping his arm around my shoulders and directing me down the beach. "We need to get you back home where it is safer. Remember that ski trip you wanted to go on? Any more of these antics, it's off."

I stumble back across the stone bridge after Dad, still shaken by everything that happened. My mind whirls in a hundred directions, and I'm not sure what to believe anymore. *Will I really be safer at home?*

Back at the house, I shrug into my thick cable-knit sweater

and head out to the car, hating myself for leaving like a coward but not knowing what to do about it. Grandfather stops me at the door, saying, "I have something for you."

He unzips a black case and pulls out the Blue Dragon bow from the cave. He hands it to me. "A gift."

The bow lands heavy in my arms, sending my heart sailing. I stare at him, a smile curving across my lips. "How? I thought you couldn't save anything!"

"I went back afterward and searched through the wreckage," he says. "Some things are not meant to disappear until their purpose has been met."

What is he talking about?

Then he draws me into a hug, and I'm so surprised I just stand there like a stuffed crane. He smells like kimchi mixed with smoke. I never imagined today would end like this. It's weird how all morning I wanted to get back to my friends. Now all I want to do is stay.

He whispers in my ear so Dad can't hear: "There is another who can help you."

If I was stiff before, I'm now a block of ice. Grandfather slides a piece of paper into my palm and then steps away. I crunch the slip into my fist so Dad can't see it and trudge out to the car.

Snow falls in heavy chunks, laying winter's blanket over the land, but my blood is pumping. It's as if I'm waking up and seeing a whole new world. I slouch down in my seat and glance at the piece of rice paper no larger than my palm.

It reads:

Master Kim 02-756-6715
47 Namsan-dong 2-ga, Jung-gu, Seoul

I tuck it into one of my jean pockets, wondering who this Master Kim is. I hope he has at least one answer to my fifty million questions.

CHAPTER 8

When we get home, Dad is inspired to ground me for eternity after my stunt on the island. I have to admit that considering what actually happened—and there's no way I'm going to tell him—he probably has a good reason for this. Fires and dark caves on forbidden islands are enough to freak out any parent, much less ancient gods kidnapping their daughters from another world.

I stand numbly in the middle of our living room, trying to process everything Grandfather said and my own experience of being pulled into the mural. My world stands off-kilter. It's as if someone has twisted each part of my life a little to the left and now nothing from my past looks the same, while my future is a gaping hole of uncertainty. I don't even understand who I am anymore. Or what I'm supposed to do.

"Where did you get that?" Dad nods to the bow case strapped to my back.

"Haraboji," I say. "It was a gift."

He opens his mouth as if to say something but then shakes

his head. Ashen faced, Dad abandons his suitcase by the door and marches directly to the hallway closet. With shaking hands, he opens the safe where we keep our smaller treasures and legal documents. I still remember how he'd taught me the combination when we first arrived in case anything happened to him.

He ruffles through the documents, literally tossing our passports and checkbooks to the floor in his haste.

"You're scaring me, Dad," I say, and watch as he pulls out a small black pouch that was tucked away in the back corner. His hands tremble as he unties the string and two tiny objects tumble into his palm. One silver. One gold. It's the gold that catches my attention. A simple band with a diamond sparkling on top.

"Mom's wedding ring," I say. My voice chokes.

Dad squeezes the rings into his palm, forming a fist. "It's all I have left," he whispers. He rubs the sweat off his forehead, but his eyes look softer, more himself.

"You still have me." I hold his fist in my hands.

"Yes. And I won't let anything happen to you, Jae." Tears fill his eyes even though I know he's trying to hold them back. "Your grandfather means well, but he's not right in the head. He hasn't been for a very long time. If he tries to contact you, don't listen to him. He can only hurt you."

I don't know what to tell Dad. That I believe Grandfather? That I see the very things Grandfather does? Will he think I'm crazy, too?

Dad's expression keeps me quiet. Color has reentered his face, and his hands have stopped shaking. It's as if just having said those words made them true for him, and everything is right with his world again.

Even when deep down I know it's not.

He wraps his arm over my shoulders, and the two of us stand there, gazing out the window as the sun sets over Seoul.

Dad and I have grown closer today. So why do I feel as if we're also further apart than ever?

At first I'm okay with being locked away from civilization.

But by hour two I'm pacing like a trapped tiger while Dad is back to being wired into his laptop and BlackBerry, totally forgetting I exist. Unbelievable.

I consider throwing my *dobok* into my duffle bag and heading over to an evening Tae Kwon Do class, but after my recent fight, I'm not sure Master Park wants me back. Besides, Dad doesn't seem too keen to let me leave the house.

Some people paint for stress relief. Others beat the crap out of punching bags (which, I might add, is very therapeutic). I do what any normal person who's nearly been kidnapped by an immortal would do. I move furniture.

First, I choose my wall color. A photography store was going out of business after Christmas, and I was the lucky buyer of his background screens, having them shipped to Korea with Dad's grudging agreement. I pull down a pale-blue color, but as soon as I do, an image of Haemosu riding through the sky in a dragon-led chariot comes to mind.

Good-bye, blue.

I yank another cord to choose the forest scene. Supposedly, green is a calming color.

Next, I drag my desk to the far corner, scraping the linoleum with a squeak that I'm sure is driving Mr. Chung below me nuts.

I know I shouldn't be happy to annoy him, but seriously, his yip-yap dog that wakes me up at two a.m. is *way* louder.

My *yo* is next. It's soft and spongy. Most Koreans roll theirs up to give them more space, but my room is big enough for me to leave it out. Still, I miss my bed in L.A., which makes my insides churn all stormy that Dad not only dragged me over here, away from all my friends, but into danger. Sure, he doesn't believe in Grandfather's stories, but aren't dads supposed to be, like, ultra-protective or something? Shouldn't he want to protect me from any threat, however implausible?

I throw the *yo* across the room.

The dragon bow catches my eye. Its bamboo curves and oak handles call to me. I pick it up and run my fingers along its smooth surface, itching to know its pull and release. Once again I hear that hum, and I press the bow to my chest and inhale deeply. The wood is soothing, like ointment on a wound. But then memories of the wall of bows, the scrolls from an ancient time, and being pulled into the mural swim through my mind. My stomach churns, and my hands start to sweat.

My cell cuts the silence, and I nearly drop my bow. I dig through my backpack, following my ringtone: "Eye of the Tiger."

It's a text from Michelle: **Missing u! Wish u were here.**

Michelle! Just seeing her text pop up calms me. She is everything that my crazy family is not. She is normal. And I realize I'm craving that.

Me: **What r u doing 2nite?**

It only takes five seconds for Michelle to text back. **Remember? Coffee Bean. Good Enough. Lily and Kumar here 2.**

I slap my forehead. I'd forgotten about the concert. Good

Enough is a band comprised of kids from school, and Michelle, Lily, and I always support them.

Suddenly I'm desperate to get out of this stuffy apartment. I've got to do something other than sit around and wait for Haemosu to show up and kidnap me like Grandfather says. Plus Kumar is there, and I want to ask him about the possibility of alternate worlds.

I peer out the window, scanning the sidewalk for anything unusual. The memory of Glittery Guy and Haechi stops me short. Supposedly Palk sent Haechi as my protector, but I still don't buy it. What if they show up again?

I hate this feeling, as if I'm some princess stashed away in a castle unable to escape. *No.* I won't let stupid immortals ruin my life. They will not control me. I don't even fully believe they're real.

I text her back: **Meet u in 20 min** and then I slip on a tight black shirt and a pair of jeans. My hair's a tangled mess, but I don't bother with it as I toss a few things into my purse: iPod, cell phone, subway card; and then on impulse I snap a picture of my bow with my phone. I can't wait to show everyone.

There's no way Dad will let me escape to Myeong-dong. He'll suggest his usual: homework, SAT prep, or college applications. I crack open my door and spot him still working on his laptop. He'll totally see me leaving if I go out the front door.

Operation Sneak Out it is.

I plop two pillows on my *yo*, toss a blanket over them, and turn off the light. Then I slide up my window until the cool city breeze blusters against me and into my room. The city is alive tonight: restaurants flashing their neon signs, high-rise apartments lit up like Christmas trees against the dark sky, and the buzz of taxis and buses honking below. Even from this high up, I smell whiffs of Korean barbeque—*kalbi*—and kimchi.

Outside our apartment hangs a balcony that stretches from one end of the building to the other. Their thin privacy walls divide each apartment from the next. It isn't the first time I've dangled over the edge, streetcars zipping below me, to swing into our neighbors' balconies.

I creep to the railing, careful that Dad doesn't catch my silhouette through the windows, and climb over the metal bars. I could fall, but I know I won't. A burst of energy surges through me as I slither around to the other side of the divider into Mrs. Jung's balcony, careful not to be spotted. I continue my escape route until I reach the end apartment where the fire exit steps are.

In seconds I'm tearing down the concrete stairs of the fire escape and outside, breathing in the night air.

The subway stop is at the end of our street. My ticket to freedom. Dad would never let me go off on my own in L.A., but Seoul's a totally different matter. Sure, it's like three times the population of L.A., but it's so safe to walk around—even little kids travel alone on the subways at night. The neighbors tend to watch out for one another, and though the police cruise the streets, it's more the honor system of the people that keeps things in order.

It's Saturday night, so the subway station is packed. I join the throngs surging down the steps, scan my card, and weave my way to the Light Blue line. In the distance I can hear the eerie screech of the subway trains, and I find myself glancing over my shoulder, half expecting Haechi or Glittery Guy to jump out. The first train's too full, but when the second comes, I manage to wedge myself between a lady with a screaming baby and a black-suited businessman.

Usually I hate crowds. The feelings of claustrophobia and being engulfed in smells of *soju*, lavender, and kimchi overwhelm me. Not tonight. They are a comfort, blanketing me from harm. There's safety in numbers, I decide as the door clamps shut and the train lurches into motion. I plug in my earphones, hoping Karp will drown out the growing worry gnawing at my chest, and let my body sway with the train. I focus on the little screens above the sliding doors that scroll the names of each stop, first in Korean and then in English.

Two more stops until Myeong-dong. I text Michelle that I'm almost there, wiggle my way closer to the doors, and wait. The train creaks to a stop, and the doors swish open. I pause before exiting, a sliver of worry edging at my nerves. But if I don't get off the train right now, I'll be in a whole different section of the city at the next stop and arrive too late to hear Good Enough.

I step off, and the doors whoosh behind me. That's when I realize why I had hesitated. What had bothered me.

The platform is empty.

Where are the lines of people? I can't remember ever being in a subway station completely alone, especially on a Saturday night. The train hurtles away, sending a blast of wind swirling around me reeking of oil and fumes.

I adjust my bag and dart to the stairs. My boots echo along the platform. *Clomp, clomp, clomp.* I focus on the posters lining the walls, studying their colors, each word. Anything other than the fact that I'm sweating. That my heart feels as if I've just finished fifty push-ups.

A burst of bright light flashes over me. Laughter echoes across the platform, a high-pitched screech, sending an ache through my bones. I freeze. The platform falls silent.

I don't dare move. The light dissipates. In my peripheral vision a shadow scampers along the pipes in the ceiling. My heart stops, and my ears start ringing.

I run.

I'm halfway up the stairs when I'm faced with two black stumps that I assume are legs. The clawed feet aren't standing on the stairs but hovering over them. The air smells like a goat stable. I grab hold of the cool railing and allow my eyes to trail up the legs, past a cotton loincloth, up its red rippled belly, and into the most gruesome face I've ever seen.

Eyes gleam down at me, and a huge mouth widens into a sick smile to reveal four dagger-like teeth.

CHAPTER 9

I recognize this creature instantly from the Korean fairy tales Mom used to read me. A *dokkaebi*. The Korean version of a leprechaun, except that these guys aren't the cute, adorable kind you see on St. Patrick's Day. They're the kind that use magic for any whim that may cross their minds. And they're butt ugly. My mind reels. Dokkaebis hate city life. Dokkaebis avoid crowds. Dokkaebis aren't *real*.

This one's black hair sticks out as if it's been electrocuted, the ends fire red. Directly on top of his head sits a single horn. He bangs his thick wooden club on the concrete stairs, and sparks of light shimmer into the air. He stares at me with a trickster's grin on his face.

"Hey, pretty girl," he says, banging the club again. "Haemosu is watching you, wanting you."

My back presses against the railing, but I lift my chin. "Really?"

"Oh, oh, you already know, pretty girl." He cackles with glee. "I help you. You help me."

Dokkaebis are known for helping or harming people depending on their whims. He steps toward me.

"What do you want?" I wish my voice would stop quivering.

"More like what you want, is it not, pretty girl? Humans always want."

"Well, I *want* you to leave me alone." I move to dart around him. His massive body blocks me.

"No, no, no. You must come with me. To special place." He cocks his head to the side, revealing oozing warts on his neck. "Skilled with the arrow, are you?"

How does he know this? "Did Haemosu send you?"

"Yes, yes, yes. Haemosu beckons you." His red eyes narrow to slits. "Before we go, we make pact."

Right. Like I'm going to make a pact with a monster. "What did you have in mind?" My pulse races as I estimate how much space there is between him and the wall. Can I squeeze through?

"Yes, yes, yes! I give you clue. You give me orb."

I've no idea what he's talking about, but I attempt a smile as I prepare to duck around him. "Sounds fair."

"The heart of the moon. Shoot your arrow into it. There your ancestors are. You can free them from their tomb."

I stop. "What do you mean by freeing my ancestors?"

"Souls of the princesses cry, cry, cry," he says. "Do you not hear?"

My head is spinning. Grandfather never mentioned anything about this. Is this a trick or for real?

The stories always say never trust a dokkaebi.

He bangs his club onto the concrete. A myriad of colors spark into the air. "Then, then, then! Get me the orb."

"Heart of the moon? Orb?" I have no idea what he's talking about.

"Yes! Yes! Yes!" With each yes, he pounds his club. "You get. I get."

The only thing I want right now is to be far, far away.

He lifts his club to twirl it again. I take that moment to duck around him and then sprint up the rest of the stairs. When I reach the main level of the subway station, I'm back in the rush of people scurrying from place to place. I skirt around a group of giggling schoolgirls and glance over my shoulder, hoping the crowds have scared him off. The dokkaebi isn't following me.

Everything is normal.

Then I stop in my tracks. Because Haechi stands just two feet in front of me. People rush along, talking on their cell phones, totally oblivious to the lionlike creature standing on four legs.

"Trouble?" he asks in a growl.

"How—how," I swallow hard, "did you know?"

"This is my city. But dokkaebis rarely roam these parts. I did not sense the danger as quickly as I should have. A rift between Kud and Palk in the Spirit World has created recent havoc."

I lick my lips, completely confused. Why is every creature so determined to talk in riddles? "What do you want?"

"Remember. Palk has commissioned me to protect you. Call my name if you should need my assistance."

I nod, getting the sense that disagreeing with a creature as fierce and strong as he would not be in my best interests. He vanishes before I have a chance to ask him why Palk even cares about a lowly mortal like me.

Although I have to admit it's a little comforting to know he's on my side.

By the time I enter the Coffee Bean, I'm out of breath, and my nerves are fried squid. The paper lanterns dangling from the thick-beamed ceiling and olive-green wallpaper give the coffee shop a cozy atmosphere. The aroma of roasted coffee and cinnamon fills the air. The room's warmth soaks into me, and I realize how cold I am. Good Enough isn't playing, but their instruments are laid out on the stage, so they must be on their break.

I stand still and take it all in. It's all so *normal*. So *safe*. I cling to that feeling, pretending for a moment that Grandfather's story is just some awful fairy tale. That immortals, Haechi, and dokkaebis are mythical.

If only.

"Jae!"

That's Michelle's voice. I catch sight of her waving with both hands from a table at the far end, near a mock-traditional Korean-style oven. She's wearing a pale-pink cashmere sweater rimmed with pearls, and her hair is pulled back into a sleek-styled ponytail.

Next to her is Lily, with her curly blond hair, beaming a lip gloss smile at me as if this is the best night ever. Lily tends to get overdramatic, but then I see why. Kumar is sitting at their table. She's been crushing on him since day one of school, and apparently she's finally gotten his attention. He's easy to spot, being the only Indian in the room. But it's Marc, also with them, who stops my steps. He looks totally hot in a dark-blue fleece pullover. What's he doing here?

His eyes leave the TV where the soccer game is playing to

find mine. For a moment our eyes lock. He raises his eyebrows as if he's surprised I'm here, and then his mouth curves into a slow smile. My heart flips. Twice.

I order a latte and head over to them. Lily pats a stool next to her for me to sit on.

"You're back early," Michelle says.

Kumar glances up from his mini tablet to nod a hello. "Escaped the relatives, huh?"

"Hey, Fighter Girl," Marc says. "Your trip go well?"

How did he know I went on a trip? As if sensing my question, Michelle whispered into my ear, "Don't hate me forever. He was asking about you, so I told him you'd be here."

Still too cold to take off my jacket, I cup my drink between my hands and watch the steam curl up from the mug. I feel my face flush. "Yeah." I hesitate and then say, "Dad had to come back early for work." I hate lying, but the truth is too bizarre.

"Perfect!" Michelle says, totally oblivious. "Now we can get back on board with our weekend plans to shop for the ski trip next week."

"I wouldn't mind checking out the shops after the next set of songs," Lily adds.

Ugh. Shopping. Just the thought of it sounds exhausting. Besides, I haven't had much luck lately in going places, with dokkaebis and Haechis and everything else freak-worthy popping up. I shiver at that thought. "No offense, but I'll skip the shopping."

"You hardly hang out with us anymore." Michelle flattens her napkin nice and neat, looking annoyed. "And now you want to quit NHS. What's going on?"

Great. All I want is to fit in and be normal. Why does it have to be so hard? I glance over at the guys, both oblivious to our conversation as they discuss something on Kumar's tablet.

"Nothing is going on," I lie. "Everything is fine. And I've decided not to quit NHS."

"Really?" Michelle asks. She looks so relieved, I only regret my impulsive decision a little. "Excellent."

"You should tell her," Lily says to Michelle.

"Tell me what?" I ask.

Michelle folds the napkin into fourths. "Charlie broke up with me this morning." She presses her lips together, and I see tears edging the corners of her eyes. "By e-mail."

"E-mail?" I ask. "What a loser. And a coward. He could've at least called you."

"I guess I'm feeling a little needy lately."

"I'm so sorry." I grab her hand. "He's a moron not to want to be with you."

"That's what I told her," Lily says. "That's why I suggested shopping. We'll get her mind off it all."

"Let's not talk about Charlie anymore," Michelle says. "Tell us about your trip to your grandfather's house. Was it as bad as you thought it would be?"

"Worse." I give a shaky laugh. If they only knew. "Actually, my grandfather gave me a gift. It's pretty cool."

I pull out my cell phone, find the picture I took, and show it to the group.

Kumar sets aside his mini tablet. "Very cool," he says.

Marc puts on his glasses. "My guess is it's at least four hundred years old."

"Wow." I study Marc, who is staring at the picture. "How do you know that?"

"My parents are archaeologists on their off time. They cart me along for kicks." He shrugs and takes a swig of his Coke as if it's no big. So why do I get the feeling he's not telling me something?

"Kumar was just practicing for his big speech at the college fair tomorrow," Lily says, as proud as a mother hen.

"Right," I say, still grappling with the fact that my friends think researching physics is one version of fun. "That's the one where the Harvard guy is coming to hear you talk about the brain thing?"

Kumar nods, scrolling through his notes. Michelle and Lily slip away for coffee refills while I half listen to Kumar and Marc talk about how humans access different brain parts and half watch the door for strange creatures. My mind keeps flashing back to when I grabbed Yuhwa's hand and was pulled into the mural. How was that possible? A parallel universe or something?

Kumar is brilliant. So brilliant that Harvard has its eyes on him, even though he's only a junior. Maybe he might have some answers for me.

"What about different dimensions?" I blurt out. "Is it scientifically possible?"

"Dimensions?" Kumar rubs his chin. "Absolutely. There are all kinds of theories on it. People have been talking about it forever. Since Pythagoras. Nothing proven, though."

"So what do *you* think?" I ask.

"Well, there's this mathematician named Dr. Revis over at

North Carolina State University. She's got this theory that there are actually six dimensions."

"We discussed this in class earlier." Marc leans back in his chair. "Where two of the dimensions are time related."

"That's the one." Kumar touches his mini and sketches out a triangular drawing. "What Revis did was bend the uppercase Greek letter *xi* until it looked something like this."

Kumar shows us the sketch.

"So you're saying that at any time, any of the six dimensions could intersect." I lean over the table to get a better look.

Kumar sets his mini on the table. "No, what I'm saying is, at any moment, all or some of the dimensions intersect, but at varying intervals."

"And according to Dr. Revis," Marc adds, "the two time-related dimensions may not be running at the same speed."

Okay, so that is so above my head, but what Marc says makes me wonder. How did Grandfather get to the cave so quickly? Is it possible that our time runs differently from the time in Haemosu's world?

The mic screeches as a guy announces Good Enough back to the stage. The band saunters up, and within a few beats the room is vibrating with guitar, drums, keyboard, and pretty decent vocals.

Lily and Michelle rush back, deposit their drinks on the table, and join the group of dancers at the foot of the makeshift stage. I sit still, watching them. A sliver of jealousy runs through me. They are having fun, while my world is falling apart. I'm in a room full of people, but I feel so alone.

I'd hoped hanging out with my friends tonight would help me feel normal, but my brain can't stop rewinding what happened in Grandfather's cave, thinking about Haechi's growl and the dokkaebi's swinging club. I press my hands over my face and push my fingers against my eyes as if that would stop all the nightmares that have become my reality.

What should I do? Ignore everything like Dad suggests and hope it all will magically disappear? Or follow Grandfather's advice and call Master Kim? I dig into my pocket and pull out the note. Master Kim's address is here in Myeong-dong. I bite my lip.

No, I think. *It's too late.* I'll call in the morning. "I'm going to get some space," I announce, standing.

"You just got here," Marc says, but I'm already walking.

I can't believe I risked eternal punishment from Dad for this. I could've stayed home and been this miserable. I weave my way to the other side of the coffee shop and slip into a booth where it's quiet and I can think clearer.

After a few minutes, I debate whether to head back to my friends or go home when Marc waltzes over with that lazy grin on his face, holding a plate with cheesecake.

"I come bearing gifts." He slides across from me. "Will this offering be enough for my forgiveness?"

I frown. Forgiveness for what? Then I remember I'm supposed to be mad at him for teasing me about my dress.

"Depends," I say. "What flavor of cheesecake?"

"Ah." His eyebrows rise, pleased. "She gives me a test. I live for tests."

His delight in academics is almost sickening. I pretend to scrutinize the cake and then pick up the fork, cut out a slice, and taste it. Chocolate. Creamy. Totally delicious.

"Okay. You can stay."

He smiles.

"You have two minutes," I say.

"You're brutal."

"We all have our specialties."

He takes the fork from my hand and stabs a bite of cheesecake.

"That fork has my germs on it," I say, loving the way his hair keeps falling over his eyes.

"It's my superpower. Eating after people and not getting sick."

"And here I thought it was your brains."

"Nope." He points the fork at me. "That's my cover."

I steal the fork and point it back at him. "So why are you really here?"

"I wanted to get a better look at your new bow."

"Are you mocking me? You'd better not be."

He raises his hands in the air, his gold ring glinting in the light. "I swear on every perfect cheesecake in the universe." But then the humor leaves his green eyes and his gaze centers on my face. I nearly forget to breathe. "I have a fascination with old things. They're far more interesting than shopping or ski parties."

"Okay. I guess you can stay for another two minutes." He's so cute. That's got to count for something. I slide my phone to the center of the table.

He puts on his glasses. "It's hard to see much from a picture. Did your grandfather tell you which period it's from?"

"No. I suppose I could ask."

"Cool engraving of the Blue Dragon." He rotates the phone, scrutinizing it. "I'd like to see it."

"You think by looking at it you could tell what time period it came from?"

He grins. "What do you think?"

I give him the evil eye as he studies it closer.

"Yep. Definitely the Blue Dragon," he says. "There's a legend about a bow and the Blue Dragon. Something about using it against an immortal."

I lean forward. "Really? Do you remember the name?"

"I don't." He hands back my phone. "I'll check it out for you if you'd like."

"That'd be great."

"It'll cost you, of course."

Before I can give him a good punch in the shoulder, my phone beeps with a text from Michelle. It reads: **Going 2 check out the shops. U coming?**

I see Michelle and Lily heading out the door, motioning me to follow.

"I think you'd better go," Marc says. "They look pretty serious."

He's right. I should go and not let crazy mythical creatures control my life.

"Shopping is serious," I say, and scoot out of the booth. "See you at school?"

He nods, and I love the way he looks at me, warm and interested. My heart does a little jig as I rush out the door.

Winter bites my face, nearly taking my breath away. The street has been blocked off from cars to allow vendors to set up tables and carts filled with jewelry, clothes, and food. The cart lanterns swing in the icy wind, illuminating the night with a ghostly glow.

Flurries of snow stick to my jacket and cling to my eyelashes. I blink them away and start weaving through the crowd in pursuit of my friends. When I come to an intersection, I swivel in a circle, searching for them through the snowy mist. Then I spot them down the street on my left. Lily's plaid jacket and Michelle's purple jacket stand out among the usual black dress of the pedestrians. I take off, yelling their names, but the music blaring from the karaoke bar drowns out my voice. Even though I'm shoving my way through the crowd and practically jogging, I can't seem to catch up to them. Are they purposely ignoring me?

They take another turn, this time down a side street where

the brick and concrete buildings all seem to have grown together in a winding warren. Where are they going? My hair is damp from the snow. I stop to put on my hat and gloves, but when I look up, they're gone. This must be some kind of trick. I yell out their names, but the wind sucks away my words.

I spin in a circle on my boot heels. The shadows shift by the automatic parking garage. Someone screams from the dark window in the hotel above. Or was that a laugh? The wooden telephone poles lining the street groan in the wind.

Voices seem to whisper in my ears. "Princess. *Princessss.*"

Terror streaks through me. I fumble for my phone. It falls into the snow and with it a familiar piece of paper. I crouch down and pick it up. It's the note from Grandfather with Master Kim's phone number and address.

Forget politeness. I'm going to find this guy.

I punch the address into the GPS on my phone. The system recognizes it, indicating it's only a block away. I take off at a sprint down the street, hoping Master Kim will be working late.

When I turn into the next intersection, the streetlights flicker. Behind me I hear something breathing. I whip around. Nothing. Puffs of cold air cloud up in front of my face as I stare into the emptiness. Or is it emptiness? I squint at what appears to be a breathy cloud under the awning of an abandoned store.

"Eye of the Tiger" slices the silence. My phone. I press it to my ear, backing away from the cloud.

"Hello." My voice shakes.

"Annyeong haseyo," a woman's voice says. I realize the voice in the phone is also coming from behind me.

I whip around to see a woman, a phone against her ear,

standing at the gate of a walled house across the street. She's wearing a pair of black pants and a thick gray shawl.

"Jae Hwa," she says. She knows my name? "I see you found your way. Your grandfather said you would come."

How does she know these things?

"Come. Come quickly!" she says, waving her arms toward the warm light of her home. "The night is full of evil spirits."

I don't need to hear anything else. I race through the iron gate, and the lady practically shoves me up the stone stairs, slamming the wooden door behind me.

Only after I step inside do I wonder if I can even trust this woman.

CHAPTER 10

I face the stocky lady, now removing her shawl, and clutch my phone tighter. She's about my height, dressed in polyester pants and a thick blue sweater. Everything is simple about her except the shimmer of gold from the ring hanging on a chain around her neck.

She seems harmless enough. Then she turns, and I see the scar etched across the left side of her face, as if some beast had ripped its claws through her skin, and I shudder, remembering Haechi's claws. Her black hair is braided and pulled harshly into place, giving her face a tight, hard expression that matches the steel in her eyes.

"I am Master Kim. I will train you in what I know."

She's Master Kim? I study the crumpled paper in my hand. Behind her is a painting of the Tiger of Shinshi, just like the one on Grandfather's note. In fact, it looks a lot like the mural in Grandfather's house. This has to be the right place.

The room has an odd scent, so strong I want to plug my nose.

"How do you know my grandfather?"

She mumbles something in Korean and then: "He did not tell you who I am, did he?"

I swallow hard, my feet rooted to the floor.

A shadow slithers across the geometric-styled window screen. I lean forward. What was that? Its shape is snakelike but much, *much* bigger. I blink at the impossible. My body goes as stiff as a breaking board with the thought of what could be outside.

Master Kim crosses the room, grabs a cloak and two flashlights. She tosses the cloak over my shoulders and jams the flashlight in my free hand. My other still holds my cell phone.

"Should keep you warm," she says, and yanks back a Chinese carpet to reveal a trapdoor beneath it. She lifts it by the attached bronze ring.

I stare down at the blackness below me. She shines a flashlight into its depths, and even though I spot a wooden ladder, I back away, unwrapping my scarf from around my neck. The room suddenly feels hot and too small.

She jerks her head toward the black hole and lifts her eyebrows as if to say "Any day now!"

Yeah right, crazy lady. Like I'm going to leap into a dark hole of my own free will. Not after everything that has already happened today.

Which reminds me, I should call Dad.

Problem. I'm supposed to be in bed.

"Now, Jae Hwa!" Master Kim yells. "He has sent his dragons!"

She knows my name. Part of something scaly from outside slides under the door. I rub my eyes.

Whatever is outside wants in.

"The ginseng is not working." Master Kim yanks on my arm, nearly ripping it out of the joint. "Stubborn child! I am taking you belowground. His powers are useless there without the light."

Claws, golden and sharp, tear apart the screen.

I dive for the hole.

The wooden ladder feels smooth and cold under my palms. Crazed Ginseng Lady ducks in right after me, her flashlight clenched between her teeth. The trapdoor slams closed, enveloping us in darkness except for the bobbing beam from her flashlight. I hear the clink of metal. I hope it's a strong lock.

Would that keep us safe?

Soon my boots hit the ground, which is slimy and gooey. I click on my flashlight and pan it around me. We're in a narrow passageway hewed out of concrete. Sure enough, the goo my boots cling to is mud combined with stuff reeking of dead fish and urine. Disgusting.

Above, claws rake across the trapdoor, and the dragon shrieks. My heart catches in my throat, and suddenly the goo isn't so bad.

Master Kim brushes past me and takes off down the passageway. The cold is bone-chilling, and I'm suddenly glad for the cloak she gave me.

I hurry after her. "What is this place?"

"An old North Korean tunnel discovered by the government six years ago. President Lee Myung-bak had it blocked off and restricted. Since the president did not want his people to know how close they had come to invasion, it was kept quiet."

Her flashlight casts creepy shadows that skitter off the rounded walls. I shiver despite the cloak, but she continues on unfazed. "My cousin's husband is the subway overseer. She mentioned it to me. I knew an underground escape from Haemosu was exactly what I needed, so I bought a house just above one of the vents. The perfect hideout. Most do not know this tunnel exists, and those who do have pretended it into nonexistence."

We reach an iron gate. I shine my flashlight through the bars and over the pebbled ground, but my beam doesn't reach far enough into the gaping blackness.

"Where does that go?" I ask.

"North Korea. You do not want to go there. Trust me."

I couldn't agree more.

Ginseng Lady focuses on a tiny square door set into the rock wall to our right. She spins the combination lock, its click echoing through the hallway. Then she leans into the door and shoves it open, the bottom scraping in aged resistance. I shine my light back the way we came, peering through the gloom and hoping my light won't catch a glint of those shiny scales I saw above.

"The dragons will not follow us here," she says, and steps inside. "They need the power of light to sustain them, and their golden claws can only keep the power for so long. Other creatures perhaps, but tonight we do not matter to them."

I gulp at the thought of other creatures and duck inside. My boots trail sludge across the concrete floor.

Master Kim sits down on a wooden bench and slips off her

shoes and enters another room. I mimic her actions, sidestepping the mud with socked feet.

The next room is the exact opposite of that dreary tunnel. The walls are lined with murals of the Korean countryside and native animals like the bear, tiger, and crane. The floor is wooden rather than concrete, and electricity lights up rice-papered lanterns attached to the walls. At one end stands a rack of weapons and Tae Kwon Do *doboks*, while the other holds scrolls and books lined up kind of like in Grandfather's cave. It's quite large, too, about half the size of my Tae Kwon Do gym.

Master Kim is already over by the rack and choosing a *dobok* to put on. She changes right in front of me. I avert my eyes and study a mural with a giant black bear.

She ties a black belt around her waist and looks at me expectantly. "Get dressed."

"So you're going to train me?"

"We have little time."

Obviously, this lady isn't into formal introductions. I riffle through the tunics to find something close to my size. Some of these look yellowed, as if they've been there for a very long time. I find one, undress, and slip it on. When I finish, I see Master Kim is talking on the phone.

"You owe me this time with her," Master Kim says into the phone.

Then, noticing I'm dressed, she holds out her phone to me, the cord tangling up around her arm, and says, "I have arranged with your father to take you home. We need all the time we can get. Would you like to talk to him?"

I stare dumbly at her. "What!" I whisper. "You told him I was here? He doesn't know I've left the house."

"He already knew. He's been searching for you for the last hour and called me to help."

I'll be grounded for eternity. I think I'll delay the inevitable. "I can't talk to him."

"Best not to mention the dragons," she says, handing me the phone. "It may not go well for you."

I push away the phone. "I'm not talking to him." Then I look at her more closely. "Wait. How do *you* know my dad?"

"Listen, young lady." Crazed Ginseng Lady takes my hand and puts the phone into it. "If you do not talk to him, I will never train you. And trust me. You want me to train you."

She's got a point. Besides, it's not as if Master Park at my old *dojang* is keen on me coming back. I put the phone to my ear. "Dad?"

"Jae Hwa," he says. "What you did, sneaking out like that, you should be ashamed of yourself!"

"I know." I twist the black belt around my waist. "I just wanted to be with my friends."

"Eun will take you home, and don't you dare leave her. Do you understand, young lady?"

Eun. Wasn't that the name Dad mentioned back at the cave? "Who is this lady? How do you know her?"

He sighs. "I should have introduced you two when we first arrived in Korea. I'm partly to blame. She's your aunt."

I gape at Ginseng Lady.

"I know this is a bit of a shock," Dad continues. "Eun and I have just gotten back on speaking terms again, even though she sides with Abeoji. Promise me you'll come home after you have some time together."

I somehow mumble out a yes before I hear the dial tone.

"You're my aunt," I say.

"Yes." And there's relief in her voice, as if she's glad the truth is out. She places her palm on mine. It's cold. "In fact, I would rather you call me Komo. How does that sound?"

"Komo." It means "aunt on the father's side." It could work. "But why didn't Dad ever talk about you before?"

"Time is against us, ticking away every breath you take," she says. "You are here to train and learn."

She moves to the far wall and bows. I bow in return, but, barely before I position myself, she charges and whips out a jumping front kick.

My instincts take over. I jerk back and then meet her front jab with a block. She spins and back kicks. I grab her leg and shove her to the ground. She leaps up before I have a chance to pin her in place and struts around me, her chin up. Well, if that's how it's going to be, I can strut, too. I might not have feathers, but I can be a peacock.

"Haemosu is all-powerful in his territory in the Spirit World," she says, and then grunts to whip out a roundhouse. I'm ready and sidestep around her quick and light. "But in our world he is powerless. He can't even maintain a physical form."

"So why should I worry about him?" I ask, bouncing on my toes.

"Because he brings small amounts of power from his world through objects such as his dragon's claws or amulets. He uses our sunlight to help him travel about. My guess is he will seek you out during daylight."

She turns to face me again. I see the attack and land a front kick, planting it directly at her chin.

She stumbles backward slightly, her eyes widening. "Not bad," she says. "The best I have seen in a long time."

But then she does a move I've never seen. It's like watching a movie. She leaps up, spins and double kicks, one foot after the other knocking at my shoulder and nose. Pain shoots through my face, and blood spurts through the air.

I fall, my turn to be surprised. I expect her to land on her butt, the way her legs are stretched out in front of her, but she folds over her torso and flips backward and onto her feet.

Unbelievable.

My nose burns, wet and sticky. But I don't care, because I've found someone who truly is a master. Someone I can learn from. My heart skips. My fingers twitch. She tosses me a cloth, and I wipe my nose clean, willing the room to focus after being knocked so hard. I'll probably have black eyes, and faintly I wonder if I've broken my nose again.

She motions with her palms upward, fingers bending for me to stand back up, and makes the ready position. "There will be no rest for you tonight. At the first rays of light Haemosu will once again search for you. And you must be ready for him."

I pull myself up and take my stance. "But what about those dragons in your house?" I ask. "They were trying to get in, and it was dark out."

She attacks with a side jab. I block. "There are three different categories in the Spirit World."

"Categories?" *Why is everything about the Spirit World so confusing?*

"Those creatures that only belong in our world, those that belong only in the Spirit World, and those that can go back and forth for limited periods of time.

"Haemosu and his five dragons are restricted to the Spirit World. But he has found a way around this. He fills their scales and claws with sunlight so they can hunt. But as time progresses, the light in their scales fades, and so does their power. They must return to the Spirit World when their power is depleted."

We spar for another ten minutes and then she has me do one hundred push-ups and two hundred sit-ups. After I've finished I lie flat on the floor, panting. She grabs me by the arm and leads me to a small table in the corner of the room to sit on a silk cushion. I'm sweaty and bloody, unlike her. Every hair is still neatly tucked into her braid. No sweat on her forehead.

"The Spirit World exists," she continues. "But we live in a very busy, noisy, and hurried world. Too modern to hear Good calling. Too rushed to feel the pull of Evil."

She pours hot tea from a tiny celadon teapot while I consider her words. So maybe Kumar's multiple-dimensions theory is legit.

"Why can't this Haemosu get over his obsession or choose some other family? Am I that unlucky?"

"Luck, fate, chance—whatever you want to call it—has nothing to do with it." She sips her tea and studies the mural of the crane beside our table. "We are given moments, and we must choose what to do with them. This is your moment."

"You're not telling me that this is some kind of destiny thing."

She laughs. "No. Your destiny is up to you." Then her eyes

become hard, like onyx. "If you are to defeat Haemosu, you must let me teach you what I know."

"You want me to defeat a demigod?" I lean forward in spite of myself. "Is that even possible?"

"Your grandfather showed you the generational chart, yes?"

I shake my head. She pulls out a charred scroll. My eyes widen. "How did you get that? It's one of the scrolls I saved from the fire in Haraboji's cave, isn't it?"

"The very one," she says. "The immortals must have guided you to save the right scrolls. Your haraboji stopped by this afternoon. He explained what happened and how you might show up. I have analyzed all the data so far, and this is what I have."

I scan the generational chart. "This is the same list I saw on the pagoda."

Komo looks at me oddly, and I explain what had happened. "So who is Sun?" I ask, pointing to her name. It has a dash next to it. "She was your sister, wasn't she? Haemosu took her."

"I searched for her and failed. But I will not let him win again. This time he will be stopped." She takes my hand in hers and clenches it with such fierceness that I believe her.

"Your mother and I kept in touch while she was alive because we were good friends," Komo says. "When I grew determined to stop Haemosu, your father forbade us to speak to each other. He is convinced that your grandfather lost his sanity after Sun, your other aunt, was taken by Haemosu. Your father is furious that I believed your grandfather. So this must be our secret. Otherwise he will never let you come see me."

Secret. I smile, liking the sound of that. And I love the idea of getting an instructor all to myself who can really push me to my limits.

"So is there a way to break the curse?"

"You will only have a chance if you fight him in our world, not the Spirit World," she says. "His powers are far greater there."

"That pinnacle that I went to," I say. "Was that the Spirit World?"

"I believe so." She takes a sip of tea and sighs. "Our ancestors discovered that only the firstborn unmarried girls are taken. They solved that by having the girls marry before fifteen, and often it worked. But then about a hundred years ago, all the grooms-to-be suddenly went missing. So they stopped that practice because two people were lost rather than one. Those were hard times for the oldest daughter, knowing she would never marry, waiting until her fifteenth birthday to be kidnapped. To have a daughter was a curse. It was almost better if she had never lived."

The image of a girl standing next to a thatched-roof house fills my mind, her *hanbok* waving in the wind and tears streaming down her face. Haemosu rides in, surging out of the clouds, his chariot led by his five dragons, all gleaming like golden rays of the sun. He snatches the screaming girl into his chariot and soars back up into the clouds, his laughter sharp and hard like thunder.

"Jae Hwa?" Komo is staring at me, her eyebrows knitted together.

My muscles are all knotted up like they get when I'm about to face an opponent in a match. I shake off the vision and nod.

Komo continues, "Many, like your parents, do not believe

in Haemosu. But your grandfather is a believer. He pored over these scrolls to save my sister. Your father thought it was an obsession, and I suppose he was right. When Haemosu came to take Sun away, your grandfather stood in front, claiming Haemosu must fight him first. Your grandfather lost. Sun was taken. Haemosu let him live because sometimes it is more painful to be alive than dead."

Komo falls silent, and one tear trickles down her cheek. I trace the geometric pattern on the table, trying not to invade her reverie. She wipes her face dry and continues. "Your grandfather sent your father away to America to study at a university and told him never to return to Korea."

"Wait," I say. "I thought Dad chose to leave."

"He did, but your grandfather made it next to impossible for your father to stay. Of course, it did not help their relationship either. But your grandfather felt it was necessary. You see, Haemosu's power cannot reach other lands. All immortals are limited to their own lands. We thought it had worked."

"Because I'm sixteen?"

"You are older than any of the other girls. He has not bothered you until recently, right?"

"It started at the museum," I murmur half to myself. "In the sun banner. He caught my arrow. I think that's when he first showed up." She doesn't say anything, so I keep talking. "Then the next day this glittery guy attacked me."

"Haemosu."

"Yes, I suppose it was him. But then Haechi stopped him and saved me."

"*The* Haechi?" Komo leans back. "Are you sure about this?"

I shrug. "He said he'd been sent by Palk to protect me."

"Palk is involved? And he has sent Haechi? How peculiar." Komo stands and clears off the table. "We have no record of any other girls receiving help from other immortals. I will have to talk to your grandfather about this. It sounds like the immortals are up to something. I am not sure I like it."

Grandfather had already told her about my cave experience, so I finish off by telling her about the dokkaebi.

"He was trying to make a deal with me." Komo frowns, but I continue. "He was saying something about saving my ancestors by opening some tomb. And all kinds of weird stuff."

Komo sits very still, staring hard into space. "These are new developments. I will have to tell the others about this."

"Others?"

She pats my hand. "You must worry about saving yourself. You are what is important."

"Komo, how did I end up here tonight?"

She smiles a knowing smile, and I get the feeling there's a lot more to my aunt than she's letting on.

"You must come to my house every night. You have much to learn. Only travel here once darkness settles in, when his powers are weak. Even still, Haemosu will send whomever he can to do his dirty work. You must be careful."

"Every night? I have piles of homework! And Dad will wonder why my grades are dropping. What about once a week?"

"Jae Hwa." Her hands are back on her hips. "I have suggested to your father that as a punishment for sneaking out, you come each night for one month and work for me. He has agreed."

"Dad agreed?"

Komo smiles. "I might have mentioned how upset your mother would have been for keeping you from seeing me while you were here."

Figures. Any mention of Mom and Dad goes to mush. As much as I don't like Dad getting involved, I still don't like being told what to do. "Don't I have a say in this?"

"Yes. You have some choice."

I glance at the door. A part of me wishes I could just walk through it, wake up in my bed, and realize this is some bizarre dream. That different dimensions coinciding side by side is some fantasy.

But this is my chance to use my training to defeat something powerful and bring meaning to my life. This is an adventure I've always dreamed of.

My aunt clears her throat.

"I'm listening," I say.

"You can leave the country, although I doubt Haemosu would ever let you on that plane. Find someone to marry you and hope he does not die before you make it down the aisle. Haemosu gets terribly jealous of suitors."

"Komo." I give her an incredulous look. "I'm sixteen."

"Or stay and fight. But whatever happens." Her eyes narrow as thin as slivers. "Do *not* let him touch you."

"Why not?"

"Because it will be the beginning of the end. When he touches you, he will leave his mark. Think of it as the engagement rings they have in America. You are promised to him, and your courting begins."

"Like when Haemosu kept trying to convince Princess Yuhwa to come with him?"

"Exactly. Each time you meet, he will pull a little piece of your soul into his realm.

"Until you are no longer with us."

CHAPTER 11

Get married? Hardly.

Flee the country? I wish.

Fight off Haemosu? I wouldn't mind nailing him with one of my side kicks.

On Monday night I ask Komo at our training session if she thinks I could take down Haemosu. She doubles over, laughing hysterically.

Who knew I was such a comedian?

Escaping my "destiny" is all I've been thinking about in the three days since my first encounter with my crazy aunt.

"Jae, you should start brushing up on your Chinese. I need your help going through these scrolls. We might be able to find clues within these ancient texts."

"Brushing up?" I say. "More like learning for the first time. There's no way I can cram that much that fast."

"Are you not taking advanced Korean?"

"Yeah. Advanced *Korean*. We hardly spend any time on Classical Chinese."

When I get home, a nagging memory has me rummaging through the closet where we keep Mom's things until I find the leather-bound book I think might give me some answers. Mom's copy of *Samguk Yusa*.

It's so old, the string binding is frayed and the edges of the soft leather cover ragged. The rice paper makes the book light and bendable. It smells aged, with hints of dust and leather. I cradle it in my hands, remembering her and her passion for knowledge.

Finally, I turn the pages with the lightest touch of my forefinger until I find the legend of Haemosu. I try to wade through it but quickly realize the language is too difficult. I need help.

The next morning I wrap the book in a padded cloth and bring it to school. I arrive at IB Korean class early; and, with *Samguk Yusa* pressed against my chest, I march up to Mrs. Song's desk.

I lick my lips and dive in. "Mrs. Song, I know I'm failing this class, but I'm determined to improve my grade."

Mrs. Song looks up over her glasses. "I'm pleased to hear this, Miss Lee. But remember, you only have three more weeks before the end of the quarter. I'm not sure it's possible."

I take a deep breath and plaster on my sweetest smile. "This book is one of my mom's treasures." I place it on her desk. Her eyebrows rise, and she sets down the purple pen she uses to grade with. I continue, "It's a rare edition of *Samguk Yusa*, written in Classical Chinese."

"I've never seen such a book," she says. "This is your mother's?"

"*Was* my mother's. She's, uh, dead now." I swallow. Even though it's been four years, it's still hard to say the words. "But I can't read it, obviously, since my Chinese sucks. I was wondering if I could translate the myth of Haemosu and Princess Yuhwa for extra credit. Maybe you could give me some starting points or a reference guide."

With delicate fingers, Mrs. Song flips through the book, every once in a while glancing up at me over her glasses.

"Fascinating," she says. "I'm impressed at your creativity in choosing such an unusual extra credit assignment. This is exactly what the International Baccalaureate Program is seeking in their students. But why, may I ask, did you choose this particular myth?"

If she only knew. I shrug casually. "It's a family favorite."

"In that case, I agree to your proposal." Mrs. Song opens her filing cabinet and hands me a packet. It's an instruction manual for translating Chinese into English. "This should give you a starting point. Read it tonight, make an initial attempt at the first page, and see me tomorrow."

I practically glide to my seat, already skimming through her packet; but as I do, I realize this isn't going to be a one-night project. This is going to take time. A *long* time.

And time has become my enemy.

Class begins, and I tuck the packet into my backpack, the elation of my small victory dissipating. I wrap up the book and gaze around the room at my classmates. With each passing day, I feel that tug, that need to stop Haemosu's madness. I don't know if Komo and Grandfather are right, that I'm the one who has to make this happen; but somewhere deep inside it's as if I've been waiting for this all my life. Still, if Dad actually believed me about Haemosu, all this insanity could be left behind. We could move back to L.A. and then I wouldn't have to learn Chinese, make new friends, or fall head over heels for a guy that Dad will forbid me to date.

Last night I'd mentioned the *moving* word to Dad while he was practicing his putting in the hallway.

"Moving?" He'd put one finger up to silence me and focused on the tiny white ball on his portable putting green. "I can't deal with that right now."

"Dad!" I'd said. "Are you listening to me? Or is that golf ball more important that I am?"

He'd gone to putt the ball, but I'd bent down and snatched it up.

"Dad, I'm serious," I'd said, crossing my arms. "We need to talk about this, and you're never around. Do you think Grandfather might be telling the truth about this Haemosu thing?"

He'd jerked his head up. "You're not still thinking about your grandfather's crazy stories?"

"I know. It's bizarre. But what if he's right? Doesn't that worry you even a little?"

"Jae Hwa," he'd said, pulling me closer by the hand, "your grandfather has been 'seeing' things for years. Ever since—"

"Sun?"

Dad had straightened, leaning on his golf club. "He told you that?"

"Sort of."

Dad stared out the window. "Sun went missing when I was a senior in high school. She was dating a foreigner. A white guy from South Africa."

Oh great, I remember thinking. *Just what I need.* "Dad. Just because someone isn't Korean doesn't mean he's bad to date."

Dad had set his club against the wall and dug into his pocket, pulling out a thick silver-linked chain. "The police looked everywhere for her. The last time anyone saw Sun, she was with him. I printed out a thousand pictures of her and handed them to everyone I came across. We alerted the newspapers, and the news channel even mentioned her. She was never found. Except for this."

Dad held out his palm. A broken silver pendant attached to a chain was cupped inside. I'd seen this before. This was the other object hidden inside the black pouch with Mom's wedding ring.

"It was the necklace I got her for her fifteenth birthday."

"You think the foreigner killed her?"

He had cleared his throat as he stuffed the chain back into his pocket. His face had a pained look, and I wanted to help him somehow; but instead I just stood there, stiff and uncertain. "Your grandfather blamed it on supernatural beings. I think it was his way of dealing with her loss. Make it less his fault for letting her go out with that guy."

"But it wasn't Grandfather's or that guy's fault! It was Haemosu. Dad, I know it."

Dad had rubbed his forehead. "I don't know what to think anymore."

"So, you don't believe any of the old stories?" I'd said. "What about that evidence Grandfather had in the cave? What about the stories from our family?"

"Evidence? I'm not sure I'd call it that. Everyone has their way of dealing with things. His way isn't mine and that's fine, but there's something else you need to know."

"Okay," I'd said.

"I'm glad you're finally getting time with your aunt. It was wrong of me to have kept you from meeting her. I was worried that she would get you wrapped up in those stories as well. Your grandfather somehow convinced her that his delusions were true. She's spent her whole life seeking a phantom that doesn't exist. And what does she have to show for it? She's never married. She lives like a hermit. Don't let either of them ruin your life, too."

Now, sitting here in class, Dad's words bounce back and forth in my head like a sparring match. There's no way Dad is going to let me leave the country. I see that now.

Komo's suggestion to convince Dad to let me get married or run away seems ridiculous, but what other choice do I have? Outside the classroom, winter howls, and the barren cherry tree branches shift and bend to its force. I wonder how much more of my family's insanity I can handle.

My eyes wander from my vocabulary list and scan the room for possible husbands to keep me from focusing on reality. It's comical to think about it. Me. Sixteen. Married.

I mean, there's Jared; he's kind of cute, but his breath always stinks. Tyler's a definite possibility, but he's too tall. I'm not an expert on kissing, but I think it would be awkward to kiss someone so high up. He'd have to have a bendable giraffe's neck to make it work. I snort at the thought.

"What are you snickering about?" Michelle whispers as she slides in beside me when Mrs. Song isn't looking. We usually share the same table so it's easy to squeeze close and gossip, but I've been sitting by myself lately.

"I'm choosing my husband." I smile deviously.

Her eyes bug out. "You're not going all Korean on me."

I choke to keep from laughing. In Korea, there are still some parents who arrange marriages for their kids. I can't imagine being set up to marry someone I've only met a couple times at a dinner date.

"Well, after you two deserted me Saturday night, I decided I needed some type of companionship. So I'm on the hunt," I say. "Where did you two go after you left the Coffee Bean? I looked everywhere for you."

Her face brightens. "You did? We thought you decided not to come. And you didn't answer any of my texts."

"That's weird."

"Okay, truth time. Are you ditching us as friends or what?"

"No!" I practically yell, which draws the attention of everyone in the class and a frown from Mrs. Song. "It's family stuff. I'm hoping things will smooth out soon."

"So does that mean you'll still be roommates with Lily and me on the ski trip this weekend?"

Guilt swirls through me. I feel as if I've totally been neglecting Michelle and Lily. Every time they ask me to do something, I'm always saying no these days.

Then I think about my aunt. She's totally against the ski trip, especially since it's outside of Seoul in the mountains. I thumb through the edges of my notebook. What should I do?

"Marc will be there," Michelle says slyly. "Plenty of chances for alone time."

I roll my eyes, but I can't stop the smile curling up. What would it be like for his hand to touch my face and our bodies to press against each other?

What would it be like to kiss him?

"Fine," I say. "I'll go."

"Now that's more like it." Michelle grins and heads back to her seat.

After class, as I weave my way through the crowded hallway to my locker, everything bad that happened last Saturday night seems to have melted away. Just the thought of leaving the city lifts a weight off me. For the last three days I've done exactly what Komo told me to do: stayed out of the sunlight and not wandered places alone. I trained with her for the last two out of three nights, even when Michelle and Lily invited me over to study for the IB bio exam. I didn't mind so much because she taught me a couple of her special moves.

Besides, if this Haemosu guy really was interested in me, he'd have come after me by now. I'm sure of it.

CHAPTER 12

The air smells like pine, and it's so fresh and clean as I step off the school bus at Yongpyong Ski Resort that my blood starts pumping. I've only been living in Seoul for six weeks, but already I've gotten used to the smog and belch of city buses. Here in the mountains it's rugged, with silver snow that sparkles like mounds of sugar.

There are ninety of us juniors pouring out of the buses and into the parking lot, so Michelle and I have to push and shove our way to the luggage pile to pick up our bags. I let my eyes stray, looking for Marc, but I don't see him. He rode in a different bus with Kumar and Lily, and I haven't seen him since. I imagine him sitting with Min and feel slightly ill.

Once we collect everything, we follow the mass down the brick walkway lined with waist-high stone walls into the hostel where our group is staying.

The hostel is a three-story European-styled building with alternating white and brick walls and peaked gables, reminding me of a Swiss chalet. With the jagged, white-peaked mountains and forested hills, it is like stepping into a European fairy tale.

Inside, the lobby is sparse, with white-tiled floors, white walls, and a wooden ceiling. I notice Mr. Carlson at the long reception desk checking us all in, so Michelle and I find a place to sit until Lily and Kumar discover us.

It doesn't take long for Lily, her long blond hair streaming behind her, to spot us. She literally runs into my arms. "I'm so glad you decided to come. This is going to be the best trip ever," she announces, practically bouncing up and down. "I just know it."

I stand there stiffly and clear my throat. My family doesn't hug (unless someone's secret cave goes up in flames), so I'm not sure how to handle this.

Kumar waves his hands in a hug-like motion while mouthing something that looks like *Hug her.* I manage to pat her back, and as she pulls away, I give her my brightest smile.

Mr. Carlson comes around and hands us the key to our room, where we deposit our bags before heading to the slopes. I've yet to spy Marc, which makes me wonder if he actually came at all. Outside, my boots crunch and sink into the snow as Michelle, Lily, and I take the shoveled path to the Dragon Plaza to rent our skis.

Michelle's eyes flick over to our left. "So when are you going to make your move?"

I follow her gaze to the Dragon Plaza. It's a mammoth ski house, designed similarly to our hostel but with a whole lot more stone, glass, and peaks.

Michelle nudges me. "Not the lodge. *Him*."

The "him" she is talking about is Marc, leaning against one of the lodge's massive white pillars and hanging out with the high school guys.

He came. But what unnerves me is that he isn't laughing and joking with his buddies. He's looking at me, hands jammed in his pockets, and his black ski jacket flaps open to reveal a gray sweater underneath.

A thrill shoots through me.

"Are you just going to stand there?" Michelle asks.

I've somehow gotten myself into such a wreck that I know if I talk to him I'll make a complete fool of myself. I scuttle ahead of the girls, now giggling at my back, doing my best not to look at Marc as I pass by. Silently I remind myself over and over that I don't have time for a relationship. Somehow I'm going to get back to L.A. and leave all this behind. No hard good-byes. No heartaches.

When I enter the ski rental shop the bell dings, signaling my arrival. It's warm in here from the kerosene heating lamps scattered around the room. The smell of it, mixed with leather and worn boots, makes me a little dizzy. I head to the counter and order my ski boots as Michelle sidles up next to me.

"Where's Lily?" I ask.

"Talking with Kumar," Michelle narrows her eyes. "You're in denial. You like him."

"I thought you were a peace activist, not a matchmaker." I pick up my skis and head to the bench to change boots.

When Michelle sits next to me, I find myself bristling even before she opens her mouth.

"I can't deal with boys," I explain. "Things are too complicated right now."

"I'm sorry." She fumbles with her boot clip. "I know I need to stop trying to control everyone's lives and putting everyone in neat, perfect boxes. I just want you to be happy. You've seemed so—"

"Stressed?"

"Yeah." She gives me a half smile. "Plus, with my love life now a complete failure, I needed to—I don't even know how to explain this."

"You want mine to be a success."

"Yeah." Michelle wrinkles her nose and shakes her head. "I know. It's lame. But if I can be a matchmaker, then I don't have to think about my love life."

"I'm sorry about Charlie."

"Tell me about it." She bends down to redo her straps, but I think she's just trying to hide her tears. "I miss him. It was the hardest thing ever to leave him when we moved to Seoul. But I thought we were strong enough that nothing could tear us apart. I was so stupid."

"Is the pain worth it?" I ask.

She hesitates. "I don't know." Then she clasps my hand and smiles at the ceiling. "Yeah, it is."

After I've jammed my feet into my ski boots, the two of us wobble outside into the sun. Komo would flip if she knew I was out here on such a clear, sunny day. But all that seems so far away. I suck in a gulp of mountain air and feel as if I've finally escaped it all.

I clip on my skis. It's been a long time since I've skied. I glide forward, wobble, and fall onto my side. Okay, so maybe it's been longer than I remembered.

Michelle and Lily laugh from behind as I brush off snow and pull my hat back into place. I join in their laughter and manage to stand up just as Marc skis over. He swooshes like a pro as snow sweeps in a wave in his wake. I absolutely can't let him see me teeter-totter. So I lean on my ski pole and try to act all nonchalant by whipping out a quick wave and a casual nod.

"Hey." He lifts his ski goggles to his forehead. "I see you decided to come after all. Don't forget you've got hot chocolate duty with me tonight."

Michelle and Lily casually glide away to the lift, which it doesn't look like I'll be attempting for some time. I notice a sly grin on Michelle's face. I want to scream obscenities at her. *No!* I want to scream at their backs. *Don't leave me here. Alone. With him!*

But I can't. I have to pretend I'm completely fine hanging out with Hotness here.

"You want to go down some routes together?"

As in the bunny slopes? Sure. That'd be a blast, Mr. Ski Goggles. "No, I think Michelle, Lily, and I are teaming up."

"Really? Looks like they're getting on the lift."

And so they are. Craptastic. I try to run after them, but my skis cross, and I face plant into the snow. I cringe, not from the blast of cold that hits my face, but from my idiotic fall. At least the snow will have cooled my raging bonfire cheeks.

I lift my head and see a black-gloved hand reaching out. Any dignity I had five seconds ago vanished with that dive. I grab his hand and let him help me up, but then my boot snaps out of the ski and I fall into Marc's arms.

He steadies me. My face smashes into his chest. He's so close, and I don't pull away as fast as I should. But then, he doesn't either. I press my hands against him to steady myself and feel his chest under my palm. My legs are Jell-O.

"You need to unsnap your ski," he says. "You're tangled."

His face is close to mine, and I notice he's got a slight dimple on his chin, too. He'd be at the perfect height to lean down and kiss me. The noise around me blurs, and all I can focus on is his lips and breath and presence.

Then I remember my aunt's words about Haemosu's jealousy. Would he hurt Marc?

I jerk back so fast, I stumble again. This time I must have turned the right way, because the ski sets me free and I can now wobble around like a normal person.

His eyebrows cock up. "Maybe I could give you a lesson."

Tempting. "Well, I'm sure you'll be hanging out at the Black Diamonds, so don't let me slow you down."

Some kids by the lodge call out Marc's name. It's Ryan and gorgeous Min of the Long Legs. Marc looks at me as if for some positive sign to stay, but I turn back to my skis and ignore him. He glides away, and somehow I manage my way, alone, to the ski lift.

Dad would've been pleased, and I should feel victorious with that sense of euphoria from overcoming temptation. I don't. My heart is like the inside of a bamboo stalk: hollow. The ski lift jerks and I slide off the bench, but the cold metal bar keeps me clamped in place. Wind rushes across my hot cheeks, and I close my eyes.

I almost kissed Marc. Out of the blue. In front of everyone. What had I been thinking? What must Marc think of me? My face burns as I remember how close our lips came to touching.

Pine tree forests spread below. They look soft and mossy, and I reach down my hands as if to brush my fingertips across the tips of them. I spot the sprawling Dragon Plaza below and the little black dots of the skiers. Wait a sec. Why does that other ski lift beside me deposit skiers off at intervals like a conveyer belt? Mine sure doesn't. It just keeps going and going and freaking going. My heart sinks.

I'm such a moron! This lift doesn't go to the beginner slopes. I'm headed directly for the black diamonds. I may be a black belt in Tae Kwon Do, but I'm definitely not a black belt in skiing.

The station to get off is fast approaching, and another thought hits me. I don't know how to get off this thing! I search through my memories. I come up with nothing. Knowing my luck, I'll break a bone by falling off the lift. I'll be the laughing-stock of the entire eleventh grade.

I brace myself as the bar lifts. The ski patroller standing there waves his arm, saying something I can only guess is "Get off, you idiot!"

I push myself and slide down the little incline. It takes me a few moments to realize I did it. But my elation is short-lived as my eyes take in the slope labeled *Rainbow Run* in front of me.

Cliff would be the more appropriate word.

People pay money to leap off of that? I wonder how they can allow condoned suicide. It can't be legal. Two skiers skim up to the edge of The Cliff, adjust their goggles, and disappear.

I glance around for another slope down, but I don't see any other way.

The Cliff it is. I suppose if I can wear a pink *hanbok* in front of a thousand people, I can leap off a cliff, too. I swish to the edge, and my heart squeezes so tight that my arms grow numb. And then my legs. And my brain.

No. I can't get scared over some stupid cliff. I'm better than that. I ease onto my bum—it's the only way—and as soon as I sit, snow seeps through my jeans and I wish I'd opted for snow pants. I focus on slithering down, my skis straight in front, and keeping my back against the ground. Inch by inch I grow closer to the bottom, which is all I can think about. Getting to the bottom. I'm at the edge, out of skiers' range, but I know any minute someone could come barreling into me.

I'm halfway down and nearly to the path below (which thankfully looks more like a ski run than my current suicide mission) when I hear someone calling my name above. I glance up. It's Marc and Gorgeous-Perfect-Body Min floating past in the lift. And they've spotted Wet-Butt Me. I wonder when this day of complete embarrassment will end. She snuggles in closer to Marc and points my way, a gloating smile on her face. My chest tightens, and I'm not sure if it has to do with the snuggling or my current situation. Probably both.

There's no way I'm letting him see me going down on my bottom. I jerk to a wobbly standing position and focus forward, but not before I see Marc's look of shock as he spots me.

There's only one thing to do to save my image. I dig my poles into the soft snow and push.

I ski straight down the last bit of The Cliff. My hair snaps across my face. The cold lashes against my cheeks. My nerves are totally fried. It's what I suppose flying might feel like, and oddly, I love it. The danger, the thrill, and the complete uncertainty of not knowing which bones I'll break this time.

I expect to flip head over heels when I hit the bottom. I bend my knees to take the impact and tuck my poles under my arms. I land on both skis, but I've got a huge problem. I'm flying in a bullet-straight path down the mountain. How do I stop? Do I cross my skis? Or plant my poles in somewhere and hold on?

There's a patch of trees to my left with clumps of bushes covered in snow. Possible landing gear, I decide. I tilt my body to the left and aim for the bushes.

I miss. A tree comes at me. I swerve to the right and then another quick left. It's like the scene in *Return of the Jedi* where Princess Leia is trying to escape the storm trooper on her speeder. Only I don't have Jedi reflexes.

I crash. And it's not in the bushes. I hit a rock that sends me tumbling and rolling until I smash into a pine tree. The forest whirls around me in blurry stars. My hand and ankle scream in agony. I lie flat in the snow, willing my body to ignore the pain like I do in Tae Kwon Do class. The ringing in my ears dulls, and I can think.

I've broken something.

No. I sit up and groan. I've broken two things: my wrist and ankle. Or maybe my ankle is just sprained. I want to hit something. I'm that angry about this stupid accident.

The wind tinkles a thousand chimes around me, and the trees waver like a mirage. I rub my eyes, wondering when the shock of the fall will fade away.

It doesn't. It only intensifies. Heat pricks my skin, burning as hot as my screaming wrist and ankle. I push against the trunk of the tree to stand, and its sticky sap clings to my hand.

A movement catches my eye through the shimmering forest. I peer up to find a man standing there, his maroon robes swirling around him in the pulsating light. The same man who stole my arrow that night at the museum.

Haemosu.

CHAPTER 13

I take in a sharp breath and lean against the tree for support. I know I should be freaking out; I know it's *him*, and he's got me trapped with my wrist and ankle probably broken. But for some reason I find myself spellbound.

"*Annyeong haseyo,* my princess," Haemosu says, a smile lighting his eyes, as warm as honey. "You are even more beautiful than I remembered." His hair is pulled back in a topknot that accentuates his high cheekbones. He has the air of a king.

Warmth drenches over me, and it's as if nothing could be more perfect than this moment. Somewhere deep in the back of my brain I remember how Komo said that my best chance to defeat Haemosu is in our world. How convenient for him that we meet when I'm practically crippled.

"You speak English?"

He chuckles. "Just one of my talents, dearest."

"Nice bow," I say, noticing his horn bow. "Hunting?" I wonder what kind of marksman he is. And if he's here to kill me.

"Ah, I knew you would like the bow. Do you wish to try it?"

"I'll pass." Why do I get the feeling he's trying to impress me? He hardly seems like the evil villain Grandfather makes him out to be. Maybe Grandfather and Komo are wrong about Haemosu. "I should be going."

I try to shuffle backward, using the tree for support. I grit my teeth, determined for him not to notice I'm injured.

"But I have been waiting so long for you." He reaches out his hand. I stare at his fingers, remembering Komo's warning not to touch him.

My breath quickens as he steps closer; his presence is overwhelming. His robe, decorated with dragons and gold-embroidered edging, brushes across the ground.

"Please. I insist." He unstraps the bow from his shoulder and holds it out to me. His smile is warm and inviting, and my defenses fall away.

"It's beautiful," I say.

The wood glimmers like gold, and I'm so intrigued that I reach out and lightly touch its surface. It tingles beneath my fingertips. I nearly forget that I should be running, not standing here mesmerized.

It won't be long before he realizes I'm injured and tries to take advantage of me. What would Grandfather and Komo want me to do?

Kill him, probably.

Could I do that? I stare into his honey-colored eyes, and I know I can't. There's a connection between the two of us that I can barely even understand. But it's there. I can feel it tug as if a hook has sunk deep within me. And even if I wanted to kill him, I couldn't possibly pull the string with my broken wrist.

"I should go," I somehow manage. Why is it so hard to say?

"Come with me. There is so much I wish to show you."

"No." Somehow I swallow down the yes that demands to be spoken.

"You will like what I have in store for you. I promise you this."

I squeeze my eyes closed as the pain in my wrist and ankle yanks at my consciousness. And something else. A desperation pulls at me.

To be with him. To follow him. To touch him.

"You don't even know what I like," I say.

"Well." He raises his chin. "Is this a challenge, my princess? Let me prove my worth."

Haemosu stretches his hand toward me. Heat crawls through my fingers, into my wrist, and then courses through my body all the way down to my toes. The pain in my body disappears.

"Now do you believe me?" he says.

I hold out my hand, my mouth gaping as I make a fist. No pain. I twirl my ankle and jump on it. Healed. Completely healed.

"Forget those lies your family has been telling you," he says. "I have the power to give you immortality. Follow me, and I will show you a place where time is left behind."

My wrist and ankle still sizzle with that odd healing sensation. I can hear Komo's voice telling me this is my chance to hurt him. But how can I hurt the person who's just healed me?

"I've already seen your land," I say, remembering that awful pinnacle. "I think I'll pass."

"What you saw was nothing compared to my palace. Come and see for yourself."

I peer around him, but all I can see is the snowy forest.

"So you will come, then. To the land of the wonderful dream." He extends his hand, and I take it without thinking. The instant we touch, it's as if a small electrical shock surges into my fingertips. With a flick of the wrist, he commands my consciousness, dragging me into darkness.

I'm falling.

Through an abyss of stars, swirling and rippling around me. And I know I'm not in the forest anymore, but in a space beyond time. Hot air brushes my face. I smell honeysuckle and strawberries, so sweet I can almost taste them.

The snow is replaced with tiny purple flowers scattered around my feet and stretching all the way to a bamboo grove. I swivel around, searching for Haemosu, and take in the rolling hills in the distance, spread with new rice, the tips spring green. He's nowhere in sight. The breeze kicks in again, and with it the scent of tangerines. The back of my neck pricks, and I know he's near. Then I hear hoofbeats and turn around. It's a buck, the sun glistening across its sleek brown coat. He bows his head and breaks into a run.

I feel oddly free in this place. And it seems so familiar. As if I've been away and now I'm home. All my pain has disappeared, and suddenly I'm a little girl again, running across the playground while Mom watches with a smile on her face.

My skin tingles, and I can feel something changing within me. I look down and realize my boots have vanished, replaced with hooves. My skin is now fur.

I'm no longer human. I'm a deer. The scents in the air are sharper: the moss below me, the smell of spring leaves.

Fear should be tearing at me, but it isn't. I feel liberated. I feel as if I was born to be here.

I take off and rush through the forest, chasing after the buck, ducking through the bamboo trees, and I'm faster than I ever imagined I could be. Soon I come to a small stream, rippling like liquid diamond. I leap over it to find that the buck has halted at a dirt path. I follow his gaze to a golden palace.

A voice whispers in my ears. It takes me a moment to realize it's the buck who's speaking.

"Just a little farther," he says.

Haemosu is the buck. And hearing him speak breaks the magic. I step back.

The buck moves toward me. "Do not be afraid," he says.

His form twists until he's no longer a buck: Haemosu again stands before me. There's a gleam in his eyes that I recognize: the look of a victor after he's won a sparring match.

He reaches out his hand again as he'd done before he healed me, but this time my vision blurs until the once-sharp scents fade and my body twists and contorts back to my human form. My stomach twists. Then my knees buckle, and I fall to the ground and throw up.

"It takes time and experience to adjust to the shift," Haemosu says. He hands me a silk towel.

"How did that happen?" I ask, my body still shaking. "I was a deer."

"Metamorphosis," he says. "Here we have the power to transform into anything we want to be. There is nothing more satisfying than experiencing the magic of my lands."

"I don't think your magic likes me very much," I say.

He takes my elbow and helps me stand. A look of yearning crosses his face as he cups my chin between his hands.

"I have searched and waited a thousand years for you, my princess, and now you are here. Finally we can be together, as is right."

I stare into his eyes and search for lies. But his voice soothes me, and I want to believe him, to sink into his arms and be his forever. All those worries Grandfather and Komo had seem silly and childish. I let them slide away.

He takes my hand, and I wonder if he said this to all my ancestors or if perhaps I am the one. The one destined to be with him. Our clasped hands begin to shine brighter and brighter, until I can see nothing else except their glow.

Images fill my mind: him carrying me in his arms through his realm, never watching my skin wrinkle or hair whiten. The thought of being his "forever" sends a thrill through me. I never thought that this was what I wanted; but now, holding his hand, I ache to be his. And the magic pulls at me. As if it's been missing from me my whole life.

The light draws itself into a liquid gold band that curls around my wrist. Five dragons bubble through the surface, contorting until they form a bracelet. I'm transfixed in his grasp as if he's numbed every muscle.

"Each dragon represents one of our meetings," he says. "Once all the eyes glow red, you will be mine forever."

I snap awake. What is *wrong* with me? Meeting him? *Forever?*

Komo said the only way to survive this was never to let him touch me. But I let him into my head. I've fallen into his freaking trap. So stupid!

"No!" I yell, and yank my arm away. My head clears, and I can see through the glow of his skin: a gray, wrinkled creature with sunken onyx eyes and a snarling mouth full of flicking tongues.

The true Haemosu without his glamour.

A monster of a man.

I scream in horror.

Haemosu disappears. The forest, once beautiful, now hangs low and gnarly; the branches are leafless.

I fell for his trap. I'm no different from any of my ancestors. Komo warned me, but I didn't listen.

I failed.

I sink to the ground, shaking. I have to pull myself together, but I can't get Haemosu's image out of my head. Those eyes. Those claws.

That's when I hear them.

Cries.

Groans.

The desperate, anguished sounds fill me with dread. I glance over my shoulder and realize the noises are coming through the brambles. I don't want to know what they are, but I feel compelled to find out.

My breath comes out heavy, cold, and wet against the gray world surrounding me. Once I pass through the brambles, I can see what used to be the palace. Its glory has vanished, replaced with crumbling stone walls, rotting wood pillars tumbled over on their sides, and the dust of maybe a thousand years.

The air reeks. A wooden gate with two doors as tall as a two-story house is still intact, and I see two massive bronze knockers: shimmering gold dragons, their tails twisted as if protecting a treasure.

A pale hand claws out from the top of the gate. Another from a crevice near a fallen guard tower. I catch a glimpse of a full arm along the tower and then a head pops up. I can't see the face through the strands of greasy black hair. Why are these people in this horrible place? Then I remember the dokkaebi's words. *Souls of the princesses cry, cry, cry.* Was he talking about these people? Are these my ancestors?

I jam my fist into my mouth to hide a muffled sob.

And run.

My heartbeat matches the thud of my boots slapping the hard-packed mud. The groans follow me as I search for where this nightmare began. Then I spot the stream. Dead fish scales and bones have replaced the diamonds that once were there, or maybe they were always bones.

I can't think about that now. All I can focus on is escape. I come to the bamboo grove and see where the light wavers and the trees appear split in half. Is that the door I came through?

A sound like something dragging through the mud reaches my ears.

"Princess! Help us. Don't leave us, Princess—"

I dive for the twisted light.

CHAPTER 14

I swallow a mouthful of snow as I lie flat, head deep in a snow-bank just beyond the ski slope. Even though the air is bitterly cold, it's fresh, and I suck in deep, chest-filling amounts. The pounding in my head slows, and I look around.

I'm back. From where? I don't know, but I want to kiss the ground I'm lying on and thank God I'm still alive.

I never believed in God or anything spiritual. When Mom was alive, she'd drag me off to church. I'd daydream. Text my friends. Anything but listen. Now I have so many questions. I'm desperate for answers. But she isn't here to give them. I'm finally ready to listen, but it's too late.

The snow I've fallen into has soaked through my jeans. I grasp handfuls of it and press it against my hot cheeks. That's when I realize I'm using my hand. I clasp it into a fist and unclasp it. No pain.

Scrambling to my feet, I jump. My ankle is healed, too. Hae-mosu really did it.

I cringe at the thought of those clawed hands touching me.

Why didn't Haemosu take me right then? Why am I still alive? What did he mean about courting? Is this his idea of torture?

Nothing makes sense. I want to scream.

Something rustles in the pines. A black form emerges through the trees, and I spin around and sprint in the opposite direction.

He can't take me. I won't let him.

"Jae! Jae!" It's Marc's voice.

The drumming in my head slows, and I stop. Marc comes around a tree, his forehead creased with worry and his eyes dark emeralds.

"Jae! Thank God, you're all right."

I back away, my hands groping for a stray branch with which to protect myself, because I don't believe this is really Marc and not Haemosu in one of his weird forms.

But he says, "Hey, Fighter Girl. It's okay. It's me."

I fall into him then, shaking uncontrollably. He runs his hands up and down my arms as if to warm me.

"I saw you crash into the forest," he says. "I thought you might have broken something, but you're okay."

I swallow hard and shut my eyes as if to block out the memories. I'd take a broken wrist and ankle any day if it means not ever having to remember that horrible palace and my ancestors' cries. When I open my eyes again, Marc's face is close to mine, his breath warm against my forehead. I notice how long his eyelashes are and how sweat beads up on his forehead.

He must have thrown off his skis and run to find me, because the forest is too thick to ski through. I should step away from him, but I am soothed by this closeness.

"I fell," I whisper my lie. "I'm okay now."

A hint of a smile crosses Marc's face. "Good. If you weren't so wet, I'd toss you in that snow mound for making me run like a banshee over here."

"How did you find me?"

His jaw works. "I heard you. Screaming."

I look away as his brow deepens again, and I find my skis, leaning the tips against my shoulder. "We should go."

He insists on carrying the skis, but I won't let him. After what just happened I need to feel as if I'm in control of something. Even if it's carrying some stupid skis. We tromp through the snow in silence when he points to the wrist that's holding the skis. The one I thought was broken.

"Some bracelet you've got there," he says as we emerge from the forest.

I see the shimmer of gold from the corner of my eye. I drop my skis and clutch my wrist. The bracelet is about two inches thick, ringed by five dragons, their golden bodies weaving around it.

Haemosu left his mark. My stomach rolls, remembering my stupidity.

Komo's words haunt me: *When he touches you, he will leave his mark . . . and your courting begins. Each time you meet, he will pull a little piece of your soul into his realm. Until you are no longer with us.*

What have I done?

"Is something wrong?" Marc asks.

I can't speak. I yank on it until my wrist is red. I think back to when Haemosu took my hand. The burning. He must have put the bracelet on me then. What does it mean? Why had he given me a bracelet? And why won't it come off?

My arm is raw. Marc puts his gloved hand over my frantic one.

"You're going to hurt yourself," he says softly.

I stop and bite my lips until I taste blood, sharp and metallic. "Yeah. We should go. Now."

The forest presses in on me as if it's watching with hidden eyes. I quicken my pace, pushing through the low branches, not caring as the boughs slap me across the face. Marc bends down and picks up my skis before running after me.

"You don't want to forget these." He waves them in the air.

"Right." But all I can think about is the weight of the bracelet clamped to my wrist like a shackle.

How long do I have until he imprisons me for good? And what about Marc? Am I putting him in jeopardy just by being with him? I remember those hands clawing to get out of the palace and the bones piled in the creek bed, and I stumble over a root. I try to swallow the hard rock lodged in my throat, because I know I don't have much time.

CHAPTER 15

After dinner I head to the private room our class has reserved in the Dragon Valley Hotel for the ski party. My one and only job is to prep the hot chocolate. Yes, it's an easy kind of job, but I can barely stir the chocolate powder into the steaming water. The sound of the screaming girls locked away in that palace fills my ears. Are they my ancestors, taken by Haemosu over the ages? Why would he even keep them there?

And then there's the bracelet. The one that won't come off despite my tugging and pulling until my wrist is rubbed raw.

I jump at every sudden noise, expecting Haemosu to strut through the door to take me away.

I deserve this. Komo warned me. Grandfather did everything he could to stop this from happening. But they made it seem as if I had the chance to beat him. That I could fight him.

Whatever. With a snap of his fingers, I was the equivalent of a stone statue.

I know my odds of survival.

Zero.

I arrange the cups in neat rows. I resolve to deal with whatever happened in the forest later. Hiding the bracelet somehow helps. It's dark out, and I remember my aunt telling me Haemosu has limited power at night. I'm about to have a meltdown, and I, Jae Hwa Lee, NEVER have meltdowns.

"Jae!" Marc says, entering the room. He's holding a stack of red boxes.

"Pepero sticks?"

"Stirring sticks." He rips open one box and starts plopping chocolate-covered sticks into the paper cups. "Tell me you're impressed."

"I'm impressed. You should audition for one of those competitive cooking shows."

We have a few minutes before the class leaders finish the games and send everyone our way, so we work quickly. Without saying anything, we've developed a system to get all the Pepero sticks in place. Marc rips; I dip the sticks into the cups.

Rip, dip, rip, dip.

I like the rhythm we have. We're a team. I'm smile to myself, glad Mrs. Freeman paired us up. I feel a surge of gratitude for Michelle's scheming, mixed with a little guilt for giving her such a hard time.

The doors slam open, and swarms of students jostle through the doorway, filling the once-quiet room with laughter. I soak it up and let myself drown in the noise. It pulls my thoughts away from earlier, and soon I'm so busy pouring, mixing, and passing out hot chocolates that the bracelet on my wrist is almost forgotten.

The line is backed up to the door; and as I pass a cup to Joey, Marc and I bump arms, and the hot chocolate sloshes all over Marc's T-shirt. His eyes catch mine, and he smiles. My heart does the same flip that it did when I was barreling down The Cliff.

I point to the word *antique* on his soaked shirt and say, "There. Now it looks authentic."

Soon the hot chocolates are distributed, and everyone is forming into small groups, laughing and talking. I wipe my chocolaty hands on a towel and look at Marc.

With impeccable timing, Long Legs shows up in tight leggings. I focus on wiping down the table as Marc pours the last of the hot chocolate into cups for those who want seconds.

"Marc! There you are!" Min of the Long Legs says, all bright under her glittery eye shadow and pink lips. "I've been looking everywhere for you. Come hang with us."

The fuzzy wrap draped over her shoulders makes her look seductive. Compared to her I must look like crap. Strands of my hair have fallen out of my braid, and my lips are chapped from the wind.

"Hey, Min," Marc says. "Sorry. I'm busy here with Jae."

"Marc," she continues in that thick, creamy voice of hers, beckoning with her hand to the group that Marc usually hangs out with. "You promised. Come on; everyone's waiting."

"Sorry, busy." He sweeps his hand over the hot chocolate stand, which is in fact all cleaned up.

"We're pretty much finished here," I say to Marc, trying to give him a way out. "You go ahead."

"Tell the guys I'll catch up with them later," he tells Min.

I freeze midstroke, the rag cold under my palm. Long Legs glares at me, spins on her Gucci heels, and tramps off.

"I think you ruined her night," I say.

"She'll be fine." Marc picks up a hot chocolate and hands it to me. Then he picks up one himself and knocks our cups together in a toast. "To us."

"Us?"

"The best hot chocolate team in South Korea."

I smile. "We should start training."

"Olympics?"

I nod and sip my hot chocolate. We stroll pass a group of kids playing cards on the floor to the giant window in the corner of the room. He leans against the window and sets his cup on the ledge.

"I did a little research on archery," he says.

I stare at him. "You did?"

"After watching you the other day, I thought how cool of a sport it was, but I didn't know anything about it. Did you know that an arrow shot from the Korean horn bow can travel the farthest of any other arrow shot from a bow?"

I lift my eyebrows. "Yes, 145 meters, actually."

"And during the Three Kingdom period the Hwarang warriors developed their archery skills to unify the land."

I crawl up on the window ledge across from him, crossing my legs. "No, I didn't. I guess I never paid much attention to the horn bow's history."

We continue chatting about the Hwarang warriors and then he finishes his spiel on the history of Korean archery, but all I can think about is how weird it is that I'm actually enjoying hanging out with him. He's the most normal thing in my life. And I need normal right now.

Outside, the snow falls heavy and thick, piling up on the trees and on the snow runs, glittering under the spotlights. It's magical and perfect, and I never want it to end.

I glance over at Marc and realize he's staring at me with those gorgeous eyes. I wish I hadn't worn a sweater, because my cheeks are burning. I'm so hot.

He studies me intently and then lowers his voice. "Do we have a chance?"

My whole body screams to wrap my arms around him and say *YES!* but Komo's words about Haemosu's vengeance stop me. What if Haemosu sees me talking to Marc and hurts him next? Could I live with that?

And even if Haemosu wasn't in the picture, Dad would totally flip.

"I don't think we do," I finally choke out.

He looks away. "Could you at least tell me why?"

"I should go," I say abruptly.

"Jae." He grabs my arm, pulling me closer to him. The way he says my name melts my insides. "Don't go. Stay."

His eyes study my lips, and all I can think about is how close we are. How his presence pulls at me. He reaches out his hand and runs his fingers through my hair.

"God, you're beautiful," he whispers.

Our faces are breaths away. I grab the front of his sweater for support because the world is swirling like the snow outside. Beneath my palms, his heartbeat thumps, alive and wild. His hands find mine and swallow them up. The gold ring on his finger cools my hot skin. He slowly rubs his thumb across my palm. My heart races.

His lips touch my forehead, and his hands slide up to my wrist. Then he shouts and jerks back, holding his hand.

"What's wrong?" I say.

"That bracelet." His face is pained. "It burned me."

I stare at his hand, and sure enough, his fingers are red. I fumble with my sweater, pulling up the sleeve to study the bracelet, touching it lightly. It's warm but not that hot. Then I notice one of the eyes of the five dragons has become as red as fire.

"That wasn't red before, was it?" he asks.

No. It wasn't.

A shiver hurtles down my spine. The iridescent ruby eye is strangely lifelike, and it is staring at me. Watching.

CHAPTER 16

"Jae Hwa!"

"Jae Hwa!"

"Jae Hwa!"

"Jae Hwa!"

"Jae Hwa!"

I spin round and round, the voices calling to me in the darkness. Where am I? I reach out my hands and grope the void, swiping empty air through my fingertips.

A breeze catches my hair. "Help me," it whispers.

I blink and search for light, but it's as dark as the deepest night.

"Help!"

"Help!"

"Help!"

"Help!"

The voices gain in volume, pressing around me, crying over and over. I clamp my hands against my ears. "Shut up!" I yell. But the voices strengthen until I find myself huddled into a ball on the rough stone floor.

Where am I?

I already know the answer. I'm locked in a tomb with the tormented cries of my ancestors' trapped souls. I want to help them. I do. But I'm no different than they are. I failed the first test with Haemosu just as they did. I let him touch me.

My motivation to fight has flown with the wind.

"Jae! Jae Hwa!"

Someone is shaking me. My head is tucked into my knees; I lift it and shade my face against the light. I'm scrunched into a ball in the corner of the ski resort room. How did I get here?

"You okay?" Michelle asks me as Lily wraps a blanket over my shoulders. "You were screaming and woke us up."

"I—I'm sorry. Bad dream." My teeth chatter even though the *ondol* heating system under the floor seeps warmth through my flannels. Lily tucks the blanket tighter around me.

"Don't worry about it," Lily says. "We don't mind. Let's pull our *yos* together for moral support."

"Yeah," I say, my voice cracking. "I'd like that."

So we drag the three *yos* next to one another and snuggle back under the covers while the snowstorm rages outside. I tuck the blanket up under my chin, willing my body to stop shaking. Lily passes out crackers, and we munch on them, listening to the howl of the wind.

"That wind," I say, then stop. They can't understand how it reminds me of my ancestors' moans. I'm alone in my misery.

"Did you and Marc kiss?" Michelle asks. I suspect she's trying to distract me from my dream.

I sigh. "I wish."

My fingers find the bracelet on my wrist. I don't tell her what it is or why we were distracted from our first kiss.

"I'm thinking of kissing Kumar," Lily blurts. "Do you think I should?"

"Well, you spent enough of the day with him," Michelle says. "I was totally the third wheel."

"You should absolutely kiss him," I whisper. "Because you never know if a kiss will be your last."

In the moonlight, I catch Lily looking at me oddly, but then she says, "Yeah, I guess you're right."

"And Michelle, you were right about Marc. I shouldn't have given you a hard time about trying to hook us up."

She smiles sagely. "That's what friends are for."

I fall asleep, this time dreaming of Marc's lips on mine, his body pressed close. But every time we touch, the red dragon eyes envelope us in their crimson light. We run, but there's nowhere to hide.

When we arrive back in Seoul, I take the subway to Komo's house rather than going straight home since Dad won't fly in from his Jeju trip until later tonight. I decide to text him and let him know where I'll be. Instead of ignoring my text or responding with an okay, he texts back.

Missed you. Do you want to eat out when I get back?

Surprised, I text: **Missed u 2. How about shabu shabu 2night? I should be home by 6.**

I sigh, knowing there's no way Dad will make it home by then. He works too hard. But I'm glad we'll finally have some time together. I text back, a smile on my face: **Sounds like fun.**

I'm dying to text Marc. We swapped numbers after we got off the bus, but what do I say? "Hey, we almost kissed last night except that annoying bracelet of mine messed stuff up. Want to try again?"

No. That would be weird and awkward.

Komo's door flings open just as I'm about to text Michelle asking for advice. Komo whisks me inside, the door slamming behind me.

"Well," Komo says with a frown. "I heard you went skiing even after I advised against it. Still alive, I see."

I don't bother telling her Dad thought it would be a good idea. Help me get my mind off stuff. Instead I show her the bracelet.

She scowls, her eyebrows knitting close together. "I told you not to let him touch you."

It's as if I'd been slapped. Of all people in the whole entire planet, I thought she'd understand. Now she's treating *me* as if I'd done something wrong. "How did you know?"

"My sister had the same bracelet." Komo starts down the hall and sits on the floor at a small table.

I want to kick myself. Haemosu made me feel as if I was special, different. How wrong I was. I fell for the same bracelet trick he's been using for a thousand years.

"That piece of information might have been helpful," I say.

After I slip off my boots, I settle onto one of the cushions as she pours me green tea. I scrunch up my nose at its sharp flavor and search for sugar.

"It is good for your health," she says. "Drink it."

I cup my hands around the green teacup. "I know I shouldn't

have touched him. It's just—" I don't even know where to begin with all the questions I have. "I need to understand what is happening to me."

"You are being gilded in preparation for the marriage ceremony." She calmly sips her tea as if we're just chatting about the weather. "Remember how Haemosu visited Princess Yuhwa five times and still she rejected him?" I nod. "It is my theory that he is reliving that rejection with each girl but hoping this time for acceptance. Those dragons' eyes on your bracelet reflect each encounter with Haemosu. Think of it as a dating ritual; but in this case he takes a little part of your soul every time you meet until all five eyes burn red and you are his forever."

"Why didn't you tell me all this earlier?"

"I was hoping it might never come to this. You had enough to worry about without knowing about the bracelet."

I wrap my arms around myself. "So he takes a little part of me each time? What does that mean?"

"I only know what Sun told me." Komo stares into her teacup, and her voice softens. "As time progressed, she felt a greater connection with the Spirit World. It was like she was half in our world and half in that world. She started seeing more otherworldly creatures. Portals between the Spirit World and our world opened up to her."

"Did that help her fight Haemosu?"

"She was distant by that point. She never talked about it much. She used to write down her thoughts in her journal, but I never found it." Komo focuses on me as if she had forgotten I was even in the room. "This is why you need to practice your Tae Kwon Do. With those skills you will have the power to defeat him. Tell me everything. Tell me how it happened to you."

So I tell her, even about my ski stunt on the slopes, the stars, and the weird deer part. She doesn't interrupt. And once I start, there's no stopping.

Afterward she's quiet. The room lies silent except for my fingers tapping the table as I wait for her to tell me what to do. I need her to have the answers. I sure don't.

The room has grown dark, and the house seems to creak under the strain of the wind. I search for a light switch to drown out the gloom settling in.

"There were girls inside a palace," I tell her. "They were trying to escape. Last night I dreamed about them, and it was so real. Maybe it was real like that connection thing you were talking about. They kept begging me to help them. I think that's what the dokkaebi was talking about. I think Haemosu's not only been taking the girls, but imprisoning them, too. I just haven't figured out why he would do that."

Komo's eyes widen. She stands, knocking over her teacup in the process, and crosses the room to stare out the window. Her hand covers her mouth, and I see she's shaking. When she doesn't say anything, I go to her and put my hand on her shoulder.

"That would be something Haemosu would do," she finally says. A tear trickles down her cheek. "Not just take them, but torture them. Never let their spirits reach heaven."

That's when I realize both of us have lost someone who meant the world to us. I think about Michelle and her thoughts about everyone having a purpose. Is this my purpose? Is that what Palk is hoping for and what Haemosu is so worried about?

That I could be the one to save them? An insane idea, but if I don't act soon, I'll join those girls.

I pull Komo into a hug because I can't help but think this is exactly what Mom would do at this exact moment.

"My sister is in there," Komo whispers. "I am sure of it. We must free her. We must." Then she wipes her face and clears her throat. "There is no time for looking back. Only time for what lies ahead."

"Is it even possible to stop Haemosu?" I ask as we begin to clear the table. "I felt so powerless against him."

"It would have helped if you had stayed out of the sunlight. Or fought him in our world." Komo is all brisk-like again. "If you had not let him touch you and pull you into his lands. If you had listened to me."

"Komo, I can't just live in some hole for the rest of my life."

"True enough."

I wander to the far wall and study the sword hanging on it. "The Spirit World has magical powers, doesn't it? Like him turning me into a deer."

"Yes, that is one component. It is called metamorphosis. The transformation of one being into another." She pulls the sword off the wall and hands it to me. "But he did not turn you. He gave you the idea, but you had to have the power within you to change. Even in his own lands, he does not have the power over you. Ultimately, it is your choice. Did he force you to run?"

I bite my inner lip. "No."

"Did he make you take his hand?"

"No. But I didn't really understand at first. It was like a

dream. And then when I realized he was touching me, I pulled away."

"Precisely. So there is your way to destroy him." She takes the sword from me and sets it back on the wall.

"I'm lost."

She smiles, which is really annoying. "When you said no, you took some of his power away."

"He let me go. I'm like his toy."

She lowers herself onto the cushion and glares at me. "Are you here to learn or to teach? Stop pacing the room like some caged animal."

I move to the window. Komo is right. I do feel like some caged animal, just waiting to be snatched up. And I hate it. "How am I supposed to fight an immortal—a demigod—with Tae Kwon Do? It's not like I have special powers or anything."

"It was through your own strength that you escaped. Perhaps you have a chance to defeat him in his world after all. You were able to shape-shift; you have the talent. Like Princess Yuhwa."

I think of how quick I'd been when I ran across that field and how I had turned into the deer. "I did seem to have some kind of power, but I don't think that will be enough."

"Disbelief is the root of the impossible."

That sounds like something Mom would say.

Can I do what Komo is asking me to do: confront Haemosu and put a stop to all this? Komo makes it sound simple. But Haemosu isn't a typical target where I aim for the bull's-eye.

My heart tells me he's far smarter and more complicated.

CHAPTER 17

As I ride up the elevator to my apartment, leaning against the cold silver wall, I wonder at Komo's explanation about the brace-let. I hold up my arm so the eyes gleam in the florescent light, and her words echo through my head: *He takes a little part of your soul every time you meet until all five eyes burn red and you are his forever.*

I drop my hand.

Forever. So final. So definite.

I spin the bracelet until I'm looking at only the four dragons whose eyes are still gold, unchanged. Somehow it makes me feel better. As if I still have a fighting chance.

Then the elevator doors slide open and I practically choke.

Haechi is standing there, his horns nearly touching the hall-way ceiling. He's as still as stone. I clutch my suitcase tighter, waiting for the elevator doors to close. They don't. It's as if they're frozen, too. Sure, he's supposed to be my protector, but there's no denying he's beyond scary. And he couldn't stop Haemosu from gilding me.

"I see you have met Haemosu," Haechi says, eying my bracelet. "If only I had the honor of assisting you in your time of need. I have no power in his land unless I am invited."

A new idea hits me. "He's imprisoned my ancestors, hasn't he? Can you help me get them out?"

"Impulsive and brave." Haechi shakes his head. "No. That task is for you and only you. But I do have a message from Palk, the great one of light and goodness."

I clutch my suitcase tighter.

"Never doubt. Never shy from who you are meant to be."

"How is that supposed to help me save them?"

The air shimmers around us like it does on a hot summer's day, and Haechi's body starts to fade. "To save them," he says, "you must open the tomb."

Then he disappears, leaving behind the faint scent of ginseng. The hallway looks empty without his massive bulk overcrowding it. Somehow I manage to unlock my knees and head down the hall to our apartment, trailing my suitcase behind me. My steps are slow as I grow closer to the door. Dad won't be home from his trip from Jeju until six. And that's if he gets back in time. Now that Haechi is gone, I wish he'd stayed.

Never shy from who you are meant to be. What had he meant?

I punch in the code and enter. The click of the door shutting behind me sounds loud against the stillness of the apartment. Beams of sunlight trickle through the windows, dust captured in its path like falling snow, and I can make out the low hum of the kimchi refrigerator as I slide off my boots and coat.

The sunlight reminds me of when I'd first stepped into Haemosu's world and it was perfect and unblemished, and suddenly

I long for that feeling. I move into the sun's path, close my eyes, and drink in its warmth. Memories of running through the forest as a deer, the wind against my face, and the power I had consume me.

A cloud passes over the rays, and the warmth vanishes. My eyes pop open, and I jump back. Is Haemosu trying to lure me back into his world? I press my body against the wall and wait, as still as stone, for him to appear.

But nothing happens. I'm flipping out over nothing. Perfect.

I rub my hands on my jeans. This isn't good. I'm dying to return to a place that I know will only bring me harm. What is wrong with me?

I've only been gone for one night and yet it feels like a lifetime. I stare at my bracelet. My whole world has changed now that I've been gilded.

I head to my desk, where I have all my notes on my translation of Mom's *Samguk Yusa*. Now that I have entered Haemosu's world, I'm hoping the myth will hold more meaning for me.

Grandfather told me about the time when Habaek, Princess Yuhwa's father, tried to stop his daughter from being captured by Haemosu. But is there more to the story? Have I overlooked something?

I skim through my chicken scratch handwriting until I get to the part where Habaek challenged Haemosu to a fight.

Haemosu descended to Habaek's palace, where they
tested each other's skill. Being deities, they tested
each other in the power of _____

What is this word, I wonder, tapping my pencil on the paper. Could this be what Komo was talking about? Metamorphosis? Like when I turned into the deer. I keep reading.

Habaek first changed himself into a carp, but Haemosu changed himself into an otter and caught Habaek. Then Habaek changed into a deer, whereupon Haemosu changed into a wolf and chased him.

I stop and realize this is the same creature I chose, too. Or maybe Haemosu influenced me to choose. Interesting. The rest of the page is unfinished. I settle myself in my chair and begin to work, using my computer and sometimes texting Michelle for help. An hour later I've finished my rough translation.

Finally, Habaek changed into a quail, but Haemosu changed into a falcon and caught him again. Habaek gave up and acknowledged Haemosu's supremacy. An official marriage ceremony was held, and Habaek sent his daughter, Princess Yuhwa, to the heavenly realm with Haemosu. Before Haemosu's chariot could leave the water, the princess escaped using her hairpin and returned to her father.

How am I suddenly supposed to turn into an animal? I rub my forehead. When I saw Haemosu as a deer, did I change into one because I was thinking about it or because Haemosu put that thought into my head?

I toss aside my notes. These aren't helping me. I turn back to Mom's box and dig some more, hoping to find something else that can help me.

Nothing.

I flip open my laptop next and do a quick search for the word *metamorphosis*. Pages of articles pop up on my search engine.

I start with the dictionary. It reads: "a change of physical form, structure, or substance especially by supernatural means."

Sounds about right. It's kind of like when a werewolf shape-shifts, but without limits. I grab my notebook and write down the definition. Then I scribble pictures of an otter catching a carp, a wolf chasing a deer, and a falcon snatching up a quail.

Seeing those images gives me pause. Why did Habaek turn into a quail and not a stronger creature? It had to be because he wasn't strong enough. As I looked through each of the animals, I saw that Haemosu always transformed into a similar animal, but a more powerful one.

Was that because of Haemosu's physical or mental strength?

I scroll down and click on an article that catches my attention. According to this author, the key to metamorphosis is "taking control of your own mind and harnessing your strength."

I write down "Control of the mind" in my notebook. So it must be mental strength. I chew my pencil, trying to piece this puzzle together.

Then the author writes about "using your cunning of the mind." What animal could outwit Haemosu?

The article ends with:

Can a bear catch a rabbit? Or a dragon outwit the tiger? Raw power alone will not win the battle.

"Know your adversary," I say aloud, remembering my Tae Kwon Do lessons. "Makes sense."

That was the problem. I didn't know Haemosu well enough. I stare at my bracelet and grimace. Not well enough *yet*. I scroll to the bottom to see whether I can find an e-mail address there. That's when I freeze.

**DR. JAMES GRAYSON,
professor of religious studies at Yonsei University.**

The man I saw talking to Grandfather at the museum ceremony. Marc's father.

CHAPTER 18

"The trip was a complete success!" Mrs. Freeman declares, and the class breaks into applause.

I take in our National Honor Society group gathered around the large table and wait for someone to start snickering or make a comment, but everyone is soaking in Mrs. Freeman's sunshine. There's no doubt that I'm enrolled in the most active, most enthusiastic, smartest group of kids around; and they're all out to create a better world.

For the first time since arriving in Korea, I want to be a part of that group, raising money for the poor and making a difference. But I have to defeat Haemosu, and I'm still wondering if I'm strong enough and smart enough to do it. Michelle thinks we all are here for a purpose. But what if my purpose is too big? What if I can't do it?

Once the cheering dies, Mrs. Freeman announces that it's time to plan our next event. She moves to the board and writes "Ideas" at the top. Michelle, of course, is the first to raise her hand.

"How about a food drive?" Michelle opens her laptop and

starts typing. "We could take food to the homeless that sleep in the subway entrances."

Mrs. Freeman writes it on the board. More ideas are generated, but I've stopped listening. I opt for twirling the bracelet around my wrist and creating my own brainstorming list.

WAYS TO KICK HAEMOSU'S BUTT
1. Lock him in his own tomb.
2. Shoot an arrow, aim for the heart.
3. Turn into a dragon and blow fire on him until he's nothing but ashes.
4. Chop off all his limbs.

"Jae Hwa," Mrs. Freeman says from across the room, "I see you've made a list, too. Care to add anything?"

I skim over her list and compare it to my own. Okay, chopping off limbs really wouldn't work. Maybe I need to pick up some of Michelle's ideas. Mine are pretty brutal. "How about a carnival for orphan kids?"

"Fantastic idea!" Mrs. Freeman beams. "How about you, Marc?"

Marc sits straighter, adjusting his glasses. "Yes, Mrs. Freeman?" he says in a tone that makes him sound like the teacher here.

"What are you drawing?" Mrs. Freeman asks, and comes around the table to pick up the pad he's sketching on.

As she lifts the paper, I catch a peek of the rough, penciled drawing. It has five dragons connected in a circle. My bracelet! Marc glances my way and covers his paper. I lower my eyes, pretending I'm looking at my notebook. Is Marc still thinking about the bracelet? He wanted to see it again at breakfast on our last day at the ski resort. I wouldn't let him.

Now I'm desperate to talk to him, because I also want to know why his dad is an expert on metamorphosis. Okay, so maybe I can't get the memory of his lips brushing my forehead out of my mind and I want more. But that is definitely bad.

Komo had said none of Princess Yuhwa's suitors lived. Haemosu's jealousy wouldn't allow it. Would Haemosu think of Marc as a threat? And then there's Dad. Last night over dinner he mentioned that someone had told him I was hanging out with a white boy and reminded me again to stay focused on my studies.

As if I don't have enough to worry about.

"I was doodling," Marc tells Mrs. Freeman. "It helps me focus. John Hopkins University School of Medicine did a study two years ago reporting that drawing stimulates the mind."

"Oh." Mrs. Freeman stares at the paper. "So has this drawing inspired anything yet?"

"I think Jae's got the best idea up there," Marc quips as if he's been mulling over this for some time. "She's got my vote."

That was smooth. I wonder if he tutors in diplomacy. If only I could skirt around issues with my dad like that. Michelle jumps up from her seat as if Mrs. Freeman has given her permission and starts a whole stream of ideas on all the possibilities of a carnival. She winks at me. I smile and sit back, feeling as if I've finally been accepted into this group.

Until a note is tossed and lands on my notebook. Warily, I open it.

Back off or I'll tell your daddy. Marc's mine.
He's always been mine.

xoxo

My eyes wander to Min. She peeks up from her tablet and blows me a kiss. She has no idea that I could break her in half.

I rip her note, wondering how on earth I haven't gotten kicked out of the school yet. Meanwhile, Mrs. Freeman absently hands the drawing back to Marc. The glow in me dies. What am I thinking? I can't be a part of all this and deal with Haemosu.

Marc has the design drawn perfectly. So perfectly that the hairs on my arms prick up as if they've been pulled by a magnet. He rubs his forehead with his thumb and forefinger, and glances up at me. Our eyes meet. My heart stops. He knows something. I can feel it.

When the bell rings, I grab my backpack and skirt around the table. I've nearly reached Marc, but Min of the Long Legs pulls him aside.

"So are we on for tonight?" she asks, draping her arm over his shoulder. "There's a new movie playing at the theater in Sinchon that I know you'll adore."

She glances back at me, a smirk playing across her red lips. I press my books against my chest and glare at her. I don't have time for Long Legs's elementary school games or her jealousy. I bolt for the door.

"So," Michelle says, breezing up next to me, "will you be on my team?"

I have no idea what she's talking about.

"Sure. Absolutely." If I'm still alive then, that is.

From the corner of my eye, I catch sight of Marc hurrying after us. I pull on Michelle's elbow and steer her into the hall.

"What's wrong?" Michelle asks, wide-eyed.

"He's going out on a date with Min." My chest aches. "Why did I think he could be interested in me when there's a girl like Min gushing over him? Crap. He's coming."

I pull Michelle into escape mode, but he rushes to block our path.

"Can I talk to you a second, Jae?"

"Marc." I'm a little unnerved at the intensity in his eyes. "Maybe later. I need to get to my locker before class. Plus, don't you need to plan your *date* with Min?"

I really think I deserve a medal or something for keeping my cool.

He holds his finger in front of my face. "One minute."

"One second," I say.

He clears his throat and looks at Michelle. She raises her eyebrows, not budging.

"It's okay," I tell her, "I won't beat him up." When she's gone, I step closer to Marc and whisper, "Someone saw us together on the ski trip. They had the nerve to tell my dad, and he's forbidden me to hang out with you anymore. I think it was your girlfriend."

Marc's chin lifts, and his eyes widen as if I've slapped him. The books in my arms weigh a thousand pounds, they're so heavy. I focus on my Converse sneakers because he actually looks devastated.

"What I wanted to tell you is to be careful," he whispers into my ear. My heart lurches over the feel of his breath against my neck.

"That bracelet you're wearing," Marc continues. "You should take it off. There's something not right about it. Tell me I won't burn myself if I touch your bracelet. It wasn't an electric shock back at the ski resort, was it?"

No joke. "What makes you think that?"

"I've been researching it." He glances around. "I think it's a symbol of enslavement."

If he only knew. He's about to say something else when Long Legs sidles up to him. Will she not go away?

"Marc," Min says sweetly, "I'm heading to class now. Care to join?"

"I'm talking to Jae," Marc says. "Alone."

"Let's talk later," I say, and then give Min my best scathing look, "when we're really alone."

She bristles and stalks away. Before I can say anything else, the warning bell rings. Great. I still haven't gotten my calculus book yet. Ms. Wood is so strict about tardies. I'll have to run to get to class on time. I say, "Listen, I've got to go."

"Right," he says. "Catch you around."

He sprints off down the hall, weaving through the crowds as if he's chasing something. I watch him for a moment and shake my head.

When I reach my locker, slightly out of breath, a piece of paper is taped onto it with an arrow sticking out from its center. What a weird practical joke. It's a picture of a full moon. Doesn't

Min have better things to do with her time? I rip it off. And then I remember.

Full moon. The dokkaebi wanted me to pierce the belly of the full moon. He must still want to bargain with me. No one else could have known about this.

I glance around the hallway, half expecting to see his giant, ugly self pop out into the hallway. Nothing happens. Either he's shielded me from seeing him or he left long ago.

The locker resists as I yank on it. I give it a hard pound with my other hand. It jerks open, and I fall backward to the hard floor. The noise in the hallway vanishes as if someone has clicked MUTE, except for a light tinkling sound. Inside the locker, my books fade away. The hook and the gray iron walls melt as golden light streams through and out of the locker. The warmth of it drenches me, tugging at my body.

I stand and stretch my hand into the iridescent light. It shimmers as if it's sprayed with gold. One step closer and my hand slips into the locker. I grope toward the back, but it's not there. I squint, and that's when I can see a glistening palace, gilded in gold and gems. My breath leaves me. It's beautiful.

A voice calls out from behind me. "Jae Hwa!" But it's so far away, like at the end of a long corridor.

A gust of wind swirls around me. My whole body glitters as I am pulled inside. And then I'm standing in a thicket of tall grass that waves against my knees, tickling them. Beyond the field is a grove of persimmon trees, laden with plump orange fruit. Fluffy white clouds sail above on a sea of sapphire sky.

Haemosu emerges from the grove with a confident stride, taking a bite of a persimmon. I can't deny how handsome he is, dressed in a red silk tunic and pants lined with gold ribbon, a giant dragon rearing across his chest. But then the light shifts, and for a moment I can see his true hideous self. A decaying skeleton of a monster.

Stepping backyard, I suck in a deep breath. He must see the fear sweeping over my face, because he stops midstride. Staring intently at me, he crushes the persimmon in his hand. Instead of spewing out juice, it erupts in a gush of red liquid like spilled blood.

"So you can see my true form," he says. "Interesting. The others never did. Perhaps Palk is right. Perhaps you are different from the others."

"So you'll let me go, then." I clench my fists, hating how my voice shakes.

"No. That would never do. A prize like you must be treasured for eternity."

He lifts his arms in the air and roars, the ground shaking in response. I stumble and fall to the ground. As I'm staggering to my feet, I watch in horror as he transforms before me. In a shiver of light, his body ripples into a black spiked beast. Smoke pours from his nostrils. A long thick tail snaps behind him.

I've never seen anything more horrifying than this.

I whip around and take off in a full sprint just as his four paws hit the earth and he leaps toward me. Icy terror streaks through my veins. My feet pound the grassy field, but I can hear his paws behind me and feel the lash of his tail swipe my heels.

I've always been fast, but here I'm as fast as the wind. Maybe faster. I think I can outrun him.

But it's not enough. Because I can't find my way out of Haemosu's world. Last time I escaped by finding the place in the air with a distinct contortion. I've no idea how I got here this time.

Then the ground falls away, leaving behind a sharp cliff that plunges to nowhere. I stagger to a stop and hold out my arms to keep from plummeting over the edge. I comb the cliff edge for the wavering light, feeling Haemosu's presence drawing closer.

Where's the flipping doorway?

"Why run from me, my princess?"

I spin to face Haemosu's perfect human face. I want to punch it until its black and blue.

"Your efforts are pointless. We are meant for each other. Even my lands respond to you. It will not be long until we are together for eternity." He's got another persimmon in his hand and takes a bite of it. Juice drips down his chin. "I thought we would spend some time together. You and I."

The cries I heard in that dark, abandoned palace echo in my memory, and a fire rises up inside me. "Time together? Is that what you told all those other girls?"

"I do not know what you speak of."

"The curse. That's what you have brought my family. It needs to end. Now."

"Do not lessen what we have." He clucks his tongue, taking my arm and rubbing his hand over the bracelet. "I am intrigued. How do you plan on ending our special bond?"

I whip out a side kick into his gut, and the fruit falls to the ground. He tries to grab my leg, but I whip around and my foot smacks him in the cheek. I throw a punch aiming for his temple, but he grabs hold of my left wrist where the bracelet is.

I scream in pain as an electric shock pulses through my body. I drop to my knees when he finally lets go. My teeth chatter from the shock. All Komo's training suddenly seems pointless and stupid. Metamorphosis magic? Transforming into another being? What had I been thinking to believe I could stand up to a demigod?

A voice calls out my name, booming from below the chasm, sounding oddly familiar. I search for the source. No one is there.

"Who is calling you?" Creases fill Haemosu's forehead. "It sounds like a boy. Did you bring someone through the door?"

The locker. My thoughts clear. Yes, that's how I got here. If I can find it, I can escape. I think about the voice. It sounded awfully like Marc's.

"You made a very poor decision in telling someone about our special place," Haemosu says, and strides to the cliff. "I will not share you with anyone. You are mine alone!"

Haemosu reaches out his hand and aims it toward the voice. "He does not understand who he is dealing with. Perhaps he should have a taste." It dawns on me that he's going to do something horrible to the person calling my name. What if it *is* Marc? I couldn't bear Haemosu hurting him.

I grab ahold of Haemosu's arm just as a burst of golden liquid shoots from his fingertips. But it's enough to throw him off guard, and his aim is flung sideways. He isn't used to girls who can fight.

"This is between you and me," I say, hoping that whoever is trying to save me is okay.

Haemosu rears back, and a mind-splitting screech erupts from his mouth, pulling at his lips until they stretch into a beak. His body contorts, the red silk twisting and bending into feathers; his legs extend into wings, and sharp claws replace fingers.

A massive bird stands before me.

The beak is larger than my head, and it snaps at me. My reflexes click into motion, and I snap out a front kick, jamming my foot into the beak. The bird screeches again, flies higher, and circles above me. The roundhouse double kick Komo taught me comes to mind.

I wait, my high block in place as he nose-dives straight at me. When the bird is inches from me, I lift my body into a spin and twirl around. I've estimated perfectly as my foot impacts against his stomach. His claws attack my face. A chunk of my hair tears out, and his beak rips my left cheek. I fall to the ground, which is no longer tall grass, but hard-packed dirt.

I scramble to my feet, but not fast enough. He's pecking at my back. I scream as the pain cuts through me as if I'm being stabbed by sharp pieces of glass.

I push out a front punch but knife through empty air as he swerves left. If I don't do something soon, he'll tear me to shreds. My mind races, trying to remember how Komo said I should transform. What did that article say?

Take control of your mind.

Haemosu soars high above me now, screeching out some battle cry. I have a few moments. I close my eyes and focus, desperately blocking everything around me. I visualize the form of a bird, something to fly me away. Didn't Habaek in the legend turn into a bird? The picture of a hawk in Mom's book comes to mind.

Another screech erupts in the stillness.

I snap my eyes open. He's in a nosedive. I break into a sprint so that I'm running in his direction, hoping to force him to redirect. My feet pound the ground, kicking up dust.

Then I realize I'm racing full speed directly toward the cliff. He cornered me.

"Jae! Jae!" Marc's voice calls from the nothingness beyond the cliff.

I must concentrate on becoming a bird. It's my only chance. I run toward Marc's voice, not thinking about the cliff anymore, only the air, its fullness and blueness stretching out beyond me, waiting to be flown through. A tingling prickles over my skin. My vision blurs as the cliff edge looms. I pump my legs harder, my muscles screaming, Haemosu screeching.

The ground falls away.

All that is left is empty air, and my heart lodges in my throat as I freefall. My chest tightens, and something inside me explodes, energy coursing to every tip of my body, from my ears to my toes. I flail my arms through the void, and that's when I realize I don't have arms anymore. They're feathered wings.

And I'm flying.

The wind fans my face. I beat my wings faster. The air abruptly changes from clear cold to warm dry. My skin bristles again, and I watch in horror as my wings twist and the feathers fall away. The sky blurs. I'm losing my focus.

Once again I'm human.

My limbs jumble around me as I fall. My arms flail, and my feet can't find the ground fast enough. I trip over a thin metal edge, and then I'm tumbling through my locker onto the floor, back at school, sprawled across the hallway.

CHAPTER 19

Slowly I sit up, my stomach heaving. I know I'm having side effects from the metamorphosis, but I can't stop shaking uncontrollably. Marc grabs my shoulders, kneeling next to me. His eyes look oddly golden and wild. I blink and stare at my locker, which at this moment looks perfectly normal.

I search the area for Haemosu. He's nowhere in sight. I slide forward on my bottom and kick the locker closed.

"You okay?" Marc asks, a sharpness to his voice. "You're bleeding. I'm taking you to the nurse's office."

Bleeding? I look at my palms, and sure enough they're scratched and bloody. I gingerly touch my back. It's warm, and my shirt clings to it. Marc helps me up, and I glance around to see if anyone has noticed. But the hallway is empty. Everyone must be in class.

The hall lies in deadly silence. Marc's shouts still vibrate in my ears. Marc's voice. It was his voice that called me back. He was calling for me. It had to have been him. Did he see me? Does he know?

Then my heart stops, remembering the golden liquid Haemosu shot across the chasm. I can't help myself. I reach out and lightly touch Marc's arm to see if he's safe. He feels warm and solid. At first glance he seems perfectly normal. Jeans. Navy T-shirt. Ruffled brown hair.

But his eyes still show hints of that shimmery gold Haemosu blasted.

My heart skitters as my fingers reach for his face. "Your eyes. Are you hurt? What happened?"

"Don't worry about me. We need to get you to the nurse. You look like a horde of fire ants has been feasting on you."

Marc draws me to him. I'm still in shock, and allow myself to lean against his chest and let my body relax. I know I should be worried about my injuries, about his eyes, but right now I'm just glad to be alive.

We shuffle our way down the hall and step outside. A light dusting of snow covers the path. I shiver, wishing the nurse's office was connected to the main building. When we enter the nurse's office, Nurse Lah and the two assistants rush over.

"What happened to her?" Nurse Lah asks, directing us to a cot lined with a crisp white sheet.

"She fell." Marc rubs his eyes.

"Fell?" Nurse Lah grabs a bottle of antiseptic and gauze, then sits on a stool and rolls over to me. "On ice?"

"Right outside the gym next to the bushes," Marc confirms.

I shoot Marc a grateful smile. Ice makes a lot more sense than telling her I was pulled into another dimension and confronted by an immortal who transformed himself into a savage red bird.

Marc gives me a hard look as if trying to tell me something. His skin looks paler than usual, but his eyes are also back to their piercing green except for a hint of golden speckles. I can almost convince myself that I imagined the gold, but there's something in his gaze that tells me he knows more than he should. Oddly, that's exactly what I want. For someone other than my aunt and Grandfather to know the truth about me.

I wince at the sting of the medicine as the nurse cleans out the scratches on my hand and then wraps them. She moves to inspect my back but first gives Marc the eye.

He shifts on his feet, saying, "I'll be right by the door."

I nod, and Nurse Lah draws back a curtain to give us privacy.

"Well, it looks worse than it actually is," she says as she cleans away the blood. I cringe and grit my teeth. "Scratches will do that. I'm going to put some ointment and large bandages on them. That should heal you up and keep them from scarring or infection."

How can I have only a few scratches after that attack?

Once the nurse leaves I take a few moments to collect myself. I peel away one of the bandages on my hand. The scratch has healed up almost perfectly. Only a thin line is left. *Impossible.*

It seems that what happens in the Spirit World doesn't apply to the real world. And there's Marc, again, right in the middle of my mess. Is it coincidental that he's been there for me both times I've encountered Haemosu? And what about that article his dad wrote? Does Marc know more than he's letting on, or am I completely paranoid?

Beyond the white curtain, I hear Marc chatting with the nurse about the weather. He sounds so normal and relaxed.

Maybe I just imagined that look in his eyes earlier. Maybe I imagined him calling my name over the chasm.

I push the bandage back in place, pressing my lips together as I slide off the bed. I can't handle anything else magical or otherworldly right now. I find Marc sitting by the entrance on a blue plastic chair, a book in his lap. A quick glance at the cover tells me it's written in Hangul: *Legends and Myths of Korea*. I know it because I have the exact same book back home.

"Looks like you didn't need to stay after all." I won't get him involved in my mess of a life. I think of Haemosu's rage upon hearing Marc's voice in the Spirit World. I can't risk Haemosu taking out his vengeance on Marc. I say, "Nurse Lah says I'm scratched up, but I'll be fine. Thanks for helping, though."

"Does this mean I can't carry you to class?" He grins.

"I'd flatten you, Brainiac. Better not."

The nurse laughs from her desk, and even I can't stop the smile crossing my face as I push open the cool glass door and step into the frigid air. How does Marc know exactly what to say to make me feel comfortable? He stands, tucks the book under his arm, and follows.

"You read Korean?" I ask.

"Naw, I just stare at the pretty characters for fun."

"Cultured and a comedian."

"I try to please. I expect to get through college on my comedy skills alone."

I burst into a ridiculous laugh, and I can't seem to stop. *This is probably what hysterics are,* I decide as I snort and hiccup like a complete idiot. At least the pressure in my chest seems to have released as we hurry up the stairs into the high school, away from the February cold. I grab the side door, but the chill from the handle seeps through my bandages. Even with the wounds healing at impossible speeds, it still hurts.

"Wait," he says, and the humor leaves his face. "I can't let you go back in there after what just happened."

"You know what happened?"

"I do. And I think you're in terrible danger."

The wind curls around me, frosty and sharp. "That was your voice calling me, wasn't it? You saved me."

"Yes."

My head spins as if I'm going to faint. I shake my head against the dizziness and suck in a deep breath. Komo and Grandfather never mentioned that humans could see into the Spirit World without those spirits allowing it. Even I saw only what they wanted me to see.

"How could you see me? Did anyone else?"

"Something wild happened back there." He massages his forehead. "We need to talk."

CHAPTER 20

We skip our calculus lesson to sit on the carpeted floor in the far back corner of our school's auditorium. I'm slightly unsettled by the rows of empty maroon-colored seats and the stage, dark and silent; but it's quiet and private here.

I lean against the dark-blue wall and cross my legs, trying to figure out how I feel about everything. Now that Marc seems to be drawn into this mess, it's getting complicated. How much did he really see? Really understand? And then there's the guilt— and the thrill—that's tugging at me because I want him to be a part of this.

Marc settles beside me, releasing a long sigh as he, too, leans against the wall, stretches out his legs in front of him, and closes his eyes.

"What happened back there was crazy," he says. "Did I see what I thought I saw?"

I press my sweaty hands against my jeans. I'm not supposed to tell anyone about this insanity. But that was before Marc had saved me. "What did you see?"

"Something that belongs in a fantasy film."

My throat tightens. *He knows,* I think, and I don't even want to think about the consequences. "What makes you say that?"

"My dad is a professor of religion at Yonsei University." He twirls his gold ring around his finger. "So I've heard all the stories and memorized all the beliefs. It's just—it's different when you actually *see* it."

I remember Haemosu's anger when he heard Marc's voice. That shot of light I thought I'd deflected. A sliver of cold slides through my body. What if I hadn't deflected all of it? Marc is rubbing his eyes again. I reach out and touch his face.

"Your eyes. What's wrong?" I grip his arm tight. "The monster hurt you, didn't he?"

"Technically, these creatures aren't monsters." He half laughs, and then his jaw tightens as he focuses on me. "Think of them more as supernatural figures. In some cultures, people call them angels and demons. Some call them ghosts and spirits."

"You can call him whatever you want, but the man you saw was a monster."

"Dad used to explain it to me as if they were more than just fairy tales. I always thought he was a bit crazy, but I went along with it to keep him happy. I guess in theory I believed him. Now I *know* they're real."

I search his face for pain or some sign of Haemosu's mark on him, but he seems fine.

"In the locker," Marc says. "You faced one."

I take a deep breath. "Yeah. I did. And I wouldn't have found my way back if you hadn't called my name."

"You disappeared into your locker. And then I remembered

my dad's stories about the Spirit World. I even remembered Kumar's theory on different dimensions, and then all that stuff my dad had taught me made sense. I tried to climb into your locker. I beat on the back wall and started screaming out your name."

I stare at him, surprised that he would be that worried about me. He could've strolled back to class, not giving me even a thought. But he hadn't.

Marc burrows his head and rubs his hands over his face. "Then something crazy happened."

Chills slide up my arms. And I'm afraid of what he'll say next. Afraid my fears are reality.

"A flash of light filled the locker." Marc stares at his hands. "It was so bright, it burned my eyes. The pain was so bad I couldn't move."

I turn to sit in front of him, grabbing both his hands. "What? Why didn't you say anything to the nurse? Are you okay?"

"I must have sat there on the floor for nearly thirty minutes. When the pain left, I thought I was blind. I knew I should call someone, but then my vision started to come back."

"You should never have stayed. You should leave right now and get as far away from me as you can."

"I'm not that kind of guy."

I yearn to reach over and touch his face and wipe away the pain in the etched lines on his forehead. "Does it still hurt?"

"No." Marc blinks and then shakes his head slightly. "You?"

"I'm okay." My hands are fine, but I can't tell him the whole truth. That I never believed my fear could reach this level. That I'm always looking over my shoulder for the next monster to terrorize me. I'm supposed to be tough and strong, but instead I am terrified to walk down the street.

"Watching you get torn to shreds—" His voice breaks, and my throat constricts, remembering.

"So at my locker," I swallow hard, "what *did* you see?"

"My dad is really more the expert on this kind of thing. But I think your locker somehow became a portal into another world. I was watching you in the hall, and then you climbed right into your locker. It was wild. Then after my vision came back, I realized there was still this golden light coming out of your locker. When I looked back inside, you were standing on this high bluff and this man turned into a red bird and attacked you. Jae, you need to tell me what's going on."

"What you saw was the Spirit World." I rub my bandages, afraid even to look at him. "Or at least that's what my aunt and grandfather call it." He's going to think I'm insane. Besides, I'm not even sure if telling him will make things better.

He twists the ring around his finger and is silent for a moment. I wait, holding my breath, expecting him to laugh or say I've lost my mind. But then he looks up and nods at my hands. "How're those injuries of yours doing?"

It's ridiculous at how those words send my heart soaring, but they do, and I'm desperate to cling to the feeling that I can trust him. I peek under my bandages. My palms are smooth. The lines from the scratches have vanished like magic. I pull off the bandages and roll them into a ball.

"After our meeting today I wanted to talk to you about something, but Min showed up."

"Forget about Min. What did you want to talk about?"

I bite my lip, slightly alarmed at how happy his words make me. It's as if I want Marc all to myself. I say, "Last night I did some research on metamorphosis, transforming from one thing into another, and one of the articles was written by your dad."

"My dad?" He sits back, brows pulling together. "I suppose it's possible. He does a lot of research on stuff like that."

"And then just now you mentioned he's an expert on this kind of stuff. Don't you think it's a strange coincidence that my grandfather and your dad are friends?"

"Coincidence?" His body tenses, and the tendons in his forearms tighten. He opens his mouth as if he's about to tell me something important but looks away. I wonder for a moment if he's not telling me the whole truth. But then he says, "Yeah. That is odd. You want me to ask him about it?"

"No," I say quickly, and then, "unless there's a way without telling your dad about me. I'm not sure I'm ready for anyone else to know about this."

"I got it." Marc relaxes, and his smile reaches his eyes as if I'm the most important person in the world. I really am paranoid to think that Marc would be a part of anything to do with Haemosu.

"Maybe since I can see this place, I can help you. Who was that guy?"

I lean back against the wall again. Can I trust him? Komo said not to tell a soul. But he knows already. He saw the whole thing. And what if he's right? What if he can help me?

Marc reaches over and takes my hand. His fingers skim over where the bandages once were, and my skin tingles at his touch; but he stops at the golden bracelet. It has become a barrier between us.

"This bracelet has something to do with this, doesn't it?"

"That bird you saw is a demigod who morphed into a bird. He put the bracelet on me. His name is Haemosu."

"The five dragons." Marc's fingers intertwine with mine. "Of course. Haemosu is known to drive a chariot led by five dragons. The legends call his chariot Oryonggeo."

So he does know a lot about mythology. "It's so twisted, though. My mom always told me dragons bring good luck."

"Sounds like Haemosu distorted everything. Why is he doing this to you?"

I pick up Marc's book and fumble through it until I find the legend of Haemosu. "Do you know this story?" He nods. I continue, "My grandfather thinks the princess actually escaped and that Haemosu is still angry at her for leaving him. She's supposedly my ancestor. He's been kidnapping the firstborn girl in my family ever since. Komo believes he's reliving the moment of courting Princess Yuhwa over and over again, hoping Yuhwa will change her mind and not leave him. Grandfather had a mural of her in his cave. I look just like her."

Marc stares at me and then at the book.

"You don't believe me," I say.

"You're the oldest?"

"Yes." I twirl the bracelet around my wrist, the gold of the dragons' twisted bodies glinting in the theater lighting.

There are now two dragons' eyes gleaming red. My chest feels as if a chain has been wrapped around it and cinched tight.

"The bracelet won't come off. Haemosu says every time we meet, another eye will glow. When all the eyes burn bright, I'll be his forever. He said he's been waiting for over a thousand years for me."

"This guy's really into you."

"So you don't think I've got a chance."

"No. That's not it." He lets out a groan. "You can't give up."

"I'm not!" I tuck my knees to my chest. "But you saw me earlier. I'm no match for an immortal."

Marc moves his body so he's facing me. His lips are so close I can't stop imagining how easily he could pull me into his arms.

"I saw an amazing girl standing up to a warrior. A girl who transformed into a bird and escaped. Don't tell me that isn't something."

I want to believe Marc. I reach for him, his skin burning against my palms. Our lips meet, breathless. His lips are soft, tender, and I've lost control. Sinking into his kisses. Drinking in his smell and touch. I trail my hands from his face down to his shoulders and follow the line of his biceps. I draw him closer. So close until our bodies are practically one.

Because I won't lose this moment. This kiss.

Haemosu can't take this from me.

I won't let him.

CHAPTER 21

After school, Michelle races up and bumps me playfully with her hip. I cringe at the sudden movement.

"Hey, girl," she says, sliding her bag strap over her shoulder. "You free this afternoon?"

"I'm heading to the archery center," I say. I don't tell her what I'm really doing. Heading off to practice #2 on my list of Ways to Kick Haemosu's Butt: Shoot an arrow, aim for the heart. "I really need to practice."

Because I must have perfect aim so I can watch his ugly grin falter when I slide my arrow through his heart.

"You're always training." She lifts her eyebrows. "It's not like you're prepping for a big tournament or anything. Come on. Have a little fun."

"Right. Fun." What a laugh that is. If only I could tell her the truth. That I'm just trying to survive. That I was torn to shreds only hours ago, and fun was tossed out of my vocabulary the day the creep showed up. Still, she's right. If these are my last days, I sure as hell don't want to be living them out as a sourpuss. "You want to come with me? We can hang out, and I can show you how awesome I am."

Michelle laughs, and I almost smile. This is good. Exactly what I need.

"It's a deal." She hooks arms with me, and we head out into the freezing cold. "But you'll owe me a movie date after this. Something fun and not involving weapons."

We pick up my dragon bow and arrows at my apartment and head to the archery center. Michelle chatters nonstop, which is a relief. I can't talk right now because my head whirls with insane images, and there's no fix for it except to prepare and plan. I can't let myself stop and think of what might happen if my plan fails. If my arrow doesn't hit its mark. If I become another of Haemosu's victims.

Before heading to the shooting area, I pop into the training center and introduce Michelle to Ahn Seong-Cheol, the head of the archery center.

"You haven't restrung your bow in some time," he says.

"I like to do it at my apartment." There's no way I'm going to tell him this bow hasn't needed stretching or new strings yet.

"Sometime I'd like to get a closer look at that bow of yours."

"Sure." I smile. I will never show anyone this bow. There's something special about it. "Maybe another time."

Michelle and I leave the center. I kick at the gravel road that winds up the mountain and listen to the latest school gossip.

"So you were right today," Michelle says. "Word is out that Min has made dibs on Marc, and he turned her down."

"Long Legs?" I smile as I imagine her disappointing pout. "Since when do we make dibs on people?"

"Did you just call her Long Legs?" Michelle stops, and at my sheepish grin she laughs, her breath coming out in white, puffy clouds. "Love it. It really fits. I think we're meant to be friends for life."

"I think that's the best idea I've heard in a long time." I grin, not bothering to tell her that our time might be slightly shorter than she thinks.

"You didn't tell me I was going to get my workout today," she says, panting.

"It's not far. Just up over the next rise."

"I feel like I'm in the middle of nowhere."

She's right. Forest lines the sides of our path, and there hasn't been a car that's passed us yet.

"Wait until we get to the Pavilion of the Yellow Stork, where the shooting range is," I say. "Then you'll see Gwanghwamun."

At the clearing, Michelle sags on a bench inside the pagoda while I unpack my bow and take in the view of Gwanghwamun below. Downtown Seoul is an eclectic mix of skyscrapers jutting tall like cranes, with ancient palaces and temples scattered about their feet. The low roar of the city floats up to where I'm standing.

I slip on my arm guard, gloves, and thumb ring, then notch in an arrow. There's a slight breeze that kicks up my hair. I wish I'd tied it back, but I'd been so desperate to get away I hadn't bothered.

The target I'm aiming for lies a hundred meters away. Most

bows couldn't possibly hit a target that far, but the Korean horn bow is known for its ability to hit unbelievable distances.

"Please forgive my archery," I whisper to the wind. This comes so automatically that I hardly even remember I'm saying the words. It's been ingrained in me ever since I first started taking lessons from my archery master in the States.

When I raise the bow, I visualize how Chumong, Korea's most famous archer, must have looked two thousand years ago as he drew back his bow. Then I begin my ritual. First, I focus my heart. Then I check to see if my chest is wide-open and my hands are in line. Finally, I draw back past my shoulder and aim slightly upward. The bow tingles beneath my palms. It speaks to me, whispering magic through my veins.

Haemosu's face is the target.

I allow my heart to guide my arm.

Release.

The arrow sinks into the bull's-eye with a thud.

Michelle squeals and claps. "Damn. You never told me you were so good. How do you do it?"

I squint against the late-afternoon sun. "I've been practicing since I was six. Plus, this bow is kind of special. It was a gift from my grandfather."

I pick out another arrow and repeat. Over and over. My goal is perfection. Anything less than perfect will mean death.

"Any progress with Hot Stuff?" Michelle asks, tearing me away from my obsession. "What's your plan for ripping Long Legs's talons off him?"

"You mean Marc?" I turn around to gather up the arrows that are being ferried back to me from the basket. My face is burning twenty shades of red, and my heart has catapulted into a full-out sprint.

"Of course, silly girl!"

"We kissed." There. I said it out loud. Just saying those words makes it real. And I already feel that ache itching to break free. I need to see him again.

"Oh my gosh!" Michelle jumps over to me. "Seriously? When did this happen? Why didn't you text me right away?"

"Girl, you really need to try out for the cheer squad."

She waves her hand dismissively.

"It was right before the end of school," I say. "I was having a bad day, and he was there to help me out."

"I bet he was."

I roll my eyes at her knowing look. "It was nice."

"Nice?"

My face is definitely on fire. It's a good thing she can't read my mind, because all I can think about is how his lips were on mine. The feel of his arms wrapped around me. The way he said my name as if I'm the most beautiful girl in the universe.

"When are you going to see him next?" She starts pacing. I bet a million bucks she's planning out my entire love life.

"I don't know. Things are kind of complicated right now."

"Then uncomplicate them." She grabs my arm. I'm surprised at how strong her grip is. "Call him. See him tonight."

She has no idea how much I want to do just that. "I don't know. Won't it seem like I'm desperate or something?"

"You must have some kind of good excuse to see him."

"Actually, I do." I rub my bow, thinking about his dad and metamorphosis. I groan. "There's no way I can call him."

"I can't believe this. You're a black belt in Tae Kwon Do and can shoot an arrow into the bull's-eye from a hundred meters away, but you can't call the guy?"

She has a point.

Michelle digs through my coat pocket and pulls out my phone. She starts texting. "I can't believe I'm freezing my bum out here for you."

"What are you doing?" I try to grab the phone from her, but she ducks away.

"Voilà!" She pushes SEND.

"You didn't."

"It's done."

I start whacking her with my glove. Then the phone chimes. I got a text. Michelle screams and eagerly stares at the message.

"Hey!" I grab the phone from her, but she's already read it. "Do you mind?"

"Not really." She grins. "You're welcome, by the way."

I read the message.

I'm free tonight to talk. You want to come over?

"He just invited me to his house," I say.

"And that's how it's done."

CHAPTER 22

"Hey there." Marc stands at the door to his house, the wind flapping his faded blue shirt and sending strands of hair over his eyes.

"You," I say.

"Me." He grins. "I see you found my house all right."

He lives in Seongbuk-dong, a nice neighborhood that climbs up the mountain behind the president's Blue House. Marc's house is tucked inside a walled courtyard, similar to Komo's place.

"Come on in." He swings the door open, and I step inside.

After I kick off my shoes, he leads me up the stairs. I stop midway, noticing the rows of photographs, medals, and awards.

"Who are these people?" I ask.

"My lineage." His tone is sharp, almost sarcastic, and his eyes darken.

I start reading off the names:

> JOHN GRAYSON—*assisted in deciphering the Rosetta Stone, 1799*
> CALVIN SHARSDALE—*inventor, 1826*

HOWARD SOCKWELL—*archaeologist, 1964*
STEVE BOURGET—*headed the archaeological find at Huaca el Pueblo, Peru, 2009*
DAMIAN GRAYSON—*assisted in discovery of ancient city near Be'er Sheva, 2012*

"Wow," I say. "That's quite the list. Are they really your relatives or people your family admires?"

"Relatives. Some are distant cousins."

"I can't believe it. You must be proud."

"I used to be." He shrugs.

"Not anymore?"

"Big shoes to fill."

"No one expects that of you, though, right?"

"Want to see the rest of the house?" Marc asks, and I know he's avoiding my question.

He leads me upstairs into the main room, and I'm blown away by its high, wood-beamed ceilings and a glass wall on the far side that overlooks downtown Seoul.

But that's not why my jaw drops. It's the artifacts that pack the walls and cram the shelves. A massive golden disk hangs from one wall with what looks like Hebrew script on it. Persian carpets cover the wooden floors, pots that look a thousand years old are scattered everywhere, and tall rectangular *hanji* lanterns pool light into the corners of the room.

Marc laughs at my expression. "Yeah," he says. "My parents are professors, but they also do archaeological digs and studies around the world. The Mongolian government loaned my mom the Sabek necklace to study in return for her work to get medical supplies to northern Mongolia."

I follow his finger to a case hanging on one wall. Tucked inside dangles a gold necklace riddled with stones.

"That's really cool." I pull my sweater over my bracelet. "But lately jewelry has kind of lost its appeal."

"Sorry about that." He runs his hand through his hair. "That was stupid of me to mention it."

I wave my hand, not really wanting to talk about it, and set my bow case against the wall. I jam my thumbs into my pockets. There's an energy buzzing in the air. It's as if both of us have so much to say, but we don't know where to begin.

"You want to sit?" he asks.

As we weave through the pots, I nearly trip over a gong resting on a wooden frame.

"Do you ring that when special guests arrive?" I grin.

"Only people we've put on high alert."

"Ah. So I don't fit into that category?"

He considers me for a moment. I can't help but notice how his eyes trail down to my lips. "Maybe you do." He grins, and I punch him lightly on the shoulder.

"Easy now." He rubs his arm playfully. "Careful with that punch. You underestimate yourself."

He heads off to the kitchen for drinks. There's a stack of newspapers and magazines scattered about on the antique coffee table. I pick up a magazine; but I'm not careful enough, and the vase in the center of the coffee table wobbles. I grab for its base, righting it before it falls, and let out a long breath.

Marc saunters in carrying two glasses of lemonade. "That's from Beijing. Xia Dynasty."

I snatch my hands away, tucking them in my lap. "Leave it to me to break something thousands of years old."

"Just messing with you." Marc hands me my glass, cool beneath my sweating palms. "Most of the really valuable stuff is in museums or in the glass cases along the back wall." He rattles off a couple of artifacts that are his favorites: a ram's horn from Bethlehem, a boomerang from the Outback, a carved elephant from Java, a mask from Africa, a tea set from Pakistan. My head swims just thinking about all those places.

He points to the vase. "I'm pretty sure that's a knockoff."

"What a relief." I sip my lemonade. "Do you ever travel with your parents?"

"Sometimes. If I can get out of school. Summers we usually go somewhere for research or to a dig."

"I'm completely jealous."

"Everyone in my family has discovered something huge." He leans back and stares out the massive window. The sun is setting, washing the skyscrapers with liquidy pinks and reds. "My parents never let me forget that."

"So they expect you to discover something?"

His jaw tightens. He sets his glass on the table a little too roughly and moves to stand at the glass wall, his back to me. "I speak and write six languages fluently, been on the honor roll practically my entire life, and even know some judo moves. But here's the kicker. I don't want my parents' lives. What I want is something completely different."

I follow him and lightly rest my hand on his arm.

"And what's that?"

"I don't know yet." He reaches out and runs his fingers along my jaw. "Or maybe I do. Have you ever felt as if you were meant for something in particular, but you don't know what it is?"

I nod.

"That's exactly how I feel. Like I'm ready and waiting, but it's not here yet. Sometimes I don't know if I'll ever figure it out."

Electricity from his touch sparks along my skin. The memory of his kiss from earlier haunts me. I want more. I reach to pull him closer. But Marc cries out, leaning back.

My sleeve must have slipped up my arm, exposing Haemosu's little gift and touching his neck.

"Oh my gosh!" I say. "I'm so sorry. I didn't mean to."

"Man." He rubs his neck. "That thing has a bite to it, doesn't it?"

Looking down, I see the two dragons' eyes are glowing, as if the creatures are watching us. I yank down my sleeve, covering the bracelet.

"Let's get some ice on it," I say.

After he's got the ice pack pressed to his neck, he says, "Remember what I told you after the NHS meeting today about that bracelet of yours?"

"A sign of enslavement. How could I forget?"

"Come here." He grabs my hand and leads me down the hall. "I'll show you what I found."

When I realize we're about to enter his bedroom, I stop. "Your parents don't mind?"

"They're still at work. Don't worry." He laughs. "You're safe with me."

There are books everywhere, piled in stacks on the floor and loaded on shelves. He's got a wide desk cluttered with scrolls, a globe, and more books. A long shelf rests above his desk, running the full length of the window, with mounds of artifacts teetering on it.

I sink into a large futon chair and point to his shelf. "Did you find those?"

"Yeah. I guess I have a trophy wall of my own." He rummages through a few books on his desk until he pulls out one. "Here it is."

He hands me the opened book. I study the illustration of a glowing man pulling a long chain. A straggling line of weeping girls with bowed heads is attached to the chain. It's obvious they're being dragged into slavery.

"Look at the bonds that keep them chained." Marc hands me a magnifying glass.

I don't want to look, because the pain on these girls' faces is all too familiar. I recognize that desperation, that hopelessness, in my own reflection in the mirror. But I straighten my back. There's no way I'll be able to defeat Haemosu by allowing myself to be sucked into the pit of despair. I take the magnifying glass and hold it over the page.

He's right. Though the ink on the page has faded, the golden luster of the girls' bonds remains. And a strange pattern. I lean closer. No, not strange at all; a sickeningly familiar design comes into focus. The twisted curl of the dragon's body.

I drop the magnifying glass.

"This book was written about a hundred years ago," Marc

says. "It's obviously a reprint, but I think the stories have some truth to them."

I push the book away and cross my arms, wanting to hide my own shackle. Pretend it doesn't exist. "Yeah, they do."

"Maybe it was a bad idea to show you." He clamps the book shut and shoves it into his bookshelf. "I seem to be making a mess of things rather than fixing anything."

I press my fingers to my temples, willing my brain to stay focused. Panic threatens to crawl up my throat, cinching it so tight I won't be able to breathe.

"Hey." Marc pulls me up and into his arms. "We're going to figure this out. Together. You aren't alone in this."

He drags his fingers through my hair, and then his hand trails down my neck. I don't stop him. He tilts my chin so I'm looking into those forever-green eyes of his, and I believe that he'll do whatever he can to help me.

He presses me to him, and my arms wrap around his neck, loving how perfect his body feels. His lips kiss my forehead, breath hot as fire, and drag along my cheeks to my lips.

I'm lost. Between earth and sky.

It's as if we've entered our own realm that belongs only to the two of us. I could live here forever.

A knock on the door.

We push apart. For a moment I can't remember where I am.

"Marc," a man's voice says from the doorway. I look over to see his dad. Frowning.

"Dad." Marc's voice comes out clipped, angry. "This is Jae."

"Hello, Jae Hwa." He smiles and reaches his hand out to

shake mine. Once again I'm reminded of how much Marc looks like his dad. Same broad shoulders, square jaw, and shaggy hair. The only difference is, his dad's eyes are blue. "We met at the museum. I'm good friends with your grandfather. How are you holding up?"

"I'm okay." I study him, confused, and unsure what to say. It seems he knows more about my situation than I thought. I peek over at Marc. Did he tell his dad? But Marc just shakes his head and rolls his eyes.

"Can I talk to you?" Dr. Grayson asks Marc.

"I'll be back in a minute." Marc squeezes my hand and follows his dad into the hall.

I bite my lip. Dr. Grayson seemed ticked off that I was here. I slide out the doorway into the hall, listening.

"What are you doing, kissing her?" Dr. Grayson asks Marc as they enter another room at the end of the hall. "You are disregarding protocol and breaking the rules."

The door slams shut, and with it my heart. Disregarding protocol? Breaking the rules? The truth hits me like a mass of concrete. His parents don't approve of him dating me. Is it because I'm Korean? Maybe I'm not smart enough. Or maybe his parents need him to find that special artifact, and I'm distracting him from achieving his destiny.

I lean against the wall, my bracelet and heart weighing me down like a brick in water.

CHAPTER 23

I'm debating whether to bolt or stay when a woman's voice says, "Hello there."

I spin on my heels, trying to look nonchalant. Definitely not as if I've been sneaking about. A woman with sandy-blond hair tied into a ponytail at the nape of her neck stands at the entrance to the kitchen. She's wearing khaki pants and a purple wrap sweater. A large rock necklace rests against her chest. I wonder if it's as ancient as most of the items in this house.

"You must be Jae," she says, smiling a warm smile. "I'm Marc's mom. I'm so happy to finally meet you. Come, let me make you a cup of tea."

I follow her into the kitchen. She pulls out a traditional celadon tea set and prepares black tea for both of us. As I watch, I can't help but notice she's the one Marc got his green eyes and dimple from.

"So you and Marc have been hanging out lately?" she asks.

I've no idea what I should tell her. Actually, all I really want to do is leave and forget about talking to Dr. Grayson, because

I'm not sure who to trust anymore. I'm guessing either Marc or Grandfather told the Graysons about me and maybe even about the whole Haemosu thing. After hearing Dr. Grayson talk about me like that to Marc, I can hardly think straight.

"Well," she continues as if I've answered her question, "I think it's great. Marc needs a challenge in his life, and this is the perfect opportunity."

I swallow, trying to process her words. "Opportunity?"

We stare at each other for a moment. She takes a sip of her tea, then says, "He's tutoring you, right?"

Before I have a chance to dig myself into a giant hole, Marc and his dad join us.

"Great!" Marc's dad says. "The two of you have gotten a chance to meet. Jae, Marc here was telling me you had some questions about metamorphosis that he thinks I can help you with."

My eyes dart to Marc. He told his dad?

"It's okay," Marc says, grabbing an apple from the basket on the counter. "You can trust him."

My eyes dart between Marc and his dad. Neither seems upset, so I'm not really sure what to think. This is something Marc and I need to talk about later. Still, what is there to talk about? It's not as if we're dating or anything. It's not even like we'll have a long-term relationship.

"Would you be comfortable coming to my office?" Dr. Grayson asks. "Marc will come with us, of course."

Dr. Grayson's office looks more like a giant library than an office. It's two stories high, completely lined with wooden bookshelves. A wooden ladder is connected to a track to reach the higher shelves. Instead of a traditional desk, a giant oval table with four stools sits in the center of the room. Two couches are situated beneath the large windows.

Dr. Grayson sits on one of the stools. He presses a button, and a panel pulls back in the center of the table. A computer screen rises, and Dr. Grayson punches in a password.

"Do sit." He gestures for us to join him. Once we're situated, he asks, "So you found my article on metamorphosis?"

"Yes, I did." I rack my brain for a reason why I would be asking about something crazy like this. "I'm doing a report on Korean mythology in class."

He nods as if this is the most interesting thing he's ever heard.

"You seem to know so much about it," I say, relieved that he bought my explanation. "Where did you get your information from?"

"Lots of old texts." He waves his hand as if it's inconsequential. "Nothing you teenagers would be interested in."

Marc huffs but doesn't say anything.

"So are only certain types of creatures able to do this change?"

"I'm not completely sure. But the myths that talk about transformation only indicate gods and demigods with this ability. These immortals use the power in battle and impersonate other humans or animals. The Fox Sister fairy tale, where a *kumiho* shape-shifts into a human girl, comes to mind."

Dr. Grayson clicks on a file. The myth of the fox-tailed woman pops onto the screen.

"So it seems like it's pretty easy to do," I say. It isn't for me, but maybe that's because I'm not immortal. Maybe I'm not meant to shape-shift.

"It appears to be a part of who they are. Even so, it takes complete concentration, focus, and skill to maintain the transformation."

"Are there side effects?"

"There aren't any mentioned in the myths. It appears that the key is remembering who you are so you can switch back. If you can maintain that mental control, then you've found what's needed to sustain the shift. Not *you*, of course, but the immortals."

"Of course. That's really helpful. Thanks."

"We've got to go, Dad," Marc says. "Jae needs to get home."

"Excellent," Dr. Grayson says with a bow of his head. "Until another time."

I smile, thinking how incredibly formal his dad is. Maybe that's all his conversation with Marc was about earlier. Maybe he's just old-fashioned.

As I get up to leave, I glance at the ceiling. It's domed, and in the center of it is a giant mural. I stare at it, shaken.

The Tiger of Shinshi.

Is it coincidental that my aunt, Grandfather, and Marc's dad all have that same painting in their homes? I stop cold at the door as something else tickles my memory.

"You okay?" Marc asks.

I turn and reach out my hand to Dr. Grayson. "It was great talking to you."

"Of course," Dr. Grayson stands, his eyebrows raised, and he shakes my hand.

My heart skips a beat. Because I was right. He's wearing the same tiger ring as Grandfather and Komo.

This isn't a coincidence at all.

CHAPTER 24

The next day I head to Komo's house after school because I'm still hoping she's thought of a way to keep me alive. What will she think about Haemosu being able to suck me into his world through my locker? And how I morphed into a bird?

I am alive, but I haven't escaped Haemosu's vengeance. Because another dragon's eye has turned red.

Marc acts as if everything is okay. I want to believe him. But Haemosu did something to Marc; I'm sure of it. I trail my fingers over my lips, remembering Marc's touch, his kiss.

It takes only thirty minutes to get to Komo's house by subway. I call Dad and tell him I'm going to hang out with her.

The truth is, I'm falling way behind in school. Third-quarter grades are only a month away, and I'm sure I'm failing everything because I'm spending my nights training rather than studying. But why worry about grades if I may not even live to see them?

I ride the escalator out of the subway and onto the busy street. I smell *hotteok*, and my stomach rumbles. Other than the bowl of *japchae* I ate for lunch, I haven't eaten anything all day.

Michelle texts me, asking when our movie date will be. I text back, promising tomorrow night.

When you don't know how long you have to live, you have to live as if every second counts.

I detour to the wooden cart where a lady drops little balls of stuffed batter into a cast iron pan. She presses the balls flat with her spatula, letting them fizz in the grease until golden. I hand over one thousand won, and she passes me a hot pancake, a piece of wax paper wrapped around it to keep my fingers from getting sticky. I lick the fried edge and take a bite that tastes of sugar and cinnamon. I smile.

As I stroll down the sidewalk, I pretend this is just a normal day and nothing is chasing or trying to kidnap me. Buses belch smoke and traffic whizzes by. The final rays of sunlight glint off the skyscrapers in the distance, and I try to memorize this feeling of freedom, not sure if I'll ever feel it again.

When I turn the corner of Komo's small street, I'm licking my fingers, the *hotteok* already gone. The sides of the road are littered with cigarette butts, paper cups, and promotional flyers. A light wind kicks up, sending the trash skittering down the alley. I freeze, hearing the tinkle of bells. It smells faintly of honeysuckle.

My vision blurs. One moment the street stretches before me and the next I glimpse a snow-capped mountain. I blink, and the vision vanishes. I tilt my head, squinting, and it reappears.

This must be what Komo means when she talks about living on the edge of two worlds. I narrow my eyes at the mountain, and as I do, it crystalizes while the street blurs. Where is that place? Is it one of those portals or connection points between two dimensions that Kumar believes in?

I force myself to concentrate on the street. Two men in black suits stroll toward the main road. A shopkeeper brushes off her stoop with a giant straw broom. Two schoolgirls in their uniforms, heads nearly touching, giggle at something on their phones. Above, tall grayish buildings jut into a sky that threatens of snow, and hundreds of wires string across from building to building, an electrician's nightmare.

The mountain fades. My vision clears. And with it the odd sensation of someone watching me in the fading daylight.

I break into a jog until I reach Komo's gate, slamming it behind me as I hurry up her steps and rush inside without knocking. If there's one thing I've learned lately, it's to trust my instincts.

I stop dead. Komo is sitting on a cushion at her low table drinking tea—with *Grandfather.*

"Grandfather?" I ask. "What are you doing here?"

"Jae Hwa." He stands and bows. "It is good to see you. I am here in Seoul with your aunt discussing how to deal with Haemosu."

I somehow manage a bow. About five million words are stuck in my mouth, and I can't seem to get one of them out. Komo sets down her teacup and motions for me to sit next to her. Slipping off my backpack and setting it on a hook by the door, I plop down on the pillow and try to brush the hair out of my eyes. Komo folds up a map of Korea along with a brochure of the Sejong Center and sets them on top of the apothecary chest.

"I was not expecting you until after dark," she says.

"I needed to talk to you now." I glance between the two of them. "Both of you, actually."

"What is it?" Grandfather asks.

"I went to Marc's house last night." I rub my forehead, overwhelmed by everything I needed to tell them.

Grandfather frowns. "Dr. Grayson's son?"

"Yeah." At first I'm surprised that Grandfather knows who Marc is, but then I remember he is friends with the Graysons. "While I was there, I talked to Marc's dad about metamorphosis."

I take in their expressions, waiting for them to be upset. But they aren't. Which indicates that my suspicions were correct. So I continue.

"I noticed that the Tiger of Shinshi was painted on his ceiling, just like it's painted on both of your walls." I gesture to Komo's painting. "And he's wearing the same tiger ring as both of you. Don't tell me that's a coincidence, because it's not."

Grandfather sighs and leans back in his chair.

"She deserves to know," Komo says. "She's affected by the order in one way or another."

"What order?" I ask. "What are you talking about?"

"So be it." Grandfather nods. "First of all, you should know that what I am about to tell you is highly secretive. No one but a select few are aware of our order's existence. Normally I would need approval for speaking so openly with you, but since you are limited for time, I think it is necessary."

"Okay." I stare at the two of them. They certainly don't seem like the type to be a part of some secret organization.

"We are both council members of the Guardians of Shinshi," Komo says.

Grandfather adds, "We are the defenders of Korea, protectors of the land, and seekers of justice. Just as the Tiger of Shinshi holds the Korean people by a golden thread, we watch over and help maintain Korea's balance with the Spirit World. Our order has been in existence since the founding of Korea."

I stare at him for a moment, trying to put together what he's telling me. I vaguely remember the folktale of the Tiger of Shinshi, the immortal tiger bound to protect Korea.

"Is this another myth?" I ask.

"Indeed." Grandfather waves his hand. "But this is not something you should worry over. Dr. Grayson is also a council member, and I trust him. The council has agreed to assist us in saving you. I should have thought to ask Dr. Grayson about metamorphosis myself."

"I don't understand." I grip the edge of the table, needing its solidity. "Why have they suddenly decided to help us now? What about Sun and all our other relatives? Where were they then?"

Grandfather's shoulders sag. "Let us just say we've learned that Haemosu might have something the council wants. Hence our plight coincides with theirs."

"The last thing she needs to worry about is the council and its needs," Komo says, giving Grandfather a raised-eyebrow look. "What you need to focus on, Jae, is yourself and how we can help you."

Then I explain what happened in my locker. Grandfather mutters a string of Korean words under his breath while Komo clucks her tongue.

"This is bad." The wrinkles around Komo's eyes deepen. "Something is wrong."

"Something? Isn't everything wrong?"

"Maybe not," Grandfather says. "She has learned the art of metamorphism. This is a step in the right direction. Jae Hwa, now that Haemosu has gilded you, we do not have much time. In less than a week you have had two encounters with him."

"We must act now," Komo says. "Tonight, perhaps."

"What are you talking about? What's happening tonight?"

"Remember the *Illumination* exhibit that your father's company sponsored?" Grandfather says. "The *samjoko* amulet is on display there. The Guardians of Shinshi have recently uncovered information that leads us to believe that it acts as a key into the Spirit World."

"Like a transporter?"

"It is not that simple. Each tomb of the ancient Koguryo kingdom was built as a gateway into the Spirit World. According to legend, if the *samjoko* is fitted into the keyhole within a tomb, it will unlock a passageway into the Spirit World."

"You're basing your whole plan on legend?" I gape at them. This is madness, putting our lives at risk based on some random story written nearly a thousand years ago.

Grandfather shrugs. "We are discovering that what we once deemed to be myth is often reality. I am willing to take the risk."

"We plan on acquiring it," Komo says, "and entering the Spirit World to attack when he is not expecting it."

I shift onto my knees. An image of a circular bronze medal with a three-legged crow flashes through my memory. The bird's body touched eight smaller points around the circle. "So you want to get this amulet so you can go hang out with Haemosu. That's—" Crazy, stupid, ridiculous.

"Shh!" Komo presses her fingers to my lips. I flinch. "Do not utter his name here!"

Now I'm not supposed to say his name? When will the rules and restrictions stop?

I say, "I'm coming with you." There's no way I'm letting them do this without me.

"No." Komo begins to clear the table, setting the teacups on the linoleum counter. "It is too dangerous."

"I can help."

"Then you shall." Grandfather clears his throat after seeing Komo's scathing look. I try not to look too triumphant. "Your aunt told me you believe that Haemosu's locked the girls' spirits in a tomb. This is also news to us. We must discover why he is keeping them there. I cannot sit idly, knowing my daughter is still trapped in his clutches."

"We must plan quickly," Komo says. "The museum closes in three hours. We need to be inside when they lock the doors. A Guardian will be there to assist us in case we run into trouble."

"Wait a second," I say. "You're not planning on stealing it, are you?"

Komo doesn't answer. Instead she picks up a scrub brush and turns on the faucet to clean the dishes. I want to scream, shake some sense into them. There's no way I can let them get hurt because of me.

I lost Mom to cancer, and I couldn't control that. I won't lose Grandfather and Komo, too. I have to think of a way to stop them.

"Come," Grandfather says. "We should not discuss this here but in a more private place."

Komo sets the teacups in the drying rack and moves to the center of the room to toss back the carpet over the trapdoor. I help her lift the hatch, and just as I start down the ladder rungs I glance at the window. Someone is standing outside, silhouetted in the streetlight against the curtained window.

I grow so cold, I nearly let go of the rung.

"He's here!" I yell.

"That is impossible!" Komo says. "Darkness already has set in."

Grandfather whips around as the front door flings open. Flashing light burns my eyes. I duck my head into my arm.

"Conspiring, I see," Haemosu says in his creamy-smooth voice. He's dressed differently tonight, in black slacks and a blue-collared shirt; but he's still his same perfectly gorgeous self, with those piercing black eyes, chiseled features, and wavy black hair. "So we meet again, old man. I cannot have you influencing my princess."

Komo doesn't even blink. She rushes at Haemosu, whipping out a roundhouse kick. Haemosu is thrown sideways and crashes against the concrete wall, cracks splintering up and down where he lands. Grandfather turns to me, his eyes wide, and pushes me farther down.

"Stay below and lock the hatch," he says.

"No!" I push against him. "You need my help!"

Grandfather leaves me, and I scramble back up the ladder. Komo is bouncing back and forth on the balls of her feet as Haemosu pulls himself off the wall. Grandfather sidles next to her.

"Not much of a welcome," Haemosu says, brushing off chunks of cement. "Especially since I have brought my friends."

He snaps his fingers. Two boars leap through the open door,

snarling. One lands on Komo, pinning her to the ground with its sharp claws. The other faces Grandfather and growls.

"Komo!" I scream, and forward flip through the air. I land next to her as the boar's fangs sink into her neck. Blood spurts up in the air, and I kick the boar in the side; but its furry mass feels like iron. The animal won't budge.

Grandfather punches and kicks at his boar, barely holding off the beast as he backtracks to the kitchen cabinets. He yanks open a drawer and withdraws a handful of knives. In quick succession, he hurls knife after knife at the boar until the beast's face is riddled with them.

"The sword," Komo screeches. Her pale finger points to the wall.

I follow her finger to the sword resting on two nails above the step chest. Before I can take another step, the bracelet on my arm flares white. It jolts me back, and I'm flung to the very opposite wall. The bracelet bolts me to the wall.

Haemosu laughs and snaps his fingers again. The boars' heads flick to him. "Leave the princess alive. She will watch you kill these two conspirators," he says. And then to me, "You shall suffer for making a fool of me. You will watch all those you love suffer until you are begging me to take you."

Then I start screaming, and my vision is a blur of anger as I snatch anything within grasp with my free hand—picture frames, lamp, vase—and hurl them at him.

In a burst of light, Haemosu vanishes. His laughter echoes through the room, spinning my heart into a raging fire.

The boars gnash their teeth, saliva drooling from their tongues, and face Grandfather and Komo again. Grandfather leaps onto the table and dives across the room toward the sword. The beast jumps after him. Grandfather's outstretched hand whips the sword off the wall, and as he falls, he swivels the sword around and pierces the boar in midair.

I pull against the bracelet, now with three dragon eyes blazing red.

Komo has squirmed back toward the couch while Grandfather scrambles to his feet, slipping on blood. The boar rakes his claw across her chest. Still she holds him off. Her hand snakes under her couch cushions and pulls out a silver dagger, and she plunges it deep into the boar's chest. Grandfather pierces the boar's rear. It wails, kicks him in the face, sending him tumbling backward. Komo yanks her dagger back out and stabs the boar again. It collapses to its side.

Komo, her face streaked with crimson lines, falls still.

And so do I.

The carnage of blood, the rank animal odor, the broken furniture overwhelm me. Sharp silence chokes at my throat, and suddenly it's impossible to breathe. The door bangs against the side of the house in the wind.

Bang, bang, bang.

My wrist is raw and throbs with pain. But that is nothing compared to the agony in my chest. A cutting wind swirls through the room, kicking up golden dust. It whirls around the beasts and Komo's body until all three are drawn into it.

"Don't take her!" I yell.

Grandfather shifts on the floor and lifts his head. "Eun," his voice whispers, and then louder, "Eun!"

Komo's eyes flutter open, and she reaches out a hand to me.

"Komo!" My scream pierces the night as she vanishes in the tunnel of wind.

She's gone. She needed me, and I couldn't save her.

The bracelet finally releases me from the wall. Sobbing, I sink to the floor, the pain of the battle battering against me like sheets of hard rain, but I crawl against the storm inside me to the door.

Haemosu took her to that awful palace of his. I'm sure of it. Grandfather pulls me into his arms, tears streaming down his wrinkled face.

"I tried. I tried." Grandfather repeats those words over and over. "If only he had taken me. If only—"

Why? WHY!

"This is all *my* fault," I say. "I should've let him take me. Then she'd be safe."

"This is the first time he has broken out of his usual path." Grandfather's eyes are wild with fear and anger. I have never seen him like this. "It is impossible, but he was here at nightfall. He no longer requires light to empower him. This means only one thing. None of us is safe. All the old rules we held on to mean nothing! I must find out how he is getting this kind of power. Jae Hwa"—he cups my face between his hands—"time is of the essence. Your father might be next."

A calmness settles over me as if I've stepped out of my body, and I know what I must do. "Then I'll hunt down Haemosu and stop him before he gets the chance."

"No." Grandfather clutches me tighter. "This is for me alone. You must convince your father to escape the country. I need you to take me to the clinic. Then tomorrow night I will get the amulet, enter the Spirit World, and put an end to this forever."

I stare at the pool of blood where Komo had been. "Okay," I say.

I don't tell him the truth. That there's no way I'm going to let him sacrifice his life for me. Not over my dead body.

CHAPTER 25

I skip the elevator and instead huff up the stairs to the ninth floor of our apartment building. My hand trembles as I push my finger over the scanner to unlock our apartment door. When it finally releases, I shove the door open.

"Dad!" I yell out as I enter.

I want to believe he'll be home, lying on the couch watching TV, but part of me is already freaking out that Haemosu has taken him, too.

"Jae Hwa," Dad calls over the noise on the TV.

He's lounging on the couch, woolly socked feet propped up on two unpacked boxes. His tie is loose, and his top two buttons are undone. I sink onto the couch next to him and allow my breathing to return to normal.

Dad's fine. Happy. Watching TV.

"Did you work out?" Dad says, pushing the MUTE button. "You sound out of breath, like you've been running."

"Running. Yes. I went for a long run."

"Your time with Komo go well?"

My mind is filled with visions of blood, barred teeth, and swirling wind.

Komo has been—

I can't think about it. Can't even *believe* it. I push my fingers against my eyelids to stop the tears, stop the images flashing before me.

Dad sits up. "What's wrong?"

"She's—she's gone. He took her. Just like he did the others."

Dad's forehead creases. "What are you talking about?"

"Haemosu *took* Komo."

Dad is silent for a moment. "Is this the same Haemosu that your grandfather keeps talking about?"

"Don't you get it?" I jump up and start pacing the room. "We need to get out of here! Like *now*."

"Jae. You need to calm down." Dad stares at me as if I've lost my mind. "What has gotten into you?"

"You don't believe me!" My throat constricts.

He stands up, his jaw set. "This is about going back to L.A., isn't it?"

"No! I mean, yes!"

"Eun has been talking about this nonsense with you, hasn't she? I strictly forbade her to bring you into any of this. That was our agreement when she wanted to see you."

When I don't answer him right away he says, "I knew it."

I say, "Call her. Now."

He raises his eyebrows and pulls out his phone, punching in the numbers. His hands are shaking, and I suspect that a part of him believes me. "This kind of insanity is exactly what I was worried about. She's got your mind all twisted with her ideas."

I rub my palms up and down my jeans until they burn as Dad puts the phone to his ear.

"Eun," Dad says. "How are you?"

I stand frozen. My head feels stuffy, as if it's full of cotton. "She's there?"

Dad nods, but continues to talk into the phone. "Uh huh. Yes. I was calling because Jae Hwa is worried about you. Are you hurt?" Pause. "Okay." Dad sits back on the couch. "Good. You need to stop encouraging her with this Haemosu nonsense. It's not healthy." He pauses. "So you agree? Good. Good. Here, talk some sense into her."

He hands me the phone. "Your aunt is fine. She said she cut her finger."

Cut her finger! I snatch the phone. "Komo?"

"Ah, my princess," a deep male voice says. *Haemosu.* My heart shrivels. "Truly I am enjoying our courtship. So much that I'd hate for it to end."

The phone drops from my fingers, clattering onto the wooden floor. The colors of the room wash away as I sink to the ground. Haemosu is one step ahead of me. Always one *freaking* step ahead!

Dad is saying something to me, but I only hear buzzing. Somehow I manage to stumble my way to my room. The punching bag becomes my sole focus. I ignore Dad's knocking, pleading to talk. All I can think about is the bag and my pent-up anger.

An hour later I'm sweaty, and my fists ache when I finally lie flat on the floor. I can't stop worrying about Komo. Is she okay?

Did Haemosu take her to that awful palace? The thought makes me so sick I race to the bathroom and throw up.

I splash water over my face and stare into the mirror. Dark shadows circle my eyes, and my hair is wild and snarled.

I will find a way to rescue Komo.

There must be something in the ancient stories that Grandfather and Komo overlooked, some secret way to outwit the monster. Back in my bedroom I pull out the dragon horn bow Grandfather gave me and rub my palm over its wooden surface.

Everyone has a weakness. Even a demigod. I will find Haemosu's, hunt him down, and use it against him.

The next morning I drag my feet down the school hallway, hoping the cream and saline has erased the puffiness from around my eyes. I even used powder to hide the flush on my face. Too many tears. Too little sleep. My only motivation for crawling out of bed was the hope that I'd encounter Haemosu.

Tonight I'm supposed to meet Grandfather at the museum at 7 p.m. to steal the amulet. Which means I've got to figure out a way to get the amulet before then. There's no way I'm letting Grandfather face Haemosu for me. Komo had. And now she's gone.

I stop short, swallowing the lump in my throat. The hallway fades, the light blurs like the headlights of a car, and Komo's face fills my vision.

Her words rush to me: "Take control of your mind; harness your strength."

"I can't," I whisper.

"You can," she says.

Then she's gone as if someone has clicked off the headlights. I'm sandwiched between streams of kids, shoving their way to lockers and classes. My stomach knots up, and there's a tugging at my chest; but I will my feet to move. Komo isn't the only person haunting me. Haemosu dangles in the forefront of my mind. And every time I look at the bracelet I am reminded of him.

"I brought you a gift." Michelle hands me a coffee cup as she falls in stride with me. "Vanilla latte. Extra hot and extra whipped cream."

I take a sip. It tastes like hot water.

"Did he give that to you?" Michelle asks, pointing to my bracelet.

"What?" How does she know about Haemosu?

"You know. Marc. He's totally crushing on you."

"Oh. Right. Yeah." The lies keep piling up. I've reached my locker and stare at it. I haven't touched the door since yesterday's episode with Haemosu. The thought of it sends my pulse racing. But I need my Chinese textbook.

My translation of the legend of Haemosu and Princess Yuhwa is tucked away in that Chinese textbook. I want to work on it some more, look for clues I haven't seen before. If only I wasn't so hopeless when it came to Chinese.

Michelle touches the gold bracelet before I can stop her. She immediately jerks her hand back. "Ouch!" she cries. "What's up with your bracelet?"

Just Haemosu's little way of saying "Hands off!" I want to say, but I don't and instead pull my sleeve over my wrist. "Nothing. Probably static electricity."

"Oh." And to my surprise I think she buys my outrageous lie. "Don't forget about our movie night," Michelle says. "Lily is coming, too."

"Crap. I totally forgot about that. Can we do it another time? I need to see my grandfather."

"You can't be serious."

I grimace. "I'm sorry."

"This is getting old, Jae. You promise you'll hang out, but you never do. It's always one excuse or another."

"I know." I close my eyes, my head pounding even louder than before. My life sucks.

"So why are you staring at your locker? Did you forget your combination or something?"

"No. I'm just reviewing my Chinese symbols in my head before class." And although it isn't true, I really should be since IB Korean is kicking my butt. Yep. I'm going to fail. All those times I'd hated studying. Now it's all I wish I could do. Curled up on my *yo* with my textbook, drinking a cup of hot chocolate, not a care in the world.

I spin the combination for my locker. My hands shake.

"I don't know why you torture yourself like that by taking advanced Korean," she says, leaning against the locker next to mine. "If you didn't spend so much time on that class, you could be hanging out with us."

"Tell me about it."

Komo and I hoped to find a clue in the ancient texts to save me. How am I supposed to get help now that she's gone? She had become the closest person to a mom for me. It was Komo who was looking out for me. Protecting me.

I can't wait to see Haemosu again. I'll show him how my punch feels, how nice my foot looks imprinted on his handsome face.

"Listen, if you don't want to be friends, I get it," Michelle says. "But I'm tired of tiptoeing around you. I helped hook you up with Marc, and now you're too busy for me. Or were you just using me to get Marc?"

My eyes widen. "That's not it at all."

"Then what's your problem? You've got a great guy who has the hots for you, and you're acting like the world has ended."

"Sorry to disappoint. Maybe my life isn't as flipping fantastic as it appears."

"Testy, are we?" Michelle shifts her books and eyes our classroom door. "Are you going to open your locker already or what? We've got like fifty-five seconds until the late bell rings."

A hand reaches over my shoulder, pushing to keep my locker door closed. "You sure that's a good idea?"

It's Marc.

My heart skips, and his touch melts the tension in my shoulders. We haven't talked since yesterday; and on so many levels I wish we were two normal kids falling in love, without immortals, magic lands, and excess baggage from a thousand years ago. I say, "No. But I should."

Our eyes meet. Mine saying "I need this." His saying "Bad idea."

I pull the metal lever up and swing the door open, holding my breath.

There's no golden light. No hidden world. Just my books

sprawled on the shelf with a plastic container of half-eaten *kim* and Tae Kwon Do pictures taped to the door. Marc runs his hands through his hair and lets out a chuckle. "You sure know how to start a day, Fighter Girl."

I breathe again, snatch up my books—all of them—and stuff them into my backpack. It's full, so I decide to carry my bio and Korean textbooks.

Michelle stops studying her split ends. "You're moving back to L.A., aren't you? Is that what this is all about?"

"No." I swing my backpack over my shoulder. It's heavy. "I just think it's best to be prepared and study for all my classes each night."

"Fine. I'll talk to you later," Michelle says. "Or not. You decide."

"Michelle," I say to her retreating back. She's upset, and I don't know how to fix it. "It's not what you think."

"She'll get over it," Marc says.

"What if she doesn't?" I ask. What if that's the last time we ever talk again, and I've completely ruined our friendship because I couldn't tell her the truth?

"Let me help you," Marc says, his gaze as tight as a drawn arrow, and I realize he's not just talking about the books.

The bell rings. We're late.

I open my mouth to say yes but find myself shaking my head. No. How selfish am I even to think of risking his life? Marc, Grandfather, and Dad. I must keep them safe from Haemosu.

Now it's Marc's turn to shake his head, but I leave him and race down the hallway toward class.

"I'm fluent in Chinese!" he yells over the rush of everyone dashing into class.

I freeze. What can that boy *not* do? He must have overheard us talking. I glance back at him before stepping into English. He's still staring at me, the hallway now empty, with his lips in a half smile. Impossible.

"After school?" I say.

"Coffee shop. At the bottom of the hill."

I nod and slip inside class, promising myself this will be nothing more than a quick Chinese lesson. I definitely, absolutely won't let him get involved.

CHAPTER 26

The strong scent of ground coffee greets me as I enter the coffee shop after school. The cozy atmosphere of cafés is one of the things I love about Korea. That and the subway system. I hate being tied down to the school bus. *There's a lot I'm starting to like,* I realize as I move to the marble counter to order. If Haemosu hadn't shown up to ruin my life, I might actually come to enjoy Korea. I order a chai tea, hoping it will calm my nerves, and scan the crowded café. Most of the tables are filled with coffee mugs and laptops, surrounded by students.

I spot Marc in a soft evergreen-colored chair in the back corner, a pile of books resting on a small coffee table nearby. He hasn't seen me yet; but his glasses are on, and his forehead is scrunched like he's reading something really good. I smile.

"Hey, Brainiac." I thread my way to him.

He looks up and motions to the empty chair. "Glad you showed up, slowpoke. I had to beat up half the soccer team to keep your seat reserved."

"Impressive." I sink into the cushiony seat and push aside

a stack of books to make room for my mug. "Got enough books?"

"You can never have enough books," he says, but his voice doesn't have that usual playfulness to it. He sounds tired, and there are dark circles under his eyes. "How are you doing?"

"I should be asking you that. How are your eyes?"

"Never better," he says nonchalantly; but he won't look at me, and I get the feeling he's lying. "But you avoided my question. How are *you*?"

I cup my hands around my mug and soak in its warmth. He deserves to know the truth. No more jokes. No more pretending everything is fine. Because it isn't.

I need to tell him everything. I'm desperate, and there's no one else to talk to about this. Images of Komo spin through my head. I say, "Not good. He took my aunt."

"What?"

"Yeah. She's—she's—" I wave my hand through the air, not trusting my voice, which is full of unshed tears. "Haemosu took her," I finally manage.

His jaw drops. "You're serious."

I nod. Silence hovers over us, and finally Marc leans back and blows out a long stream of air.

"God. I'm sorry, Jae."

"Yeah. But I'm going to find her. Bring her back. He isn't going to win this fight." I had promised myself I wouldn't get him involved any further, but one request couldn't hurt him, right? "I need your help."

I set my mug between two stacks of books, dig through my

bag until I find Mom's *Samguk Yusa* and my unfinished translation of the legend of Haemosu. "I'm hoping we might find a clue here. But my Chinese kind of sucks."

Marc takes the book with such reverence that I know he understands its value. Barely touching the pages, he flips through it, scanning the contents. "This is old," he says. "I shouldn't even be touching this book without gloves." He takes my translation next. "Looks like the myth of Princess Yuhwa and Haemosu."

My insides wiggle. Since Mom died, I'd promised myself I wouldn't let anything hurt me like it had when I'd felt her hand grow cold in mine. I had always tried to be smartest, strongest, and toughest, never relying on other people for help. But here I am, practically pleading with Marc to help me deal with the biggest problem I've ever faced. And that scares me. Big-time.

Marc starts reading through the myth, pointing out each Chinese character. Our heads nearly touch as we lean over the text. It's hard to focus on anything other than his scent and the sharp lines of his profile. I jot down notes in my notebook, hoping that will keep me focused.

"There's nothing new here," I say once we're finished. "Haemosu kidnaps Princess Yuhwa, takes her in his chariot, she escapes using her hairpin, and he never stops looking for her." I toss my notepad on the table.

"If I remember correctly, there's another legend somewhere here about Haemosu." He takes off his glasses and starts rummaging through his pile. "Here it is. It says that Haemosu, a demigod, wanted to become as great as the immortals." Marc chuckles. "This worried the immortals, so they asked the

Guardian of the East, the Blue Dragon, to create a bow that could kill Haemosu. Just having this weapon kept Haemosu in check, because it was a reminder to him of his mortality."

"Wait a second. I remember you mentioning this the night Good Enough played."

He nods, his brows pulling together as I dig through my backpack for my phone. I scroll through my pictures until I come to the one with the bow Grandfather had given me. The one that survived the fire.

"You think you own the Blue Dragon's weapon? That's a big deal. It's not like you can just go down the street and pick one up."

"I think we should take this myth as fact," I say.

"It's a stretch. A crazy stretch."

"When Grandfather gave me the bow, he seemed to think it was special because it didn't burn in the fire."

"It does have the Blue Dragon's image carved in it. . . ."

I skim my fingers over the engraving as an idea forms. "What if my bow really is from the Blue Dragon? What if the next time I see Haemosu, I pierce him with an arrow from that bow and kill him? Without him in power over his land, my ancestors would be free, and so would Komo. And even if this isn't really the bow of the Blue Dragon, Haemosu doesn't know that. I could use it as leverage."

"Now you're thinking."

"It's a long shot." I grin. "No pun intended."

Marc studies my bracelet. "Listen, you have only two more chances before the last of the five eyes turns red. What if you fail? It's a huge risk."

"You sound like Komo. She wanted me to leave the country. I just need to be ready for him the next time he comes. But I can't go around carrying a bow all the time."

I pull up the Sejong Center website on my phone and scroll down to the exhibit items from the Koguryo kingdom. Sure enough, the amulet Grandfather was talking about is displayed, the *samjoko* resting in the bronze circle, touching the eight ball points around the edge. My pulse races as I show it to Marc.

"The *samjoko*," he says. "Considered to be more powerful than the dragon or the phoenix."

"That's what the plaque at the museum says." I stare at the photo for a moment. "Remember when you found me in the forest at the ski trip?" He nods. "That was right after the first time I entered the Spirit World. When I was there, there was a palace filled with—"

My throat tightens, and my eyes fill. Marc slides his hand over mine, his fingers warm compared to the cold memory.

"I think they were the souls of my ancestors. They called after me. 'Princess,' they said."

"So they think you're his next Princess Yuhwa? That's creepy."

"Yeah, I guess it is. The thought of my female relatives throughout the generations locked up in that awful place. I can't stand it. And now Komo, too. I have to get them out. Grandfather wants to steal the amulet because he believes it's a key into the Spirit World. He plans to go and kill Haemosu himself. I can't let him do that. Haemosu will kill him."

"No." Marc crosses his arms, shaking his head. "I know what you're thinking, and it's a bad idea. You should leave the country like your aunt suggested. Nothing good comes from messing around with the supernatural. Trust me."

"It's the only way. There's something about Haemosu's world that connects with me, like I'm a part of it in some way. And every time I enter his world, I get stronger." I shudder, thinking of the real reason. *I'm slowly becoming more a part of that world than this one.* "I think I can stop him."

"I don't like it. My vote is for you to move back to the U.S."

"Convince my dad of that," I say. "Besides, it's probably too late anyway. Haemosu always seems to be one step ahead of me."

I stare out the window, where a fog has settled, heavy and thick as if it's about to rain. "And after he took Komo, he threatened to do the same thing to everyone else I love. I have no choice."

"No one is asking you to be the heroine." Marc pushes away his coffee mug and leans so close I can see golden specks in his eyes. "You don't have to be the one to save the day. Besides, we're all here for you. You don't have to do anything alone."

"My aunt believed we make our own destinies. I've been making this my destiny my whole life. Which is why I should attack first. He'll never expect me to come on my own."

"One problem, Fighter Girl. The museum will never lend you that in a thousand years."

I smile. "I wasn't planning on asking."

CHAPTER 27

"No," I tell Marc. "You've been a huge help, but I need to do the rest of this on my own."

He crosses his arms. "There's no way I'm going to let you do this by yourself."

"And I can't let you get kicked out of school. Or watch you get hurt like everyone else who gets within ten feet of me. So no." I start shoving books into my backpack.

"You need to think this through."

This is the problem with brainiacs. They want to plan, analyze, and speculate. "There isn't time. I have two hours to do what I need to do." I sling my backpack over my shoulder and head for the door.

"Jae Hwa!" Marc calls through the coffee shop. He runs, sliding past me as I'm pulling open the door, and blocks the exit.

Unbelievable. He's going to force me to knock him flat on the ground. "Last chance to move."

"What if I've already got a plan?" He stretches his arm across the doorway so I can't exit. Cold air rushes into the coffee shop from outside.

"That'd be interesting if there *was* a plan," I tell Marc, "but there isn't."

"Listen. I'm going to help you, whether you like it or not. I have connections from the times I worked there. And a season pass to the museum."

"A season pass to jail, you mean."

"Funny." He isn't laughing. "I know where they keep their keys. I know where the back door is. And I know where the power box is."

Power box? I tap my foot, thinking, and bite my lip as the reality sinks in. I can't do this theft alone. I've got no plan. No experience. I need his help, and I'm desperate to rescue Komo.

What if I could make it so Marc is out of sight, away from me when I take the amulet? Then Haemosu wouldn't even know Marc was a part of this.

"Fine," I finally say. "You can come."

Marc grins, but it quickly turns into a frown as his eyes center on something behind me.

"What?" I follow his gaze.

"Let's get out of here." He grabs my arm, practically pushing me out the doorway.

"Wait," I say. "What about your stuff?"

"I got my backpack. I'll get the rest later."

His jaw tightens, which sends my own pulse racing, and then he breaks into a jog down the cobblestone sidewalk. I peer over my shoulder, and that's when I see him.

The same dokkaebi that met me in the subway station, coming out of the coffee shop, his red, bulging eyes focused on me. He saunters after us, so slowly that it seems he'd never catch us; but as I turn back around, he's suddenly ahead of us, standing by the bus stop and twirling his club. Both Marc and I jerk to a stop. No one in the bus line notices the troll.

"Don't look at him," Marc whispers into my ear. "He's been stalking you at school all day."

"What? How are you able to see him? I know for a fact that the dokkaebi isn't interested in you."

"Let's just say my eyes don't hurt, but I'm seeing things in a whole new light."

I can't stop my mouth from hanging open. "What are you saying?"

Marc slides his hand in mine. I don't pull away. "I'm saying I can see *things*. You know, supernatural stuff. Whatever happened to me back at the locker did something to my sight."

"No. Tell me you're lying."

"I wish."

"Pretty girl," the dokkaebi says. I can hear him perfectly from ten feet away even with the traffic buzzing by us. "Haemosu wants pretty girl now. Before we go, remember our deal?"

"You made a deal with him?" Marc gapes at me like I'm insane.

"Absolutely not!"

"The belly of the moon, pretty girl," the dokkaebi says. "Belly of moon. You get my treasure."

The dokkaebi reaches out his oozing arm to grab me. A growl cuts the air as Haechi dives over my head and pounces on the dokkaebi. The dokkaebi shrieks, and in a torrent of colors, he disappears.

The bus screeches to a stop at our curb, slush spewing. There, painted on the side of the bus, is a giant picture of Haechi that the tourism office has been plastering across the city.

If they only knew.

"Get on!" Haechi tells wide-eyed Marc and me.

Marc is the first to break free of his stupor. He pulls me forward, cutting in front of everyone else in line, and the two of us clamber onto the bus.

"What the hell just happened back there?" Marc says. "That was Haechi helping us, wasn't it?"

I nod in a slight daze. The gremlin's words echo through my mind: the belly of the moon, belly of the moon. What is he talking about? And what has happened to Marc?

"Why is the Haechi helping you? And why does the dokkaebi think you made a deal with him?" Marc whispers over my shoulder as we work our way to the back of the bus.

"Who knows?" I plop into a seat, distracted by the furniture shop across the street. Its door disappears, and instead of there being furniture inside, there's a beach with a traditional Korean temple on a cliff. I press my palms against the cold window and stare at the temple as the bus rolls away. What was that? Was that where the dokkaebi was going to take me?

"Jae," Marc says, wrapping his arms around me. "You okay?"

"Um—yeah." I shake my head. "I don't know what I would've done if Haechi didn't show up."

"The dokkaebi didn't hurt you, did he?"

"No. He's more interested in some orb thing."

Marc's head jerks up. "What did you say?"

As the bus lumbers down the street through the city, I tell him about the time I encountered the dokkaebi in the subway.

"You know that dokkaebis can't be trusted." Marc twists his golden ring around his finger. He looks off into space as if mulling over something. "All they want is treasure. I'm surprised Haemosu would even trust the creature."

I rub my forehead, a headache pounding my temples. I can't deal with Haemosu and dokkaebis and break-ins and weird places popping up. One thing at a time. "Tell me more about this sight of yours."

"Let's just say the past twenty-four hours have totally sucked." He slides on a pair of sunglasses even though it's cloudy and overcast. He nods at me. "Seems to make the Others fade away. Plus, if I've got the glasses on, they don't seem to notice *me* noticing them."

I suck in a deep breath. "Marc, I'm so sorry. This is all my fault."

"No, it's not, Fighter Girl. Besides, my parents have been helping me. Apparently my *gift* might become useful." Marc snorts. "That's what my dad called it, you know. A gift."

I cringe at the bitterness in his voice, but then how many times had I heard that same tone come out of my own mouth? "I get how you're feeling," I say. "At least your dad didn't freak out."

Then I remember how Grandfather and Komo said Marc's dad was a part of the same order as they were. Which is probably why Dr. Grayson took it all in stride, unlike my dad.

"So why does your dad think seeing strange creatures can be useful?" I ask.

"It's a long story." Marc sighs. "The sunglasses were my dad's idea. I bet you a million dollars all he's been doing today is researching this whole thing. You have no idea how excited he is."

"At least he's being supportive." I think about how my dad is in total denial over Haemosu. "Maybe it's temporary. Maybe it will go away if we can kill Haemosu."

"Yeah, that's a possibility. I'm crossing my fingers. I know this sounds weird, but I'm actually glad. Maybe my dad is right. Maybe this will be useful in helping you out."

"Nothing good can come out of Haemosu's sick tactics."

"Forget I even mentioned it. My problems are nothing compared to what you're going through." Then he lifts his sunglasses, raising his eyebrows, and gives me a devious smile. "So, are you ready to hear what I've got to say?"

"Spill. I'm dying to know the details of this cryptic plan."

Marc whispers it into my ear so no one overhears us. He's so close that if I turn my head our lips would touch. A warmth spreads through me just thinking about it.

When he finishes, I almost smile. We actually might be able to pull this off.

At the next stop we part ways. Me heading to the museum to get a feel for the place while Marc heads to his house to pick up a couple of things.

Unease churns through my stomach at the thought of Marc being involved after what happened to him yesterday. But I'm so desperate to get Komo back that I can't even think straight. This plan has got to work.

CHAPTER 28

It's five p.m., the time of our planned break-in, and Marc is late. I press my face against the frosty glass door of the museum and scan the plaza for him. Outside, a preschool group lines up in a neat row beneath the dragon flags of the *Illumination* exhibit. When they march away, the plaza's concrete slab lies empty, nearly matching the gray sky above.

I flip open my phone and speed-dial Marc. If all goes well, Marc and I will get the amulet before Grandfather does, and I can still meet Michelle at the movies.

He answers on the first ring, saying, "Almost there."

"The place is dead like you expected."

"Good. Got my pliers ready."

A minute later I spy Marc coming up the stairs and across the pavement. He's got his hands in his pockets, strolling toward the front doors, acting as if he hasn't a care in the world. As if he's not about to assist with a theft. My heart quickens at the thought of what he's doing.

For me.

He pushes open the glass door and my chest aches, wishing this could be an innocent date, where we look at boring old stuff and maybe kiss in dark corners. But today is nothing like that.

Marc gives me a slight nod as he passes me in the entryway before continuing inside. That's my signal. But before I turn I see *him*.

Haemosu.

Standing alone in the center of the plaza, his crimson cloak whipping in the wind, in sharp contrast to the washed-out world around him. He looks at me with those dark-pooled eyes. His eyebrows rise an inch. Another school group passes by, oblivious to the man wearing a traditional Korean tunic and a circlet crown across his brow. One step, then another, he comes.

I back away, pulse throbbing in my ears, across the museum lobby and into the weapons exhibit. Should I call off the plan? Or go ahead with it?

I squeeze behind a panoramic silk screen and duck inside one of the traditional Korean houses in the next room. I drop to the dusty floor and crawl to a window slit to catch sight of Haemosu striding into the weapons exhibit. Perfect. He doesn't realize I'm not there anymore.

The Koguryo kingdom exhibit lies directly in front of me. After a few minutes I skirt directly to the amulet encased in the glass cabinet. The *samjoko* stretched out in the center of the bronze disk pulls at me.

I stop for a moment. What if taking the amulet is exactly what Haemosu wants me to do? What if we get caught and sent to jail? What if—

Laughter fills the room. I swivel around, thinking I'll be

face-to-face with Haemosu, but it's only a bunch of middle school girls flirting with a museum tour guide.

"You are so smart," one of them tells the guide in Korean. She flashes him a coy smile. "My school project would have been just awful without your help."

I'm ready to gag when Marc comes up behind me.

"Stay focused, Jae," he whispers in my ear as he slides a hammer into my palm. "I've unlocked the rear exit."

I peer over my shoulder and catch him heading down the stairs to the basement. A map of the museum now rests on the glass display next to me. I pick it up. Marc has circled the back stairwell as a reminder. That will be my escape route. I scan the room for Haemosu. He's still nowhere in sight. I will Marc to hurry.

"Oh!" one of the girls screeches, loud enough, I'm sure, for the passengers on the buses outside to hear. "Is it gold? But it must be. Look at the shine, the color, the way it sparkles under the lights. If only I could try it on."

Whatever the guard mumbles under his breath as he glances around doesn't seem to be to the girl's liking. She pouts her lips and bats her eyelashes. "But don't you think it would look perfect on me? Please, please, please open it."

Her whiny voice grates on my nerves, but it doesn't seem to bother the guard. He starts apologizing profusely that he cannot open the case for her. I duck behind another glass case that holds a mannequin replica of Princess Yuhwa wearing her wedding dress.

The lights blink out. The museum falls into darkness. Marc has cut off the power. I flick on my flashlight in time to see the girl clinging to the guard and screaming as if her life depended on it.

I race to the glass cabinet, and in one swoop I smash the hammer down onto the glass, shattering the glass into a thousand pieces, setting off alarms. I grope through the glass for the amulet, a slice of gold against the darkness. The sharp glass edge cuts my fingers. The amulet slips through my hands, and it drops with a clatter to the marble floor. My flashlight beam skitters across the floor until I find it, but before I can grab it, a hand reaches out and picks it up.

My tongue feels thick and dry as I slowly lift my head. The girl smiles at me.

"You have no need for bronze, my princess, when I can deck you in gold." And then her body twists and her skin pulls until the girl has been replaced by Haemosu.

I can't move. Right now my crazy hunt-down-Haemosu-and-kill-him sounds like the stupidest idea on the planet. Problem is, I have no other ideas.

Guards shout from the far end of the exhibit, and beams from flashlights roam a few feet away.

"Come," Haemosu says. "These men are of annoyance."

Footsteps pound the marble floor toward us. It's Marc, careening around the corner, sprinting toward us.

"Jae!" Marc says, waving his flashlight. "Run! It's a trap!"

Haemosu's eyes narrow, and his mouth dips into a frown. "You!" he says to Marc. "You are supposed to be dead. You will pay for your interference."

No! I leap on Haemosu's back and wrap my arm around his

neck, choking him. Haemosu gags, but grabs hold of my braceleted arm and pulls. The electric shock from the bracelet sears me, and I scream in agony. Still I fight against him. There's no doubt I'm stronger than he in our world, and I taste victory.

But then the bracelet begins to glow. Wind surges around me, and my hair whips at my face.

Marc picks up the hammer and raises it over Haemosu's' head.

And an explosion shatters all the glass cases in the room.

I scream through the darkness but manage to kick the amulet out of Haemosu's hands. Marc cries out my name, but a void tears at my lungs and sucks away all sound before I can respond. The floor vanishes, and I'm falling. The guard's flashlights become stars, and they churn around me as if I'm in a vortex. I grope empty air, searching for the amulet. Something! But it's gone.

And with it my hopes.

CHAPTER 29

The wind dies. The stars fade. My feet find solid ground amid the nothingness, and the darkness pulls away like a curtain, allowing light to pour through. It washes over me, and I'm blinded. I cover my eyes as heat penetrates my skin, warming me—such a contrast to the bitter cold of Seoul. The sweet tang of tangerines fills the air.

I move my hand away from my eyes and squint against the brightness. I'm in a great hall, and it looks vaguely familiar. The floor and walls are lined with shimmering gold, etched with battle scenes. Eight red pillars create a line from the throne to a wood-beamed ceiling. Rice paper lanterns are attached to the pillars, glowing even in the daylight. The ceiling is painted in traditional green, red, and yellow vertical stripes, with chrysanthemums at either end of the design just as in the palaces in Seoul. A golden pedestal with the impression of the *samjoko* in its center stands in the center of the room. I eye it, wondering if the amulet would fit inside it. Was that the portal?

And then I catch sight of Haemosu, lounging on a bright,

golden throne on the red platform before me. Massive red pillars rise up on either side of the platform, holding a pagoda-style roof. He's resting his arms on the dragon's head armrests, and his feet are propped up on the dragon's tail footstool.

"This place is far more romantic than that musty old museum, do you not think?" Haemosu says, rolling my flashlight across his palm. "And plastic?" He shakes the flashlight in the air. "I have prepared a beautiful palace for when you become my queen. You deserve more than this rubbish you have been given. You deserve gold."

"What I deserve is freedom," I practically growl, holding up my gilded arm. "Where is my aunt?"

"Now, dearest, do not be terribly boring." Haemosu tosses the flashlight, and it smashes into a celadon vase, shattering it. "Your aunt is tucked away in a safe place. Let us not worry over her."

If only I had the dragon bow. I could pierce his heart with an arrow in seconds. I look around me and notice I'm standing next to two wooden racks where long-handled fans are stored. The long stick part of the fan reminds me of those European lances. *Useful.*

Casually I stroll toward the racks, but something pricks me in the hip. I glance down and realize I'm no longer in jeans and my black hoodie but wearing Princess Yuhwa's dress from the museum. My stance wavers as I grab a handful of silk. It's slick against my rough hands. *A dress?* I glower at Haemosu, but he only smiles.

I lift my hand and touch twisted braids and loops. Moving my fingers farther, I realize I must be wearing a crown, too. I squirm my hips, hoping to dislodge whatever is stabbing me, but moving only makes it worse. There must be a needle stuck in the skirt.

"Something wrong, my princess?" He grins as if reading my mind. "A dress like so is far more appropriate than the rubbish you were wearing."

I have about a million things I'd really like to say to the creep, but I bite my tongue.

"You have a point," I say, putting on a princess smile, all the while imagining him as my punching bag. I slip a fan out of its holder. "We got off on the wrong track. Why don't you come down and show me the queen's palace you were talking about?"

He raises his eyebrows as if wary but then flashes me a movie star–worthy smile. "I am pleased you have finally decided to see things my way. You must wish to see what soon will be yours. Everything is easy. Perfect. You will be so happy here."

Happy when you're dead, that is.

"You know, you are my favorite," he says. "Far more interesting than any of the others."

He slides off his throne, and as he reaches for me, I leap at him and ram the long handle end of the fan into his chest. He totters back, surprise lighting his face. I twirl the stick again and smack him across the temple.

But when I raise the stick to whack him again, my gilded arm freezes in the air like stone. He snatches the long-handled fan away and snaps the handle in half, tossing it to the side.

"Really, Jae Hwa," he says. "How are we supposed to live a life of bliss if you are always trying to kill me?"

"Seriously? How about you tell me where my aunt is and *then* we can discuss bliss."

"Your aunt was poison to your soul, Jae Hwa. You needed to be free of her influence."

"You know"—I'm shaking I'm so angry—"I can't take your crap anymore. I wish I was good at playing games or conniving enough to outwit you at them. But I'm not. I haven't forgotten how you tried to gouge my eyes out as a bird. I haven't forgotten what you did to my aunt and Marc. And I remember this place as it really is: a stinking vision of hell. So this is what you're going to do. You're going to take me to the queen's palace and let Komo and my ancestors go."

I spin on my heels. My gold belt clinks as I march across the hall. I keep my chin high, trying to ignore the pricking feeling under my dress, and head toward the double wooden doors that span higher than a two-story house.

A snarl cuts the air.

"Where do you think you are going?" Haemosu growls.

I glance back. Haemosu's glamour has disappeared, and I can see him for the wasted creature that he is. His sunken eyes glow red like the eyes on my bracelet, and all his tongues flick out of his mouth like hungry snakes.

"Open the doors!" I throw as much force into my words as I can muster, hoping he won't hear the fear behind them.

"Never," he roars at me, sending my hair flying.

"Open them!" I jab my finger at the doors.

A rumble pulses the ground and shakes the doors. With a moan, they swing open.

My jaw drops. I never expected them to obey *me*.

I rush outside, down the steps, passing stone statues of dragons and phoenixes, and into a grassy courtyard. There are at least ten other buildings circling this courtyard, with more tucked away behind those. They are miniature versions of the great hall in Gyeongbokgung Palace, wood structures with stone pillars and fluted roofs. When I took the tour of the Gyeongbokgung Palace with Dad, I remember there being at least three hundred buildings. I'm sure this place isn't much different. It could take all day to find the queen's palace.

Just beyond the courtyard is a stone wall nearly twenty feet tall, with convex and concave tiles alternating across the top. Out here that sweet, fruity smell is even stronger. Jagged mountains just like the ones that surround Seoul rise up through an evergreen forest beyond the wall.

"Where are the prisoners?" I spin in a circle and scan the courtyard.

"I told you, Princess. I do not hold prisoners."

"Stop calling me princess!"

I spot a small bridge that crosses a stream, the water sparkling like diamonds. There's something familiar about this stream. Is it the same one that had been filled with bones earlier? I stride out to the bridge, where I lean over its side, holding on to the thick wooden-beamed railing. With my eyes closed, I listen.

I expect to hear the gurgle of the water as it slips over the rocks, following the current. Or maybe the twitter of birds, calling to their mates. Or the song of cicadas, a lullaby to the trees.

But I don't.

Instead I hear the coursing of wind sifting in and out of barren trees. The rustle of dead leaves across the ground. The cries of girls in anguish.

I snap up straight and face Haemosu. He's strolling toward me with a lazy grin and smooth olive skin, his glamour back.

"Forget the bracelet, my love," he says in a low, even voice that curls around my heart and pulls me to him. "Stay with me now. You do not need to wait until the last dragon burns red to become my queen."

I back away to the other side of the bridge. How is it that after all he's done, after I *know* the truth about him, my heart still aches to believe him? To slide into his arms and join him in his perfect world. I shake my head hard to get rid of his voice seeping into me. Poisoning me.

"Queen?" I say. "What about all the other girls? Won't they be a little jealous?"

"There are no others. Only you."

He stretches out his hand, fingers extended, and slowly makes a fist, squeezing so tight his fingers whiten. My chest constricts, and I double over in pain.

Can't breathe!

I push my hand out against the pressure, and for a brief moment it's as if I can touch his grasp and push him back. His hold lessens, and his eyes grow wider. Maybe I do have some power in his world. But as soon as the surprise of this fades, I can feel his fist overpowering me again.

I stagger backward and, turning, break into a sprint down the path and through a small side gate. I must find the queen's palace. I might not be strong enough to beat Haemosu; but if I can open the queen's gate to save my ancestors and Komo, then all this won't be for nothing.

I race into an evergreen forest, tripping over my skirts and landing face-first in the dirt. I claw at the ground until I'm up and stumbling along the dirt path through the forest.

At the end of the forest I spy the palace. But it isn't crumbling or gray like before. It's golden, with sharp rays of sunshine and blue flags waving in the tangerine-scented breeze. The gates gape open, as if inviting me inside. I slow my pace as I step out of the forest.

Why is the gate open? Is this the right place?

No one is inside. No hands claw over the edges. No cries for help.

Yet I'm sure that this is the place. I remember it perfectly.

Had I been wrong about just needing to open the gates? But that's what Haechi had said.

Haemosu materializes in front of the entrance, hands clasped and feet apart as if he's out here to enjoy a lovely day in the sun. I clench my teeth, hating him all the more.

I shuffle closer, eying him. "The gates. They're open."

"Of course."

I dig my nails into my palms and suppress the storm inside my chest. Because my grand plan to open the gates and release my ancestors is obviously the stupidest one in this dynasty.

"Where are they?" I say.

His forehead bunches up, and he cocks his head to the side.

"I said, where are they!"

"Do not be foolish." He stretches out his hand, gesturing me to walk ahead of him. "Please, come with me into the palace. See your new home."

A lilting song reaches my ears. It sounds like someone is singing inside. The voice sounds like Komo's.

I brush past him to stand at the entrance of the palace, inches from the open gate. Only the strangeness of the situation keeps me from entering.

"Komo!" I call out. "Are you there?"

"I'm here, darling," Komo's voice says from inside. "Come and join me."

I frown. Komo would never call me darling. Something isn't right here.

A gazebo rests just inside the gate, decorated with flowers, ribbon, and rows of wooden ducks. It reminds me of traditional Korean weddings. I shiver at the thought. A golden building stands at the far end of the courtyard. A massive pearl, as plump and round as the moon itself, sits inside its wall, and I feel the overwhelming urge to touch it. I step closer. My slippered feet lie inches from the groove in the ground where the gate must lock in place.

"Please, my love," Haemosu says, "your aunt waits for you inside."

I balk, my legs wooden. I nearly skipped into his trap willingly!

"No," I say. "It's a trick."

With effort I step back. I've failed. Again. Merely opening the gate won't release my ancestors' spirits. And I've no idea where Komo is either.

I need to get out of here. The pull from the palace intensifies, like a metal chain has been wrapped around me. Tugging. Heaving.

Haemosu grins. He's saying something, but it's taking every effort to keep my legs from prancing straight through that gate.

But the pearl. Smooth and pure. Just one touch.

"Jae Hwa!"

It's Marc's voice. I blink and realize I am almost inside the courtyard. Haemosu scans the forest, a scowl on his face, and suddenly I'm terrified for Marc and what Haemosu might do to him.

"Marc!" I yell. "Stay away!"

I pick up my skirts and sprint back to the forest, back to where Marc's voice came from. A growl splits the silence. I glance over my shoulder just as Haemosu leaps through the air, transforming into a tiger.

He pounces on top of me, snarling as he throws his body against mine. I fall hard to the ground, and his paws pin me down. I choke on dirt and squirm under him, my chin screaming in pain.

I twist so I'm facing him and push against his chest with my palms. He flies off me and crashes into the bushes. If I wasn't so panicked or hurt, I'd be thrilled at the power I'm discovering.

"You are a difficult one," he says. "Stubborn." He's a man again, standing and brushing the dirt off his clothes with a look of annoyance. I struggle to my feet, and the realization hits me. He wants me to enter the queen's palace. He tried seduction. That sure didn't work. He tried brute strength, but in the end he can't force me. Something is stopping him.

I must enter of my own free will, I realize.

"You know I won't do it." I lift my throbbing chin higher. "I'm going to find a way to save them."

"Oh, you will enter, my princess. Trust me. You will."

CHAPTER 30

"And if you will not go inside on your own"—Haemosu steps away, and a sly grin forms on his face—"I have my ways of enticement."

He claps his hands. A thick shadow slides across the ground between the two of us. I crane my neck back and stare up at the most gruesome, horrific monster I have ever seen: a Minotaur look-alike with horns, fire-breathing nostrils, and clawed feet larger than my entire body. His skin shines in the sun like plated metal. He stands on hind legs and roars. The ground vibrates as the creature clomps closer to me.

I dart for the tree line, but a bolt of fire from the creature's mouth rains down, creating a wall of searing flames. I duck, covering my face from the heat, and stagger backward. The creature clomps closer. There's no other choice: I have to backtrack and race to the other side of the gate. But even there I'm blocked by another wall of fire.

My path is now blocked on both sides. Behind me is the

queen's palace entrance and before me stands Grossness at its finest, drooling green slime.

Sweat beads on my forehead. My legs tremble. I take a deep breath and spread out my arms as I focus all my thoughts on morphing into a bird like I did once before. The sky is my only option.

A tremor shakes my body. *It's working.*

As if sensing my intent, Godzilla's cousin roars. He arches his back to the sky and spews out a ball of fire. It rolls across the blue—a swirl of crimson, yellow, and orange—and curves to meet with the wall on either side of me.

My focus shatters. My body pulls in twisting agony, and I collapse to the ground, morphed back to my human self. My stomach is heaving again. My body shakes uncontrollably with the aftereffects of the metamorphosis.

Then the creature blasts another burst of flames behind him. The two of us are now in a dome of fire. The only escape lies behind me—through the gate.

My skin burns, my eyes burn, my throat burns.

I should be dead. Incinerated. But no, that would be too convenient for Haemosu. No dying for me today. Because he doesn't want me dead.

He wants my soul.

"You can't have it!" I scream. "You can't—" But my voice crumbles.

I can feel my skin bubbling. Pieces of my hair are burning, falling out. I cover my head with my skirts, wanting to cry, except my tears are dried up. And then I hear it, deep within me. A voice.

Believe, it tells me. *Believe in the power within you!*

Marc? Or Komo?

No, it's something beyond even them. I think about Mom and how she'd say that God gives us strength in our valleys of death. I used to think she was just saying that to help me recover after she died. Now her words make sense as a power wells up within me, ready to burst. I throw back the skirts from over my head and stand. The monster snorts and stomps closer. Would the monster lose its power if it was distracted?

I reach for my crown and rip it off.

I lock onto the image of the beast as my target. My crown is my arrow. I toss hard. The crown hits the creature smack in the eye and bounces off. He wavers, blinking, while I'm there catching the crown and tossing it up at the other eye. The creature roars and moans. My own eyes blur until all I can see is yellow. I ignore it as the beast doubles over in pain.

Then the fire walls fizzle and so does the brimstone ceiling above me. The monster's concentration is connected to his power. Spitting flames rain down on me. I duck beneath the monster's staggering legs for protection.

Once the fire walls dissipate, I bolt for the forest, pumping my legs and arms. I cut through the trees, letting the branches swipe my face. The forest blurs past me in a world of yellow. My slippers are gone, probably a pile of ashes by now, but I'm racing at a speed faster than I ever imagined. The sharp prick in my hip I felt earlier is back, jabbing into me.

I stop at a pond. Lily pads are scattered across the surface, and a golden pagoda rests in its center. I slosh into it, and though my skin screams in agony, I keep moving until my whole body is submerged in its cool depths.

"Jae!" It's Marc's voice for sure this time. I pull my face out of the water and look around. I think it's coming from inside the pagoda. Should I trust it, or is this another one of Haemosu's tricks?

A growl erupts in the stillness as something dives into the water and lands on top of me. I scream and then choke as the water surges into my lunges. It's Haemosu in his tiger form. I shove against him, swim underwater. and wade to the shoreline, my dress's heavy weight dragging me down.

His claw rips down my back. My vision blurs with pain. I roll in the mud away from him and stumble to my feet, gritting my teeth. His fangs are bared. He paws the ground, eying me.

I reach deep within myself to shape-shift again, but I don't have the strength.

I make the ready stance, but I can hardly hold up my arms, and my body sways.

He leaps again.

I draw up the last of my energy and jump. I slice the air and hit a side kick at his jaw. My skirts whip around me as I twist and punch. He grunts, knocked off guard. But I'm weakened by the effort and fall, tangling myself in the dress. I scramble back up and punch again, harder than I ever did when breaking through my wooden boards in practices. His jaw snaps back, but with a pounce he's on me again. His weight is too much. I'm pinned to the muddy embankment. All that power I had earlier is gone.

A desperate thought comes to me.

"Haechi!" I screech.

As if waiting for my call, Haechi soars out of thin air, knocking the tiger off me. The two tumble across the pond bank. I get up to help Haechi, but Haemosu stands before me.

"How dare you allow him into my world," Haemosu says.

I gape at the two of them, not sure how or why I'd have the ability or power to let in Haechi.

"You have summoned me," Haechi says. "Now flee to the pagoda! Flee!"

I stumble toward the bridge that leads to the pagoda in the center of the pond. When I reach the pagoda's wooden door, I hesitate. With my hand on the door latch, I look across the pond as Haechi and the tiger battle, fangs barred, claws raised. Haechi lets loose a loud roar.

Must move. I slide back the door, cringing, not knowing if this is a trap or an escape, and step inside. There's no ground. Only emptiness.

I fall. My shredded dress whips around my body in the void.

Down,

  down,

    down.

CHAPTER 31

My cheek is plastered against the cold marble floor, bright lights glaring in my eyes. I lift my head and debate whether to play dead or jump to my feet and fight off whoever is surrounding me.

"We've found her," a policeman says into a walkie-talkie. "Yep, she's wearing the dress. It's been damaged."

I drop my head down. It wasn't a trap. I've returned to the same room at the museum where I'd left. I groan. Why couldn't I have popped back here in a less obvious place?

A guard yanks me up. I check myself quickly and notice that the cuts along my arms are now thin scar lines. My blisters are smoothing out before my eyes. And the blood smeared over me is fading. It's as if everything I'd experienced was some awful nightmare.

The policeman is right. I'm still wearing Princess Yuhwa's dress, soggy and torn. That knife-like pain I felt in the forest is still there, too, and I rub my hip. I need to change. What happened to my jeans and hoodie?

I spot my phone lying on the floor, the screen cracked. I pick it up numbly. There's a text from Dad asking where I am and another from Michelle saying: **I'm at the movies. Where the xxxx are u? U better not have forgotten.**

Crap.

The guard picks up the bent crown at my feet and snatches my phone from me. He gives me a rough push forward. Marc, handcuffed, is standing next to one of the shattered glass displays to my right. I rush to him and wrap my arms around his neck.

"Be careful," he says. "Got shards of glass all over me."

I start checking his neck and face for glass. He grins and shakes his head. "You had me worried, Fighter Girl. And you look terrible, by the way." He leans his chin on top of my head.

My heart spins. "You don't look much better." I grab his shirt, ignoring the guard yelling at me. "I failed."

"At least we tried."

Any other guy would be calling the insane asylum right now or looking at me like I was some alien from Jupiter. Not Marc. Maybe that's why I've fallen so hard for him.

"You should've told me my plan sucked," I say. "Aren't you supposed to be a genius or something?"

"Obviously I'm not."

"I told you to move, miss." The guard wrenches me away, shoves my hands behind my back, and starts handcuffing me. "This should help you listen better—Ah!" he cries, and cradles his hand. He calls one of the other police officers, and the two inspect my bracelet. They decide to forgo the handcuffs, and resort to gripping my forearms and propelling me forward.

He has no idea how easy it would be to get out of that grip, but I don't need any more trouble than I'm in already. I glance down at my dress, almost dry, and wonder how that is even possible.

"Looks like your bracelet may come in handy for once," Marc says as the two of us are herded to the main lobby. "And the dress isn't all that bad, but my vote is still for the Pepto-Bismol one."

This is another thing I love about Marc. He knows just what to say so I don't lose my mind. He makes my most horrible moments bearable.

"If I wasn't so sore," I say, half laughing, half crying, "I'd clobber you."

"No problem. I could totally take you on." Then his forehead creases as we are marched down the corridor. "What happened to your skin? Did you get sunburned?"

"Sunburned?" Then I remember the dome of fire, and my mouth dries up. "Yeah, I guess I did."

Emergency lights wash the museum lobby where the police are swarming every corridor, blocking the doors and patrolling the exhibits. One of the policemen standing at the lobby desk waves us to him. From the badge on his jacket, I'm guessing he's the chief of police.

"Your names and parents' contact information," he demands.

After we give our information, I attempt to smooth things over. "I wasn't trying to steal anything. I just wanted to try on the dress." Sort of.

"This isn't a shopping mall," he barks, passing our names over to another policeman, who calls in the report. Then he stares at us. "We believe terrorists may have set a sound bomb that shattered all the glass cases in the museum. Unfortunately your little prank happened at the same time. Let me see the dress you've damaged."

He scrutinizes it, scratching the side of his head with his pencil. "I do not see any damage, Chung Su," he says to the museum curator.

"I am sure once the historians take a look at it," the curator says, "they will find the damage. You do know, Miss Lee, your father will receive a nice bill for repairs."

I glance down at Yuhwa's dress, thinking about how angry Dad will be; but I'm distracted by the transformation in the dress. It had been soggy, muddy, and shredded; but now it's in perfect shape.

"Looks fine to me," I tell them. "In fact, I think the color is brighter."

Something moves in the shadows by the door. I peer around the chief as a cloaked figure ducks unobtrusively between two policemen and scurries outside.

The chief's eyes narrow as he follows my gaze. "Who else was involved?" he asks.

"No one. Just me."

He jerks his head toward Marc. "What about him? He was screaming your name into the grate in the floor."

Oh, Marc. You crazy boy.

"He was trying to stop me from trying on the dress, but I wouldn't listen. He's innocent."

"That is yet to be decided," the chief says.

I look at Marc and press my lips together to keep the tears

from forming. "Thank you," I whisper to him, because I see everything clearly now. I wouldn't have found my way back without him. He sacrificed himself to get me here and now he's being arrested.

The chief clears his throat, and I push away all thoughts of Godzilla monsters, running through mythical forests, and being torn to shreds by a ferocious tiger.

"Take them to the police station in separate cars," he says.

The curator points at me. "She'll need to take that dress off."

"And wear what?" I interrupt.

"Your clothes, of course," the chief says.

They're probably floating around in the void outside time with my luck. "I don't know where they are."

The chief gives me a measured look. "Are you always this difficult?"

You have no idea.

The chief pulls at the cuffs of his sleeves and clears his throat. Then he motions to one of his men, saying, "Find something this girl can change into." Then one of the workers runs up to us holding my jeans and hoodie. "I found this on the mannequin that held the princess's dress."

The chief rolls his eyes, muttering something about kids and pranks, and orders one of his men and a museum worker to escort me to the back room to change. I suppress a snicker. Haemosu has a sense of humor.

Once alone, I lean against the wall and let out a long breath.

What will Dad think about this? Somehow I must get him to believe we are in danger and need to leave the country. I lift the dress over my head and wiggle out of it, but something slices the skin along my ribs. What was that? A red cut now runs across my side.

"What is taking so long?" the museum worker asks from behind the door.

"Just a second!" I say as I snatch my hoodie and pat it against my ribs to stop the bleeding. "It's stuck."

I twist the dress inside out to inspect it. A patch has been sewn into the side, and poking out of it is a thin, golden hairpin. I tug on it carefully. The material will need to be cut for me to retrieve the whole pin. Why would someone go to such trouble to sew a hairpin into a dress?

"Miss Lee," the policeman says, knocking on the door. "Hurry up."

"Almost ready," I say, staring at the pin, because all I can think about is Grandfather's tale of how Princess Yuhwa escaped. How she had taken her hairpin and cut her way out of the dragon's chariot. Is this the same pin? Had she secretly stowed it inside her dress for future use?

I tap my fingers on the blue material. There's something about this pin that screams "Take me!" It's a very, very bad idea. But I jam my finger in the tiny space where the pin has ripped it open and tug, hoping they won't look inside the dress for damages. The material tears, and a two-prong pin falls onto the tile floor. I lightly touch the pink-blossom design at its end, my heart beating faster than a hummingbird's wings.

After I've changed I tuck the pin inside my hoodie's front pocket. I step into the hall and hand the dress to the museum worker, who promptly starts lecturing me on all the wrongs that I've committed today.

I can't stop shaking during the ride to the station as I relive my horrifying experience in Haemosu's world in my head. My brilliant idea to steal the amulet, enter the Spirit World, and wound Haemosu with the Blue Dragon bow had been the stupidest idea *ever*. No wonder I can't keep up with my classes. I'm a complete moron.

I stare at the bracelet. All five dragons' eyes are red now except one. How many days will I have until Haemosu comes for me? When the final eye turns red, will he force me to enter the queen's palace? Will I be able to escape? Or will I be helpless against its pull?

I wish I knew how to solve this mess I've made of everything.

When we pull into the police station's parking lot, my thoughts turn to Dad. He'll be through-the-roof furious. I bury my face in my hands. Monsters are one thing. Parents are a whole other level.

They fine me for tampering with valuable museum artifacts. Apparently the police have determined that the explosion was caused by terrorists, so they never thought I (or Haemosu, though they'd never believe *that*) was the culprit.

The holding cell reminds me of a giant hamster cage minus the cool wheel and soft, fluffy bedding. I grab the cell bars, cold and hard against my palms, and peer out, hoping to catch a glimpse of Marc. I haven't seen him since we left the museum except for a brief glimpse when we passed each other in the puke-green concrete block hallway. I want to talk to him, because I don't know if I'll have another chance.

And then there's the thought that Haemosu could waltz in here at any moment and cause havoc. I lean against the cell bars. It had been so much easier when his power was limited to daylight.

"Jae Hwa!" Dad says as the policeman brings him to my cell.

"Hey," I mutter, and focus on the concrete floor. Counting cracks is far more appealing than dealing with Dad when he's furious.

"Are you okay? The police told me there were terrorists at the museum," he says as the policeman unlocks my cell. "I nearly had a heart attack."

Dad worried about me? I can't remember him ever indicating that before. I've always been the tough one. Since Mom died.

He pulls me into a fierce hug, and for a moment everything feels like it used to be before we moved, before she died. When I didn't have monsters chasing me or curses haunting me.

"I don't know what I'd do if I lost you, too," he whispers into my ear.

As soon as he lets go and we head out to the car, the full weight of the curse bears down on me once more. I'd thought I could fix everything. That I could save all of us. How wrong I've been.

CHAPTER 32

Back at the apartment I pace the room, wearing out the carpet between the futon and the TV, and ready to pull out my hair. For the entire ride home I've been trying to convince Dad of Haemosu's existence. I even show him my bracelet.

"Don't you see it's happening all over again?" I say. "What happened to Sun is happening to me, and you're just pretending it all away!"

Dad whitens. "Don't bring Sun into this."

"Dad," I say, "you can't pretend it away. It's real."

"This is all Eun's fault. She's filled your mind with lies." Dad sags onto the couch and buries his face in his hands.

Just hearing Komo's name shoots tears to my eyes. "I wish we'd never come to Korea." Yet even as I spit out those words, I know how untrue they are. Grandfather, Komo, Marc, and Michelle's faces flash through my mind. And that feeling of being connected to something bigger than myself. Somewhere along the way, I've come to love it here.

"Jae Hwa," Dad says, "moving back to the U.S. is out of the

question. You need to stop this obsession and concentrate on being here. And I was right about that boy. He's a bad influence on you."

"What? You mean Marc?"

"Yes. He's encouraging all of your impulsive ideas, isn't he? I've already spoken to his parents and told them that I strictly forbid you to speak to him."

"Dad!" I can't even see straight, I'm so angry. "You called his *parents*? None of what happened is his fault! This was all my idea. He was trying to help me!"

"Exactly. He was helping you. Stealing valuable dresses and getting yourself thrown in jail is hardly helping," Dad says.

I'm actually at a loss for words.

His BlackBerry chimes. When he pulls it out I see he's got Sun's broken necklace in his hand. How long has he been holding it?

I can't help but wonder if some part of him believes me.

"It's your principal." He rubs his forehead. "I need to take this," he says, and moves to his bedroom and closes the door.

I stalk into my bedroom and kick my door shut. The wall shudders, but I don't feel any better. I set Princess Yuhwa's pin on my desk, pick up the dragon bow, and send a string of arrows into my bull's-eye. But Haemosu's face still leers into sight, taunting me.

How do I stop him?

Dad knocks and opens the door. "I just got off the phone with your principal," he says. "The police called the school. You're suspended for three days. You're lucky. You could have been deported."

"I don't care." I pull the arrows from the target and prepare to shoot again.

"The good news is, you're allowed to return to school if you agree to see the counselor."

"That's fabulous. Yay, me."

"You've got to work with me, Jae."

"Right. Just like you're listening to me."

Silence. Dad shakes his head and leans against the doorframe.

"Do you have Grandfather's phone number?" I ask. "I need to talk to him."

"I told you—"

"Dad," I change to my pleading voice. The one he can never resist. "I need it. Will you do this one thing for me? If I promise to see the counselor?"

He sighs and then reaches into his pocket and pulls out his cell. He writes down the number on a slip of paper and passes it to me.

"I hope talking to him will—will help."

I stare at the numbers, blurring from tears threatening to fall. "Thanks, Dad." I know he still doesn't believe me, but this is how he shows that he cares.

"It's been a long day," he says. "Let's give all this a rest for now. We'll talk more about this tomorrow."

The door clicks closed. His last word hangs with the silence that follows.

Tomorrow.

I don't know if I'll see it. Outside my window, the sun dips below the sky, scratching the apartment buildings with its golden rays. How long will it take for Haemosu to lick his wounds from his fight with Haechi and come after me? He'll be ripping, flipping furious.

Run or sit. Flee or wait. Then it hits me.

Tonight.

I must get Dad and Haraboji out of the country before morning. Because tomorrow might be too late.

My heart jumbles in a twisted mess as I search the Web for flights that leave Seoul first thing in the morning. My fingers suspend over the keyboard as I realize I don't have a credit card. Then I think of Grandfather and the slip of paper in my hand. Could he help me? I punch in his number.

"*Nae,*" a deep voice answers in Korean.

"Haraboji?" I say.

"Jae Hwa! Your father told me about your arrest. You should have waited for me."

I pick up my backpack. "After what happened to Komo, I couldn't stand losing you, too."

"You put yourself and your friend in danger. It was a terrible, terrible idea."

Yeah, that pretty much sums up my fiasco. "I'm sorry, Haraboji. I ruined everything. There's no way we can steal the amulet now with the museum closed until who knows when, as well as the added security. There's only one thing left to do. Escape."

Grandfather is silent on the other end so I continue, "Haemosu promised to hurt everyone I loved, which is why you and Dad need to leave the country."

"Your father will not do this. You know that."

"What if I force him to?" I stuff a change of clothes and some of my snack stash into my pack. "If I leave the country, Haemosu can't follow me since he'll have no power once we pass the border."

"Your plan might work. But I am worried that Haemosu's power is growing and stretching farther than even our family."

I stop my packing. "What do you mean?"

"After our encounter with Haemosu last night, I talked with the Guardians of Shinshi. This is the first time in our family's recorded history that Haemosu has fought in our world at night. We think Haemosu has found another source of power. He must be stopped before his power continues to increase."

What a mess. I'd hoped to use the Blue Dragon bow, but I needed that amulet to get into the Spirit World without Haemosu knowing. He'd never let me bring that bow into his land.

"I know I failed you, Haraboji, but if we leave now and wait, the museum's security will calm down. Maybe we can come back and steal it another time."

"You did not fail," Grandfather says, his voice oddly tight. "In fact, I think your plan is a good one. We will try again."

"I've been looking online for flights that leave in the morning."

"No time for airports. You must travel by boat. It is the best and quickest method for leaving the country. Haemosu will not be expecting it."

"That might work." I type in a new search query. My eye catches on an advertisement for a speedboat called the *Beetle*. "Have you ever heard of the *Beetle*? It's supposed to be the fastest boat around."

"Of course." Grandfather is silent for a moment. "It might work, Jae Hwa. But there is something I need to do. Can you take the train alone to Busan?"

"Yes!"

"Good. I will make some calls. I have connections." His voice sounds out of breath, as if he's walking quickly. "Go to Seoul Station. At the ticket booth, show them your passport, and I will make sure they have a ticket for you. Take the 9 p.m. KTX train to Busan. Are you writing this down? I will meet you in the Busan Station south terminal when you arrive. If we plan this correctly, you will be well on your way to Japan by dawn."

"Japan?" I check the *Beetle*'s itinerary. It heads directly to Fukuoka, Japan. My throat tightens as the reality sets in. "Okay. I can do this."

"And Jae?" he adds. "Bring the dragon bow."

CHAPTER 33

I hang up and sit still for a moment, leaning my forehead into my tucked-in knees. How had he known I wanted to use the dragon's bow? Then I think about leaving Dad and forcing him to come running after me. Sneaking off at night to downtown Seoul and leaving the country without his permission is even crazier than my usual schemes. This makes my museum prank look like child's play. But what choice do I have?

I find a piece of paper to scribble out a note, hoping Dad will read it and come after me.

> *Went on a trip with Grandfather to Fukuoka, Japan. Call him if you need me.*

I place it on my desk next to Princess Yuhwa's pin, which I then decide to stick into my ponytail. I don't usually wear hairpins, but somehow having a piece of her feels like part of her determination to escape him will be with me.

As I zip up my backpack, the pictures of my friends taped

to the wall gaze down at me—Michelle, who wouldn't hesitate to join me if I had a fighting chance to save my family. Lily, who believes the best of everyone.

I can't just leave the country without telling them good-bye. I punch in Michelle's number. It rings four times and I'm sure it'll go to voice mail, but she answers.

"You stood me up," she says without a hello.

"I know, and I'm sorry. Things have been complicated lately."

"I can't do this anymore, Jae. I can't just sit around and hope you'll hang out. I can't deal with your crazy moods."

"I wish I could explain—"

"The moment I hooked you up with Marc, you vanished on me," she interrupts. "You used me to get a boyfriend. That's not what friends do."

"I'm in trouble," I finally admit. "I'm leaving the country."

"What?"

"I'm leaving right now." I bite my lip, wishing I could tell her everything; but the less she knows, the safer she is. "I'll call you when I can."

"What's going on, Jae?"

"I can't say." I finger the backpack straps. Maybe I shouldn't have called her. "You've been a great friend. The best anyone could have. Tell Lily I said good-bye."

I hang up as she starts with a barrage of questions that I can't answer. A sick emptiness fills my stomach. This is why I shouldn't have made friends. This is why I should never have let anyone get close to me.

My eyes fall on Marc's picture, smiling with that grin of his and the hair that's always falling into his eyes. I study the way his skin crinkles when he smiles. The dimple in his cheek. And his lips. I lightly touch mine.

It's a very bad idea, but I speed-dial his number. My heart quickens, thinking about the disaster that was my conversation with Michelle. It's selfish, but I need to hear his voice one last time. Besides, after everything we've been through, he deserves to know.

"Jae?" Marc answers.

I let out a long breath just hearing his voice. "Yeah, it's me. You okay? Did your parents flip?"

"I survived the gauntlet. You?"

"Yeah, the works. I called to make sure you were okay."

He's silent for a moment. "I'm good. You?"

"Not so much."

"I'm sorry things didn't work out like you wanted."

"Tell me about it. I'm sorry about—" Where do I even begin? "Everything."

"Don't be. I'd do it all again," he says.

"I'm leaving the country. It's the only chance I've got left. So I guess this is good-bye."

"There's something I need to tell you."

I close my eyes to push back the tears that really, really want to spill out. I can't listen to what he has to say, because he's become the best friend I've ever had and I can't say good-bye to that. I grab my wallet and bow case, glancing around the room one last time. "Good-bye, Marc."

"Wait!"

I hang up before he says another word. He calls back, but I ignore the ring and set my phone to silent mode. Then, clutching my bow case, I crack open my door, peeking into the living room. Dad's bedroom door is closed, but I can hear him talking on his cell phone.

Now or never.

Tiptoeing, I head to the closet where we keep the safe, hoping Dad doesn't open his door and find me rummaging for my passport. He's never going to give me the combination to the safe in the future after this stunt. But why worry about the future if there probably isn't going to be one?

I am sneaking across the room with my blue USA passport in hand to the entryway when I hear Dad's bedroom door creak. I scurry back across the living room but only make it to the kitchen.

"Jae," Dad says, and I notice his face looks worn and years older. "I know this has been a rough night, but I thought I'd order us some food."

"Um—I'm not really in the mood," I say, and then grab a box of cereal and a towel. I try to ignore the flash of disappointment that crosses his eyes or how his head hangs as he sags onto the couch. "I'll just eat some of this after I clean my bow."

Quickly, I close my door and toss the cereal box and towel on the bed, hoping he'll buy my lame excuse. If I can keep Dad from following me until after I've gotten on the train, then he'll be forced to take the next one and always be one step behind me. The last thing I need is for him to catch up with me and keep me from leaving the country.

I haven't used the balcony escape route since the night I went to see Good Enough. I slip out the window, my nerves on edge, imagining Haemosu lounging against the railing with that awful grin on his face. But he isn't, and I let out a sigh of relief.

Sneaking across the balcony is pure torture. At every creak I stop and stare at the sliding glass doors that lead to our living room. I'm half expecting Dad to slide it open and storm out. He's going to be off-the-charts mad when he finds out I've run away. I want to think it serves him right for not believing me, but even still, a twinge of guilt slides around my stomach and up into my chest.

Once I reach the other end of our balcony, I know I still have two more balconies to cross. I adjust my bow so it won't throw me off balance and take a deep breath. Then I swing over the railing and around the thin privacy wall—nine floors of distance stretching below me—and onto Mrs. Jung's balcony.

But this is the first time I've been carrying a backpack and my bow case. Their weight throws me off balance. I tumble onto Mrs. Jung's balcony and land on one of her potted plants, knocking it over. The clay pot shatters beneath me.

I freeze on the concrete floor and look into Mrs. Jung's apartment; she never closes her sliding glass doors. "*Mwuh?*" she says, getting up from her mat where she watches her TV. "Who is there?"

I scramble to my feet and lean against the divider, my breath coming out heavy. I wait in the shadows, hoping she won't come out onto the balcony. Laughter erupts from the TV. She picks up her phone. Great. She's calling the police. I check my watch. I have only forty minutes until my train is supposed to leave. There isn't time to go back to my room and wait.

It's too high to jump, but if I get closer to the ground I could. I swing my legs over the railing and crouch down, my face pressed against the bars. I lower one leg and try to touch the balcony railing below. It's just out of my reach.

Mrs. Jung comes closer, squinting through the screen door at the broken pot. I tighten my bow case against my back.

The balcony light flicks on. Holding on to the bars on Mrs. Jung's balcony, I propel myself down into the balcony below, my heart racing. I land safely.

This has to be Mr. Chung's apartment, because his yip-yap dog is there barking and pawing at the sliding glass doors. I can hear people talking behind the divider on the next balcony. The one that has access to the fire escape stairs.

There's only one thing to do. Once again I leap over the balcony railing and in one swift motion swing myself down onto the seventh floor; but this time my balance is off-kilter, and I miss the balcony. Midair, I claw for the railing, and at the last minute my fingers wrap around its cold surface.

Dangling over the edge, I pull myself up to standing on the thin outer edge of the balcony. My pulse thuds in my ears. I can hear my neighbors talking to each other above. The police will arrive at any moment. I glance below me. Six floors. Can I jump that far?

Crap no.

I notice a building with a flat roof two balconies away. I shimmy myself along the outer edge of the balconies until I'm directly over the building. I toss my backpack down first and then strap my bow to my back. Taking a deep breath, I jump onto its roof, landing hard on my knee and rolling across its surface.

Sirens cut the air. I don't have much time. I leap to the ground. Finally feeling the concrete sidewalk sends a thrill through my body despite my throbbing knee. *I need it.*

I snatch up my backpack and limp straight to the subway station. My left leg aches from where I landed on it, but I ignore the pain. My senses are on full alert. Now that I know Haemosu's appearances aren't limited to the daylight hours, I can only hope I make it there without being kidnapped. Even though it only takes me fifteen minutes to get to Seoul Station, by the time I reach the ticket counter, I only have twenty minutes left to board.

I show the ticket attendant my passport while scanning the crowd for Haemosu's face. Still no sign of him.

"Is there a ticket reserved for me?" I ask, drumming my fingers on the counter. Moments later I have a ticket in hand. Grandfather came through again. On the big electronic screen to my right, words pop up in red: LAST CALL: BUSAN.

I hurry past the groups huddled on plastic benches and head toward the turnstiles. The Korean fast-food vendors are pulling metal shades over their shop fronts, closing up for the night.

As I scurry down the concrete steps to the train platform, an icy gust whooshes across my face and blows my hat away. I turn to run after it, but I stop short. Marc, standing there in jeans and boots and with that mischievous grin, is holding my hat.

CHAPTER 34

"Looking for this?" Marc is holding up my hat.

I falter. "How—how did you know I'd be here?"

"Your grandfather." He steps closer, wary. "That's what I wanted to tell you on the phone. He asked me to accompany you to Busan. Said you needed someone mature and responsible to help you get there."

I lift my eyebrows. "Mature and responsible? I think Grandfather has grown senile."

I can't deny that I was hoping he didn't want me to leave. That he was here to tell me he loved me. I say, "What about the museum and your parents being furious?"

"I wasn't totally clear on the phone. They were upset about me breaking into the museum, but they're 100 percent supportive of me helping you out."

I open my mouth. Shut it. Stare at the train. Then back at him. "Why? Why would they want you to help me?"

"I take it you're not excited to have your own personal body-guard."

"I hate to break it to you, but you're not exactly bodyguard material."

"Looks can be deceptive." He grins. "Come on, let's get on the train. I'll explain everything."

"You're not coming."

"I already have my ticket." He waves it in the air, smirking.

"You are insane." I snatch my hat back. "Besides, this doesn't exactly agree with the terms of our suspension. You might not get into Harvard."

"I wasn't planning on going there anyway."

He's so close I could reach up and push his hair out of his eyes.

I check my watch. One minute left to board. I frown at Marc as he gestures for me to board first, but I clamber onto the train. Once inside, I begin searching the compartments for my seat, trying to ignore the fact that Marc is behind me. I'm conflicted over being relieved that he's here because I don't want to make this trip alone and feeling selfish and wrong for putting him in danger again.

The train lurches forward as I find my seat, and I let out a long breath, relieved that I'm at least one step ahead of Dad. Marc jams his backpack into the overhead compartment before settling down next to me with a stack of cards. "Want to play?" he asks.

I cross my arms and glare at him. How is it that in the most insane moments he's able to stay so calm? "Coincidence that you get the seat next to mine?"

He slides the cards through his hands, shuffling. "I don't believe in coincidences. Especially when your grandfather bought both tickets."

Outside, the gray concrete buildings of the city flash by as we flee to the southern tip of Korea. I'm trying to figure out why Grandfather and Marc's parents want him to help me. Somebody isn't telling me the whole story.

"Spill it," I say. "I want to know what's really going on."

"I guess it doesn't matter now if you know or not." Marc deals out the cards while I narrow my eyes at him. "Remember how I told you that my dad and your grandfather are friends?" I nod. "Well, they are friends because they are both part of the same organization."

"Right. I knew that already. Guardians of Shinshi or something. I can see how my grandfather has a part in all this, but your dad isn't Korean; and if it's all so secret, then why do you know all this?"

"My dad is an expert in religious studies, and he's an archaeologist." Marc's voice turns to a whisper. "Because of his expertise, he gained the trust of the Guardians. From his research, he was able to discover the location of something they wanted."

"Which was?"

He peeks over our seats, glancing at the other passengers in our car before continuing. "The legend of Korea's origin says the immortals dropped six Orbs of Life on Earth to form Korea. For centuries those orbs were kept hidden, guarded by the Hwarang warriors within Korea's great mountains. But over time the orbs slowly disappeared. My dad discovered the location of two of those orbs and returned them to the Guardians. That is why my dad is a member."

He twirls his ring, staring at it. There's something familiar about that ring. It's a simple gold ring without the tiger like

Grandfather and Komo wear, but it's still a ring. My eyes widen. "You're one of them," I say.

He looks up in surprise and then runs his hands through his hair. "I'm kind of in training."

"Oh my God."

He looks away. "There's more. My dad has been working with your grandfather for a long time trying to stop Haemosu." He swallows hard. "I was assigned to keep you safe."

"Are you saying you knew about this the whole time? From the very beginning?"

"Just that I needed to protect you. I had no idea about anything else until you told me. And then after what happened at your locker, the Guardians filled me in. They also took my new sight as a sign. A sign that I was supposed to watch out for you. That I was meant to be a Guardian."

"I don't need protecting," I remind him.

"After the incident at the museum, my dad filled me in on their side of things. Since I can, you know, see the Others, the council thinks I'm even more valuable."

I draw my knees to my chest and wrap my arms around my legs. It all makes sense now. How Marc was always there when Haemosu turned up. How he always seemed right in step with me.

I'd thought we had a connection, but I was really just a special assignment. "So that's all this was between the two of us," I say. "An assignment?"

His eyes grow wide, and I almost believe him when he says, "No! That's not what I meant."

"Well, you don't have to worry about protecting me anymore," I say. "I can take care of myself."

"You have to believe me, Jae. And yeah, you're right. You don't need protecting. You can take care of yourself. I guess I want to help somehow, that's all." He tries to take my hand, but I pull away. "This has always been more than an assignment. From the first moment I saw you. Remember that night when you came to my house, and you asked me what I wanted in life? Yesterday when we were talking in the coffee shop, it all became clear. This is it. I want to be a Guardian. More than anything. I have all the skills, and now that I can see the creatures I only want it more."

"I'm glad you've found your thing." I know I sound bitter, but I can't help myself.

Marc says, "Being a Guardian is like studying archaeology and myths. But instead of digging through dust and crumbling worlds, I'm digging up something real, alive. My work could make a difference in people's lives. I could help save *your* life."

I look into his eyes. I want to trust him because of everything he's done for me. All those moments together. Every touch. It's all meant more to me than I should've allowed myself to feel. I let my guard down, and now I'm paying the price.

But this isn't the time to get emotional. "So what does all this orb stuff have to do with Haemosu?" I say, and look him hard in the eyes.

"Haemosu's power has grown. The Guardians suspect Haemosu might have gotten an orb, which would grant him this additional power to materialize in our world so often. Or maybe he's in league with another immortal. Or worse: both."

We sit in silence, and I listen to the hum of the train flying over the tracks. Marc picks up the stack of cards and flips them through his hands. "Dad is away a lot for late-night meetings at the university. He says the spirit forces have divided Korea in half, and until things are made right, the country will only continue to fall apart."

"He thinks North and South Korea are divided because of things in the Spirit World?"

"I don't know what to think," he says. "But I get the feeling that Haemosu is one part of it. If we can solve this, maybe we can deal with the bigger picture later."

I close my eyes. I can't deal with the big picture right now. Everything seems out of place, and here I am making every bad decision in the book. Maybe there aren't any good decisions.

I decide to check my phone, and see that Dad called. So he's discovered I'm gone. Good. I turn off my phone and lean my head against the green vinyl seat, wishing I could shut out all my problems just like turning off my phone.

"What if leaving Korea is a bad idea?" I say. "How can I stop Haemosu if I just run away? What if there was a good choice, and I never saw it? Or what if there isn't a good choice, and I can only choose the bad?"

He sets down his card and takes my hand. "It's there. You just haven't found it yet."

"I don't know how to defeat him." I pull away my hand and squeeze the armrests of the chair.

"I brought my notes. Do you want to go over them again?"

"I suppose that would be better than breaking your seat apart."

I roll my eyes and snatch the papers from him. We study his notes and review the legend for the next three hours as the train whizzes through rice fields and past jagged mountains. Out here in the countryside, snow covers the ground and lies heavy on the pines, reflecting brightly in the moonlight. We fly by a small town bordered by a low stone wall. The fluted-roof house lights wink at us as we speed by.

"I want my family to be safe and for this to be the answer," I say as we put away the books and turn off the reading lights. "But I have this awful feeling that I'm missing something."

Marc wraps his arms around me and pulls me against his chest. I stiffen. I'm doing it again. Letting my guard down. I shouldn't allow him so close to my heart.

"I'm here for you, Jae," he says, his chin resting on my head. "You have to know that by now."

His words melt my resolve. He's right. He risked his life twice for me, once at the locker and once in the museum. How can I throw away that kind of devotion? I lean my head back, my lips brushing over his neck, drinking in his delicious smell. His body burns warm against mine, and my muscles relax in his arms. Assignments and myths fly away as my lips trail up his neck and over the light stubble on his jawline until our lips meet. His breathing quickens. I run my fingers through his hair, pulling him closer. We kiss, hungrily this time. Needing to be closer.

Because this might be our last night.

Our last kiss.

CHAPTER 35

"Wake up," Marc says.

I blink away the sleep from my eyes and reluctantly leave Marc's arms. Everyone in our car is standing, grabbing bags, and shrugging into their coats.

The air is warmer here. Salty. My watch reads midnight. No wonder my muscles ache. I take a deep breath and step out of the train. The sky looms dark above, but the white floors and chrome pillars on the platform are lit up bright. I truck myself up the concrete steps and into the lobby. The outer walls of the station are all glass, and I imagine it must be beautiful here in daylight. I scan the area for Grandfather and wave when I spot him. He frowns. Figures.

"Jae Hwa. Good to see you. Well done, young man," Grandfather says to Marc as we walk up.

"Haraboji." I lower my chin, giving him a solid glare. "I don't *need* an escort. I'm perfectly capable of traveling on my own."

Grandfather lifts his eyebrows. "Indeed."

"I'm glad to help," Marc says, a twinkle in his eyes. "Can I come with you to the ferry?"

Grandfather frowns deeper but nods. "Only to the ferry. Your parents will be worried otherwise."

Grandfather cocks his head, an indication for us to follow him, and marches outside to the taxi stand. In a clipped voice he tells the driver to head to the port and jumps in front while Marc and I scramble into the back.

"The boat leaves at six a.m.," Grandfather explains as we pull away. "I've arranged for us to stay for the next four hours in a resting house next to the ferry terminal until we head to customs."

"Dad has been leaving me five million messages," I say. "I think it's going to work. He says he's taking the first bullet train in the morning. I told him to meet us in the Fukuoka terminal. That way he can't talk us out of leaving Korea."

Marc and Grandfather chat in Korean for the rest of the taxi ride. Marc is more fluent than I am, and I tune them out, wondering if I can pull this off. Will Dad take my bait and show up? Can I get him out of the country in time? I wonder if Haemosu will show up unexpectedly. I hope Haechi took care of him.

The closer we get to the port, the faster I twirl the golden bracelet around my wrist.

I have only slept for three hours in the tiny rented room Grandfather found before he wakes me and Marc. I munch on dried squid as we hike the two blocks to the ferry terminal in the misty, purplish glow of dawn.

The roadside is lined with tarp-stretched shacks where

fishermen are already slapping the wooden tables with this morning's catch. I sigh. An orange juice and bagel would be perfect about now. I try to focus on the ocean and the fishing boats bobbing near the shore. Beyond them the big sea tankers drift, outlining a skyline now soaked in indigo and dark, rain-puffed clouds. A storm is approaching.

We enter the parking lot of a giant building, and I immediately notice the signs in its aqua-colored windows displaying the *Beetle*. The boat in the picture is unremarkable, white with a black hull, but Grandfather says this boat flies over the water as if it has wings.

When we enter the terminal, I grip my dragon bow's case tighter, hoping this plan will work.

Grandfather already bought our tickets and left one on reserve for Dad. We're hoping he will arrive in time to catch the next boat. I peek through the glass windows that look out to sea at my escape boat bobbing in the water. My heart lightens as I realize that if Haemosu wanted to show up, he'd have done so by now. He wouldn't make a scene in such a crowd.

"I guess this is good-bye." Marc stuffs his hands into his pockets. "Skype me, Fighter Girl."

Tears fill my eyes, but I don't care. For the past six weeks, all I've wanted to do is leave Korea, but now I feel as if it's a part of me. It's brought me friends, a great school, my relatives, and now Marc.

I throw myself into his arms.

He stumbles back, surprised, I think; but he wraps his arms around me, squeezing me tightly as if he knows how I'm feeling.

"We'll meet up again," he says into my hair. "You'll see."

My head pounds as he releases me. What if I'm making the wrong decision?

"Come," Grandfather says, motioning to the turnstiles. "It is time."

I don't have any words for Marc so I just kiss him. Right there in the lobby in front of my grandfather. He pulls me to him tight and cups my face in his hands and kisses me again, softly this time.

"*Saranghae*," he whispers.

An announcement blares over the speakers, but I don't move as I stare into his green eyes. He just said "I love you."

He loves me?

Loves *me*?

I stumble after Grandfather to the gate. As I hand over my passport to the attendant, I glance back at Marc.

His hair is wild and sticking up everywhere, and he looks so alone that I want to run back to him and tell him I'm going to stay. Suddenly Marc's eyes change. He's looking at something behind me. He reaches out his hand and yells, "NO!"

I whip my head around, and I realize I'm holding out my passport to Haemosu, in a black button-down shirt with dark slacks, his hair slicked back.

Haemosu grins. His skin flickers like a thousand stars under the fluorescent lights. "You thought I would forget about my princess?"

All the air has left my body. I drop my passport and stumble backward. I glance around at the people chatting, talking on their cell phones, totally obvious to the Korean demigod standing in their midst. Of course. No one can see the immortals unless they allow it.

No one but Marc.

"Haraboji!" I shout, but Grandfather has already gone through the turnstile and can't hear me over the crowd.

Haemosu lunges for me. I lurch away, his fingers brushing my arm, and Marc barrels through the crowd, shoving people out of the way. He dives and crashes his body into Haemosu. The two tumble to the floor. Those in line circle Marc, yelling and pointing at him.

One lady cries out, "Seizure! The boy is having a seizure!"

I push my way to Marc, but a security guard catches my arm and drags me back. "Marc!" I scream.

"Run, Jae!" Marc yells.

I kick and squirm in the guard's arms until I wrestle my way free with a back elbow punch, turn, and knee to the groin. This guard messed with the wrong girl. I race into the empty circle where I last saw Marc. Neither Haemosu nor Marc is there.

"Marc!" I shriek, spinning around, distantly aware that I must look as insane as a banshee. "Marc!"

My screaming is pointless. Haemosu has taken him.

CHAPTER 36

I stand on the gangplank, indecision pulling me in both directions. Get on the boat with Grandfather or back to land to find Haemosu and Marc? The wind cuts against my face, salt water spraying my legs. All I can think about is how Marc is gone. Can I save him? Is he still alive?

"Jae Hwa," Grandfather says, "get on the boat!"

"But Marc," I say, and my heart squeezes. Grandfather drags me onto the boat deck, and I don't have the energy to fight him. My feet weigh a thousand pounds as the gate lowers and the plank rises. I've never felt so weak and helpless in my entire life.

It's all my fault.

I shove Grandfather's hand off me and run to the edge of the boat. Should I jump? I'd have to jump just right so as not to hit the deck or the propeller. A guard pushes me backward, but all I can think about is how Marc saved me and I did nothing. There must have been *something* I could've done.

My vision blurs as Grandfather guides me into the boat's

cafeteria. My insides feel numb. The door slams shut behind us. The boat engines rev up.

"No!" I say. "We can't leave Marc. Haemosu took him. I have to help him."

Everyone is sitting at tables to watch the departure, but my shouting has obviously gotten their attention. I suppose that's because I sound like a raving lunatic.

"You are safe. That is all that matters right now," Grandfather says, leading me to a table with padded chairs that look out to the water. "There is nothing that you could have done to stop what happened. He saved you. We will be in international waters soon. Haemosu has no power over you there. This is what Marc wanted."

I stare blankly ahead while Grandfather's hand grips the side of the table, knuckles white. He's visibly upset, his lips tight and hair tussled. Even now he's so confident that we're doing the right thing. What has happened to me? What kind of person am I to stand by and watch as Haemosu takes all the people I love?

The boat slides away from the dock. I study the massive terminal; the roofline swoops down like white waves over the aqua walls. People wave from the observation dock as a heavy mist settles in. Marc isn't there. Of course he isn't there.

I should've known Haemosu would try to take him. Ever since that day I entered the locker and Haemosu heard Marc's voice, Haemosu has been jealous. I knew I shouldn't have let him come, but I'm so freaking selfish. He'd be safe at home if it wasn't for me.

I spot gulls in the distance flying toward the boat like gold coins in the sky. Slowly I stand. No, not gulls. Those creatures glinting in the morning sun are not from this world.

I know what I must do. I pull out my quiver and the Blue Dragon bow from its case. The wooden arch vibrates as if it's alive in my hands.

"What are you doing?" Grandfather's hands form fists. "Sit."

"I have to go." I strap the bow to my back and the quiver on my hip.

"No, you do not! Think of all those who have sacrificed to save you. To stop the curse."

"I hear their voices every night crying for help, Haraboji! I can't live knowing he has Marc and Komo. I can't live knowing Haemosu will come and take you and Dad next. And it's all my fault. So, yeah, I have to!"

I dash up the stairs to the upper deck before he can respond. The air rushes around me, whipping my hair across my face, and I weave my way past the lifeboats to the bow of the boat. No one is standing outside; it's too cold, which is all the better. I step onto a metal box, slip on my gloves, notch an arrow into place.

And wait.

Not for long. They come, riding the morning rays, as red as the sun's flames themselves. Haemosu's dragons.

I aim, pull, and let my arrow fly. It hits the first dragon in the eye. The creature screeches and pulls back. The second is an easy mark; for its belly hovers just above me. It makes a sound like thunder rumbling as the arrow pierces it. Before I can notch another arrow, the three remaining dragons have landed, their golden claws scratching the surface, radiating streaks of light.

"Listen, Dragons of Haemosu!" I yell over the rush of wind. The boat has picked up speed, riding along the hydrofoils and skimming over the ocean toward Japan. But that isn't my destination. I say, "I wish you to take me to your master."

The dragons blink their wide red eyes in surprise. The largest, cocking its head and flicking out a forked tongue, speaks in my mind. *We bear a message, Princess. From the glorious Haemosu.*

"I know. That's why I want you to take me to him."

You betrayed his love. Now all whom you love will pay.

My vision blurs, I'm so angry.

The message has been delivered. We must fulfill the master's desire.

One lets out a piercing screech and wrenches the dragon bow from my grasp. The largest dragon whips his head to stare at Grandfather, who has just come onto the deck.

"No!" I lunge for Grandfather, but I'm too slow as the dragon's talon snatches the back of his jacket.

"Run, Jae Hwa!" Grandfather says.

He doesn't realize that they aren't here for me, that this is one of Haemosu's awful tricks. They're here for him. Haemosu knows me better than I thought. He knows I'll do what he asks to free everyone I love.

I leap down and seize the bow as Grandfather's body is lifted airborne. I pull back and release an arrow, aiming for the talon holding Grandfather. With a cry, the dragon drops Grandfather, but then the second dragon swoops in and snatches him again in midair.

I take off running across the deck until I'm at the boat's edge. I launch onto the railing and jump up in the air, the ocean below me, and grab ahold of Grandfather's leg.

"No, Jae Hwa!" Grandfather shouts.

Too late. I'm soaring through the air with the dragons as I hold on to Grandfather, watching the boat speed away. It looks like a toy now, surrounded by a sea of blue.

We rise higher and higher. Above, I can hear Grandfather groan from my weight pulling on his leg. He shrugs off his backpack and hands it to me. "Take this," he says. "It will lighten my load."

I don't understand how that will lighten his load, but I'm in too much pain from holding on to argue. I slide the pack over my shoulder and clutch Grandfather's leg with every ounce of strength I have left. Below, I can see we are flying back toward Korea, the beaches below us and then the sprawling city of Busan, with its tall buildings and the mountains rising in the distance.

A cloud moves in and cloaks us in a world of white. I realize we're about to leave this world. I grow light-headed; waves of nausea push at my stomach. My arm aches. I just need to hold on a little longer. Pressure pushes on me from all sides.

You are not allowed to pass.

Talons take hold of me, and I'm yanked from Grandfather's leg.

"No!" I scream.

Then I'm flung across the sky, far from the city. The wind

rushes around me, screaming in my ears and tearing at my clothes as I plummet. The ground looms closer with every second. I know I'm about to die, but all I can think about is Dad, Grandfather, and Marc. What will happen to them?

A golden light envelopes me along with the sound of tinkling bells. I black out.

CHAPTER 37

My bones ache and my head feels like a hand grenade exploded in my brain. Slowly, I lift my eyes and wait for my vision to clear. After seeing the golden light and hearing the tinkling of bells, I'm expecting to be in Haemosu's world.

I'm so wrong.

The sky hovers above, smoky blue, and little block houses, some modern concrete style and others with the traditional tiled roofs, rise up toward it. Cars rush by, spraying slush on the sidewalk, splattering my face. My clothes are soaked, and my hair is slimy from whatever I'd been lying in. Probably vomit from the smell of it.

I'm not in Haemosu's lands. He saved me so he could torture me. My hands start shaking. I punch the ground, and mud and sludge splatter all over me.

Three people I care about have been taken because they believed in me. I failed them. My stomach churns, thinking about what Haemosu might have done to them. I stumble into an alley and throw up.

I check my watch for the time, but my vision is still fuzzy, and it takes a few moments for me to read it—eight a.m. I reach up gingerly and find a golf ball–sized bump on the left side of my head. How did this happen? I should be splattered across the pavement.

I do a quick inventory check, hoping I somehow managed to take more with me than the huge bump. Sure enough, my bow is still strapped to my shoulder, miraculously undamaged, and my backpack is still on my back. I spy Grandfather's pack at my feet. I pick it up and stumble down the side of the road, avoiding the mud and puddles. Shop lights flick on, and the roadside sellers make their way to their carts, tossing off the thick brown tarps in preparation for the day.

It's a normal morning for them. Unlike me. My latest grand plan has gone wrong.

I touch Princess Yuhwa's hairpin, still tucked in my slimy ponytail. I sense a connection with her just by having it on. She found a way to escape. Maybe her good fortune will rub off on me. This calms me somehow.

I need to call Dad. Without a guardian I can't leave the country. Oddly, the thought of staying in Korea is comforting. The truth of it all sets in. I don't want to leave anymore. I can't leave my friends or my family. This is where I belong. This is home.

But I can't call Dad. Haemosu is just waiting for me to lead him to Dad, so I can watch Dad get kidnapped. Haemosu will only do it if I'm there. Keeping Dad as far from me as possible is the only way I can ensure he's safe.

I search my backpack for food and finding none; I dig through Grandfather's. My hand brushes against a silk drawstring pouch. Curious, I pull back the golden strings and dump the object into my palm. It's cool to the touch, and the gold catches in the early light.

Oh. My. God.

The amulet.

Grandfather had it the whole time! I think back to when I was talking to the police chief and I thought I'd seen someone slip out. Had that been him? He'd probably planned to get me out of the country and then secretly come back to defeat Haemosu himself.

The three-legged crow looks at me as if it's itching to tell its secret. I run my finger around the circular edge, remembering how Grandfather said that each of the ancient Koguryo tombs was a gateway into the Spirit World.

If I can find one of those tombs, I can enter the Spirit World just like I'd originally planned. Because now I have the key. I can rescue Marc, Grandfather, and Komo.

Haemosu thinks he's got it all under control, but I'll show him. I clench the amulet in my fist and head over to a shopkeeper rolling back her tarp to reveal piles of socks loaded on her cart. I smile just at the sight. If I could take a picture of it and e-mail it to my friends back in L.A., they would die laughing.

But those times are gone. Life has become way more complicated than taking pictures and hanging out with friends. I swallow back tears.

"Excuse me," I manage to say to the sock lady in Korean. "Do you know where the closest Korean king's tomb is?"

She glances up, and her weathered face grins. I suppose my

L.A.–accented Korean is laughable, but she points to the bus stop across the street.

"The closest tomb is King Munmu's," she says. "Bonggil Beach is a one-hour drive away."

Only one hour away? *Yes!* "*Kamsahamnida*," I say, and skirt around her cart to a public bathroom next to the bus stop.

There I wash the grossness out of my hair in the sink, brush my teeth, and splash water over my tear-streaked face. It wasn't a hot bath, but it would have to do. Feeling a world better, I head back outside to the bus stop.

The map hanging on the bulletin board shows that I'm not in Busan anymore. I'm actually farther east up the coast between Busan and Kyongju. Interesting. I suppose the dragons were trying to throw me as far from the port as possible.

An hour later I stumble off the bus and onto a sand-streaked brick road. Every muscle aches, and my head hurts even worse. Wandering down the street, I breathe in the salty air and listen to the low rush of the waves as I search for someone to show me the way to the tomb. Even through my pounding headache, I notice there's something strange about this town.

Empty tarp-covered stalls fill the beach side of the road, and even the concrete lean-to restaurants that line the other side look forlorn. The only signs of civilization are the telephone wires strung along the road like sagging tightropes. The restaurants have fish tanks out in front and large signs tacked onto their roofs to lure visitors.

Where is everyone?

I'm so weak right now, it's hard even to think straight. A

peak-roofed restaurant with the words KING MUNMU painted on a wooden sign across the front catches my eye.

Inside, smells of cooked rice and sesame oil send my stomach growling. The restaurant's walls are slabs of unfinished wood, with old-fashioned sconces holding candles and the far end is lined with windows that overlook the sea.

Scenic paintings of Korea fill the walls. My shoulders relax as I collapse onto one of the low table's floor cushions.

A lady with long dark flowing hair glides to my table and hands me a menu.

"Hello there, young one," she says in a lilting voice that reminds me of crashing waves. "You look weary and hungry."

"Yeah, I'm starved." I give the menu a quick scan and order noodles.

I don't wait long before she drifts back with a huge bowl of thick rice noodles, steam coiling up.

"You have no idea how wonderful this looks," I tell her, and slurp up a spoonful. "I noticed your restaurant was named after King Munmu. Do you know where his tomb is?"

"Indeed." She flicks her manicured hand toward a painting of a rocky island. "One of my favorites of the king's final resting place."

She sighs and takes a moment to study each of the paintings in the room. I slowly lower my spoon as I follow her gaze. Every painting in the restaurant is of that same island. It's kind of creepy.

I say, "The tomb is on an island?" Why does everything have to be so impossible?

"Down the path just outside my restaurant. Not far." She pats my hand and pushes my bowl closer to me. "Now eat up, my dear. You look like a few pounds would do you good."

The noodles warm my body so that by the time I drain the last of the broth, I'm so tired I could curl up in one of the restaurant's corners and sleep for a decade.

"You should rest, little one," the lady whispers into my ear. I start and knock over my cup. She must have magic feet, she's so quiet. "I have a room in the back. Rest for a moment until you are refreshed."

A little rest would be nice. How can I face Haemosu when I can barely walk? I pick up my packs and bow and follow her to a back room. A *yo* with a soft white comforter lies on the floor, and in the corner there's a bathtub with fluffy white towels resting next to it. It will be heaven to soak in a warm bath and really clean this stinky sludge off me. I move to step inside. The woman's arm blocks my entrance, jerking me from my fantasy.

"The weapon," she points to the dragon bow with her eyes, "stays outside."

I'm not sure if it's the glint in her eyes or the steel tone of her voice, but I reach for the pouch holding the amulet I've looped to my jeans. The blurriness of my vision, the ache in my muscles, the pound of my head all vanish as adrenaline charges through my veins. The amulet is practically screaming *Danger!*

"I can't part with it," I say. "It's a family heirloom."

The room crackles with static electricity. The woman standing before me is caught up in a windstorm, her hair and red skirts whirling around her. Her body contorts, and like fire, a red coating of fur spreads from her toes, moving up her body until it reaches her face. I stumble backward as her ears twist out slightly and stretch until they're pointed. Then her nose elongates and sharpens until I'm standing under the beady black gaze of a woman who looks just like a fox.

CHAPTER 38

The fox-lady leers with sharp, dagger teeth. "I suppose you have never seen a *kumiho*," she says. "Yes, we exist. It is just that no one lives afterward to tell the tale."

How did I not recognize the magic of this place? After all I've been through. I should have known better.

She whips out a clawed paw, snarling. I drop the packs and hurl myself in a back flip, kicking out my legs as I do so. My feet snap-kick into her snout and send her sprawling through the open doorway. As I land, I'm already pulling the bow off my back and notching an arrow into place.

She charges at me, her tails—a bunch of them!—lifting up behind her like a peacock, ready to strike. I loose an arrow. It strikes her in the chest. She totters, her eyes roll once in her head, and then she lets out a shaman-like scream and dives at me. My pulse pounds through my veins, my vision crystallizing as I wait for just the right moment. Then I smash her with my front kick, then side kick, and I finish her off by twisting around for a jumping back kick.

She crumples at my feet and I breathe in relief, but one of her tails snags my leg and yanks me to the floor, pulling me closer to her snapping jaw.

"I must have it," she whispers. Her black eyes have turned murky white. "Give it to me."

If I remember the ancient stories correctly, *kumihos* must feed on human livers to survive. I grab the leg of one of the tables to pull myself closer and snatch up one of the lit candles. I'm so focused on it that I don't realize how close her mouth has come to my side until I look back.

I scream, kick her salivating mouth away from me, and toss the candle at her tails. Howling, she lets my ankle go as her tails burst into flames. I count them now. Nine.

The putrid scent of burning fur and skin fills the air and that, mixed with her screams, sends me gagging and running to my bags and bow. I grab them and glance quickly at the painting next to me. It's an aerial view of the tomb. The rocks create more of a ring than an island, because inside the rock ring is seawater.

The *kumiho* rolls across the floor, screaming, and starts to crawl my way. I race out the door and don't stop running until I hit the beach. Once there I sink into the gravelly sand and take long, deep breaths to calm myself.

The deep-indigo ocean builds up and crashes on the shoreline. I stare out at the water, remembering the time I stood at Grandfather's beach and first heard the story of Princess Yuhwa. I'd thought it was just a fairy tale.

I squint out at the ocean at something and catch my breath. There, rising out of the water, a golden palace appears. *Haemosu's palace.* I know it. I take off running across the beach, sliding my backpack on and slinging my bow over my shoulder. The soft sand slows me down, and I stumble through it in my boots until I reach the water's edge. The palace wavers in the sunlight like a mirage. Am I imagining it? I stretch out my hand, willing it to come to me, but instead it begins to fade.

"No!" I yell. If I could just get to it, I'm sure I could enter Haemosu's land. I start wading through the water, the surf splashing up around me.

I dive in. Ice-cold water shocks my nerves. But when my head surfaces, the palace is gone. Treading water, I scan the horizon, but nothing extraordinary is there.

I missed it. Freaking missed my chance. If I'm supposed to have a connection with this stupid Spirit World, then why can't I just walk into it? I punch the water and swim back to shore.

At the beach, I start walking down the shoreline. I'm so ticked I nearly pass a huge rock with a metal plate drilled onto it. I pause to read the plaque:

KING MUNMU'S UNDERWATER TOMB

King Munmu (661–681 AD) unified the three kingdoms to become the thirtieth ruler of the Silla kingdom. At his death, the king gave specific instructions to be buried in the East Sea so he would become the dragon that would protect the Silla from the Japanese.

An underwater tomb? I stare out at the ocean again and realize that there's a rocky inlet not more than seventy feet in length about a hundred yards from the edge of the shore. It looks just like the fox-lady's pictures. The barren rocks stick up out of the water with no apparent buildings or structures. But how am I supposed to get out there?

I take a handful of sand and throw it, frustrated, but the wind catches it and blows it right back in my face. I cough and spit out the grains. I start trudging down the beach until a small house with a low stone wall surrounding it catches my eye. Actually, the kayaks lined up on the lawn did. A boy about my age sprays them down.

"Hey," I say in Korean. "Do you give boat trips out to the island?"

The boy, his black hair hanging low over his eyes, stops spraying and cocks his head, assessing me. "No one is allowed on the island," he says, tapping the end of the hose against his jeans. "It's sacred ground."

"Really?" I rummage through Grandfather's backpack until I find his wallet. I pull out a one-hundred-thousand won check, about a hundred dollars back in the States. I try not to think about how it's all the money I have left. "How sacred?"

He takes the check and stuffs it into what looks like a water-proof jacket. "Can you paddle?"

I shrug. "Just get me to the island, okay?"

"I can take you for a quick trip. The island is nothing but tall rocks. But it's sacred, so you can't walk on it." He points to a banana-yellow sea kayak. "Take an end."

I empty my backpack of everything except my arrows and leave it all on the beach along with Grandfather's pack. Then I kick off my boots, slide on my backpack, check to make sure the amulet is secured to my waist, and roll up my jeans to my knees.

The dragon bow is last. I strap it to my back, hoping the water won't ruin it.

Sand slides between my toes, cold and wet, as we drag the boat into the surf, fighting off the waves that crash and churn at our feet. Once we're deep enough we shimmy inside, me in front, the boy in the back. I position my feet against the footrests and take the paddle the boy passes me.

I haven't done any kind of paddling since elementary school camp, which ended with me capsizing the canoe, along with three other girls from my class. Since then I've stayed clear of water sports.

The boy digs his paddle into the sea, yelling at me over the waves to do the same. I grip my paddle and plunge deep, trying to push back against the waves. I don't even look up for a while but focus on plunge, push back and lift, plunge, push back and lift. Then, from the corner of my eye, I notice black rocks jutting up in front of us like shark teeth.

My heart sinks. I should be excited that I've been able to paddle so far out, but I'm not. How am I supposed to climb those rocks? What if I have it all wrong and this amulet will do nothing? Or what if I am right and it works, but then I fail when I find Haemosu?

"I thought you said you could paddle?" the boy says, frowning at me.

"Right." I push away my negative thoughts and think about Dad's obnoxious poster back home: "The best way to predict your future is to create it." *This is me creating my future,* I think as I dig my oar in deeper. Sea kayaking out to scale impossible rocks and trespassing on a sacred burial site.

Yep. I've so got everything under control.

We're at the edge of the island, the volcanic rocks jutting up sharp and impenetrable. Water gushes against the island wall, spraying me, the salt burning my eyes. We float closer, and I examine the slopes for some way to get up on them. It's not until we make the final turn before heading back to shore that I spot it. One rock section slopes just enough that I think I could climb it.

"Let's get closer!" I yell.

"Too dangerous!"

"I didn't give you a hundred thousand won for nothing!"

He shakes his head but shovels his paddle into the left side of the boat to turn us closer to the island. After a few yards the current makes it impossible to get any closer. I'll have to jump for it.

I set down my paddle and adjust my bow.

"What are you doing?" the boy says.

"I'm going to swim to the island."

"What?" His eyes widen as if I'm crazy. He has no idea.

"If I can't climb on, will you wait for me?"

"This is a very bad idea."

Tell me about it.

Before he can talk me out of it, I pencil-jump into the ocean, icy water stabbing my skin, and pop back to the surface, coughing up water. The current pulls, and I realize I'll be swept out to the beach before I even have a chance to touch the rocks. I stretch out my arm and start swimming, fighting against the current, hoping I'll reach the rocks before my strength leaves me.

I'm not sure how long I've been swimming, but when I scrape my palm against the rock face, I know I've made it. The current bears down on me as I press my body against the rock and fumble for a handhold. My fingers are numb and white from the freezing water. The incline I noticed on the boat is just beyond my reach. I wedge my body into the rock, straining against frothing waves. I scream.

And somehow, in a haze of insanity, I reach it. Notches are grooved into the rock face, and my fingers fit into them perfectly. Maybe I'm not the only one who has been on this rock. I pull myself up, and my feet graze the razor-sharp lava rock until I find a tiny ledge for them to stand on. Slowly I work my way up the slope.

My muscles burn.

My arms shake.

I climb higher.

The wind whips around me; my hair sticks to my cheeks, wet. I bite my lip, tasting a mix of blood and salt, and keep moving until I'm at the top of the rock. I cling to its surface and gaze around. The boy is still sitting in his kayak, waving his oar at me.

It's not exactly a happy wave. More like a you-better-get-over-here-or-I'm-going-to-get-you-in-big-trouble type of wave. I wave back.

Back at the shore, the sandy beach, so safe and calm, feels like forever away.

Looking around, I realize these rock walls form a ring. From the sky they would resemble a crown, and in the center of the crown is a pool just like the one in the *kumiho*'s painting, oddly calm in comparison to the surging waves on the other side of the rock walls.

I swing my leg over the tip of the rock, which I'm sure is sending the boy into total panic mode. Slowly I climb down the slope, careful to place my feet so I don't fall into the pool of water in the center of the rock crown. I stop midway, searching for anything that would look like the *samjoko* on the amulet.

A cloud parts above me, and rays of sunlight trickle into the smooth pool. That's when I see it. A golden plate, submerged beneath the water's depths, ingrained into the side of a rock. I scale farther down the rock until I can find a ledge on which to stand. Carefully, I slide the amulet out of its pouch. I hold it up to the sun, comparing it to the golden plate below.

How does it work? Only one way to find out. I slip the amulet back into its pouch and wrap its string around my wrist.

I jump in.

This water is slightly warmer than the surf outside of the rock crown. I push my way back above the surface for a quick breath and dive back under, swimming to the golden plate. Once there, I slip out the amulet and press it into the circular space on the plate, pushing against the water until the amulet sets in place. A perfect fit.

Nothing happens.

My breath is nearly gone. I press both hands on it, willing it to work.

Begging it to work.

It moves, slightly. I push harder. My lungs scream for air.

The plate sparkles like diamonds shattered into a thousand pieces. It's so bright that I'm blinded and lose my breath, choking on water. The plate revolves faster and faster, until the inside bursts open. The light explodes, and I'm dragged within. Once again I find myself sucked into a spinning, star-riddled vortex. Into another time and another place.

CHAPTER 39

This time I'm prepared when the swirling stops. I reach for my bow, relieved it's still with me, and notch in an arrow.

But I am wrong again. So wrong.

The place into which I step is like nothing I've yet experienced. Stars glitter around me, as if I'm suspended in the middle of nowhere. Before me is an enormous tiger, sitting on his haunches, as orange as the deepest sunset, with black stripes darker than the darkest night. I drop my bow in surprise. It floats by my side.

"Where—" I stutter, my breath comes out heavy. "Where?"

The tiger's deep ginger eyes consider me, and he tilts his head to the side. Behind the tiger stretches a long thick golden thread, shimmering as it trails to forever. He roars, "I am the Tiger of Shinshi, the Warden of Three Thousand Li, the Defender of the Chosen, and the Guardian of the Golden Thread." I clamp my hands over my head. "Who are you?"

I lower my shaking hands. "I am Jae Hwa."

"What is your purpose, daughter of Korea?"

I gape at his massive paws. "I am going to confront Haemosu."

"What of Haemosu?"

"He has stolen the spirits of my ancestors and kidnapped my aunt, grandfather, and friend. I have to help them."

"The Spirit World is not for the living."

"But aren't you supposed to protect us?" I don't dare look at him. I've overstepped my boundaries. "My family hasn't had peace for hundreds of years. Please allow me to go into Haemosu's land. I have to stop him."

"Hmm." His voice rumbles. "Impertinent girl. You know that no dream comes without a price. Are you willing to sacrifice?"

My heart clenches like a fist. I lift my head. "Yes."

His eyes bore deep into mine. "Then go."

"Can you make sure my bow and arrows come with me?"

"Your weapons will not save you."

"I have to try."

"So be it." His paw reaches out and touches my hand, as soft as a cherry blossom. "Take this." I open my palm, and he places an amethyst the size of my fingernail in it. It pulses warmth through my skin.

"The soul of Korea. Let it guide you through the darkness."

Before I can thank him, he transforms into a giant topaz sphere. It rolls across the golden thread and disappears.

I stand still for a moment, trying to grasp what I've just seen. There's nothing around me but stars and emptiness. I'm lost. What now?

Then I remember the tiger's words about the gem. I strap

my bow to my back and open my palm. The gem glistens, ribbons of light cascading from its surface.

I follow the light, my feet touching nothing, and it's as if I'm flying. The wind picks up around me, and I move closer to something in the distance. It's another golden plate, just like the one at King Munmu's tomb. When I reach it, I set the amulet into the hole as before, and I'm sucked inside.

CHAPTER 40

The darkness fades, and wavering before me is Haemosu's throne room. I glance over my shoulder, but the plate I walked through has disappeared. The air shimmers, and as it settles, I slide the amulet back into its pouch and stuff the amethyst into my jeans pocket.

I swing my bow and arrow into place in one fluid motion and wait. Holding my breath, waiting for Haemosu to leap out in one of his strange forms. But nothing happens. The room is empty. I lower the bow, glad it's in perfect condition. Maybe it really is the true Blue Dragon bow.

I race outside the throne room into the courtyard. All I can think about is Komo, Marc, and Grandfather and if they're safe. If they're still alive.

"Jae!"

Marc's voice.

I skid to a stop and swing around to see Marc and Grandfather trapped in a bamboo cage at the other end of the courtyard.

I race toward them. Their clothes are shredded, and the side of Marc's face is caked with blood. Grandfather is lying still, curled up in the small space. My heart slams inside my chest like someone kicked me. This is what they get for helping me? I should never have allowed this to happen.

"Jae Hwa!" Marc says, falling to his knees, his hair a wild mess. "What happened? You're supposed to be in Japan."

"I'm so sorry, Marc." I hunch down and grab hold of the bars. "How is Haraboji?"

Marc shakes his head. "Not good. Haemosu brought him here only recently. He hasn't woken up yet."

I swallow back tears and lift my chin. "I'm going to get you out. I'm going to fix all this." I run my hands over the cage's edge in search of the lock, but the bamboo runs smooth and unending under my fingertips.

"You won't find any locks," Marc says, "if that's what you're looking for."

"Have you seen Komo?"

He looks away. I grip the bars tighter to stop myself from going into complete panic mode. I can't think about what that look means.

"He's been using the life energy of your ancestors' souls to become more powerful," Marc says. "And he thinks that with you as his queen, no one can cross him."

"That's why he was able to come out at night?"

"I got the feeling that he wasn't telling me everything."

I stand up. "Move back," I say.

"What are you doing?"

"Getting you out." I bring my hand up and slice it down on the top bamboo pole of the cage, pulling all my energy into the motion. The bar splits, but not enough to break. I prepare for another thrust.

"Hide!" Marc whispers, his eyes focused on something behind me. "He's coming."

A tingling sound fills the air, and I know Haemosu is near. He's already sensed my presence, I'm sure of it, so hiding isn't an option. I swivel around, pulling out my bow and arrow. I take my mark.

"Well, well," Haemosu says, appearing from nowhere and strolling up to us casually, his red cloak billowing out behind him. "My princess has arrived. I have been expecting you."

Apparently he has, because he's all dressed up. His silk tunic shimmers in different shades of blue as the light reflects against him. The tunic, with wide sleeves that flare out at the wrist, flows down to his feet, the front and back cut apart; and I can see he's wearing black pants underneath. The white sash around his waist holds the tunic tight against him and accentuates the five golden dragons twisting to form a circle on his chest. On his head he wears a golden band with a mini crown resting on his topknot, a dragon-headed pin sliced through it.

"I am pleased to see you have realized your destiny is with me," Haemosu says. "My kingdom is more complete when you are here."

"You have two choices," I say, my string taunt and ready.

He raises his eyebrows and rubs his chin. "Choices? How intriguing."

"Let Marc and my family go and release the spirits of my ancestors, or I'll send this arrow through your heart."

"Dearest, *dearest* princess. You must know you cannot kill me. I am immortal. A spirit of the wind."

To demonstrate, he lifts up in the air, golden dust spiraling under him. His image seems to grow larger and larger until it fills my whole vision and all I can hear is his booming laugh. And then in a blink he's back to his normal smirking self, standing in front of me.

"And do not worry your little head about that bothersome Haechi. I have made sure he will be too busy to join us."

What has Haemosu done?

"Look carefully, Haemosu," Marc says, his fists clenched by his sides. "Her bow bears the symbol of the Blue Dragon. An arrow released from it will kill you."

"Who are you to know of such things?" he says, staring at Marc, eyes blazing like dragon-fire. "You are nothing to me. Besides, I have a great ally, one who has shown me how to increase my power. And with my princess at my side, I will be indestructible."

"I will never be *at your side*," I say. "Now give me your answer!"

"You want an answer? Experience my answer!"

Sparks burst from Haemosu's body, crackling in white and gold. His figure writhes and twists until he's morphed into a wingless dragon as tall as the palace walls, golden scaled with large, crimson eyes. His four golden claws scrape the brick path and rip it to shreds.

A blast of fire shoots from the dragon's mouth, and I know what to do.

I hold out my hand and *push* the fire around me.

I'm so shocked at what I had just done, I nearly drop my bow. I reposition it, notch in an arrow, and let it loose. Too late. The tip flicks off his scaly armor just as Marc's and Grandfather's cage catches fire. The flames feast hungrily on the bamboo.

"Marc! Haraboji!" I race to them.

Marc pulls Grandfather into the corner while I thrust the side of my hand at the bamboo until a chunk breaks off the top of the cage. My skin singes from the heat. Marc rips off his shirt and starts beating the flames with it. Finally the cage breaks. Marc grabs Grandfather under the arms and drags him off to the side.

"Keep him safe!" I yell to Marc.

Haemosu's dragon body shakes, and he whips his head around, looking for prey. He rears over Marc and Grandfather.

"No!" I scream. As my words echo through the courtyard, the trees bend and shiver as if responding to my voice.

The power of the land draws to me. Haemosu blinks. I notch an arrow into my bow and send it flying. It hits his face. With a screech, the dragon rears, eyes focused on me. I don't stop.

One arrow.

Then another, and another, fast like the wings of a hummingbird until my *goong dae* is empty. The dragon lifts up a four-clawed paw and swipes at me. I leap backward.

The dragon shakes once, and the arrows fall to the ground. A growl-like laugh erupts from the dragon's throat. His scales must be steel.

It appears you were wrong, my princess, Haemosu says in my mind.

I lower my bow, frowning. Am I wrong? Is the Blue Dragon bow only a myth?

CHAPTER 41

The dragon sucks in air and blows. Flames stream from his mouth. I tumble to the ground as the fire chases me. I can't control it. His power is too much for me. And after watching the bow fail I don't know where to turn next.

The rules of metamorphosis state that I must become stronger than the dragon to defeat him. But every time I'm morphed I've screwed it up somehow. Doubt tears through me, weakening my knees.

If I lose this time I lose everything. Komo, Marc, Grandfather, my ancestors, myself. And the curse will live on in the next generation of my family.

What is stronger than a dragon? *Nothing,* I think. Nothing can possibly be stronger than a dragon.

And then a new thought strikes me, and I stand up straighter, half frozen. I hold up the amulet by its chain and stare at the figure on it. It rotates slowly, its bronze glinting in the sun.

The samjoko.

Marc's words come back to me: *It is considered to be more powerful than the dragon or phoenix.*

I clutch the amulet in my hand and spread out my arms, lifting my head toward the sky. I think of Mom and her steady belief in God. Of Komo saying that disbelief is the root of the impossible. Of Marc's faith in me. I need to believe like they do. Can I?

Closing my eyes, I feel the power grow within me, stretching and pulling and twisting like fire rushing through me until it's larger than I could ever imagine. I open my eyes.

And blink.

I am a crow, as black as midnight. A crow with three feet and glittering diamond claws. I stretch out my wings; they're as wide as a small building.

A *samjoko*.

The impossibility of what I've just done drags at my mind and shakes my belief. My body trembles, and I feel the morph reverting back to my human self. *No.* I can't let myself change back. I will myself to hold on to this image.

Haemosu roars and charges at me in his dragon state. I screech back, my voice shaking the ground, and sail up in the air. The dragon skids in his tracks and follows me into the sky. More flames shoot from his mouth. I twist and turn, lithe and strong, until I'm behind him, safe from his fire.

He swipes his long scaly tail against my wing. I'm flung through the air and smash onto the tiled roof of the palace, its clay pieces splintering and shattering as they fall to the ground. Everything blurs. My stomach slides along the roof as I plummet toward the ground. The tiles scrape my skin, and I can feel myself bleeding.

I lie on the ground, writhing, unable to get up. Have I lost already? My vision darkens, and that tingling, morphing sensation ripples through me once again. I'm shape-shifting back into a human. I try to pull myself up, try to stop the transformation, but I can't focus.

You are hopeless against me, the dragon says.

Then another voice speaks. *Rise up, Jae Hwa! Rise!*

Those words snap my brain into focus. A rush of adrenaline surges through me. I can push through the pain. I will not let Haemosu win. I pump my wings and rocket up in the air, throwing myself into an aerial over his oncoming tail. He turns to fly at me.

It's exactly what I expected him to do. Remembering the fire-breathing monster I had faced before, I twist around and ram my beak at his eye. He screeches in agony, fire flaming from his mouth. His scream is so loud, the buildings shake.

My wing has caught fire. I refuse to stop. I jam my beak into his other eye.

Haemosu flails and then drops to the ground in a heap, thrashing across the dirt. I fling myself to the ground, too, rolling across it to put out the fire on my wing. Pain shoots through me with such intensity that I can only think of the burn. But the pain gradually subsides, and by the time I'm back on my three clawed feet, it's gone.

So this is what immortality is like, I think.

Then it hits me: if I'm healing this quickly, so must Haemosu.

His head rises; I dive at him and rip apart the scales covering his heart with my diamond talons.

Then I close my eyes and focus on my own form. My body contorts and alters. A chill sweeps over me, then a racking twist.

I'm my human self again. I stagger and fall to the ground, gagging on bile. My body shakes and my vision shifts, but I must complete the task I know now I'm destined for. I reach out and mentally command the dragon bow and an arrow to come to me. They fly into my hand. I grind my teeth together to stop my trembling. I notch in the arrow, draw the string, and aim directly where the scales have been ripped away.

At Haemosu's heart.

I let loose.

The arrow sails through the air and sinks into the dragon's soft skin. He cries out and crumples into a heap at my feet. In a funnel of wind, Haemosu whirls back to his human form. His body turns pukish green.

So the legend of the Blue Dragon is true.

"Kud! Help me!" Haemosu cries out, his voice echoing across the palace grounds. "You promised this time it would work. You promised."

I glance around, wondering why he's crying out to the Immortal of Darkness. But no one else is here, just Haemosu and me. Haemosu moans and looks at me with glazed eyes.

"How could you, Yuhwa?" he asks. "You were the one. We were destined to be together forever. It was to be our wedding day, my princess."

He stretches out his hand toward me. It shakes with the

effort. A light wind kicks up, and I look down to see I'm wearing a *hanbok*. The skirt is cherry red, with green and gold edging along the bottom. I reach up and touch a crown set where my hair is parted down the middle and pulled back into a bun. So this is Haemosu's last act. Determined even in his final moments to make me his bride.

"I am not Yuhwa, and I will never be your bride," I say, watching his body shrivel.

"So be it." His words come out slow and shaky, and full of resentment. "But your aunt and ancestors will always be mine."

"What did you say?" My heart begins to race because I know what he means. Komo and my ancestors are still trapped in that awful queen's palace. Perhaps forever.

"Mine." He grins painfully. "Always mine."

A gargling sound emits from his throat, and his hand drops. His eyes grow wide, no longer dark but filmy white. His body stills.

I grab his tunic and shake his body. "Don't you dare do this to me!" I yell. "Let them go. You have to let them go!"

But it's too late. Haemosu's skin fades to a pale white and crumbles into dust. A gust of wind sweeps past, catching up the dust, and carries it away. The dragon bracelet on my wrist breaks in half and falls to the ground. The skin underneath is chaffed and raw, but I'm free.

I sink to the ground, my red dress puffed up around me as I watch Haemosu's ashes drift away.

I can't believe that Haemosu has won.

Marc staggers toward me, supporting Grandfather, who is now conscious. Both their faces are ashen, and Grandfather's eyes are wet.

"I am so proud of you, Jae Hwa," Grandfather says. "You did what no other woman in our family history could do."

Marc sits next to me, takes my hand, and squeezes it hard. "You did it."

I stare at them. "Komo is in the queen's palace, isn't she?" When neither of them answers, I bury my head in my hands. The sobs pour out of me. It's like Mom's death all over again. I'm reliving it. The pain. The defeat. The emptiness.

"No." I shake my head and stand, clenching my fists. I strap my bow over my back and snatch up my arrows strewn across the ground. "This isn't how it's supposed to be. When Haemosu dies, so does his power. I'm sure of it."

Grandfather and Marc look away, as if they can't bear the truth either. I take off through the courtyard and down the path that leads to the queen's palace.

"Where are you going?" Marc calls after me.

"To the queen's palace," I say.

I'm going to free Komo.

CHAPTER 42

The queen's palace lies in ruins, just like the first time I entered Haemosu's world and saw its reality. Groans and cries fill the air.

My ancestors are still trapped inside. Haemosu was telling the truth. I was wrong. Again.

My knees buckle, and I sink to the grass. I'm pulled back to the day Mom left. She wanted her last hours to be in her own bed, holding Dad's and my hands. She got her wish. She died in peace. But I never found peace. I clutched her hand until it grew cold, promising myself I'd never allow that kind of pain to tear me apart again.

And here I am. Komo is in there, and I can't bear the thought of losing her, too. Komo had believed there was a way to release our ancestors. I have to believe she was right, because I won't just leave her. Because, unlike Mom's illness, this time I have the power to fight it.

I hear footsteps behind me, and I know Marc and

Grandfather have finally caught up with me. I stand and take Marc's hands. "I have to go inside and find Komo."

The Adam's apple on his throat moves, and his green eyes are set on mine. "You can't," he says. "You'll die."

"If I don't come out, go back home. Don't wait for me, okay?" I stand on my toes, brush my lips against his, tasting salt. I press the amulet into his hand. "In the throne room you'll find the imprint of this amulet on a stand. Press the amulet in it, and you'll get back home."

"I'm not leaving without you." As if to prove his point, Marc strides toward the gate, but he's thrown backward to the ground as if there's a giant force restraining him.

"You and I cannot enter," Grandfather says. "I have tried before."

I stare at Grandfather. "You have?"

He nods. "Sun. With Sun I tried." Then he pulls me into a hug. In that moment we understand each other perfectly. All this is so much more than just the two of us. It's crazy how different today is compared to our first meeting at the Silla Hotel. He pulls back, and even though there are tears in his eyes, I can see fire in them, too.

I face the palace, but Marc grabs my arm. "No." His voice sounds panicked. "Don't. There's got to be another way."

I think back to the Tiger of Shinshi's words. He said my weapons were meaningless here. That there's only one way for me truly to defeat Haemosu.

Sacrifice.

I shiver at that thought but push it away. I couldn't bear living the rest of my life leaving Komo behind.

"There isn't." My face is wet. "I have to save her. Save all of them."

The gate's presence tugs at me.

This time I don't resist.

CHAPTER 43

The air whooshes past my ears, and as I'm pulled into the queen's palace, all color is replaced with grays and blacks. The space through which I was pulled is now a massive wall. I touch its cold stone, so similar to a tomb.

I start to panic. This is exactly what Haemosu wanted me to do. What if Haechi and Palk were wrong about opening the tomb? What if this is just one more thing I've been wrong about?

"Komo!" I yell, my voice echoing against the ancient walls. Is she still here? Grandfather and Marc seem to think she is. I scan the toppled pillars and dead bushes for her. Where might she have gone?

The fountain is corroded and crumbled. The path has sporadic gaping holes in it, and when I peek into one, all I see is endless darkness. A weeping willow stretches its barren branches over the courtyard, as still as stone.

At the other end lie the round-pearl double doors that lead inside another building. It's the only part of the palace that still shines as if it's polished daily. Could this be the tomb?

"Yesssss," a familiar voice that's half growl, half hiss says. "Open the moon."

I spin to face the voice. It's the dokkaebi, stinking like a wild animal. His red chest heaves in and out, and his eyes blaze a fiery red that matches his spiked hair.

"Pierce its belly," he says. "Pierce its belly, pretty girl."

"How do I know I can trust you?"

"Wasting time!" He bangs his wooden club on a stone statue. It crumbles at his clawed feet.

Then as if he summoned them, a skeletal shadow creeps out from behind the stalks of the dead bamboo grove to my right. A hand gropes the edge of the fountain, the skin decayed with bones peeking through.

"Open, open, open!" he says. "Or they tear you apart."

I swallow hard, my heart thudding in my chest as I ready my bow against these creatures. A bony hand from behind me yanks back on my arm holding my bow. I spin around to stand face-to-face with an empty-eye-socketed face. I scream, kicking it back. Another is at my other side; it too claws at me, tearing at my dress. All the while the dokkaebi's laugh echoes through the courtyard.

They pull on my hair, grab my crown, fight for the bow. I kick, punch and yet they still swarm me, as if they're angry I'm alive. I focus on the door, the pearl one as round as the moon at the other end of the courtyard.

The dokkaebi believes it holds a treasure. What if the treasure is actually my ancestors' souls? Could I pierce it with an arrow?

I break out a roundhouse kick, sending the skeletons staggering back, and jump onto the edge of the fountain. I aim, draw back, and let my arrow fly. It cuts the still air and sinks into the center of the doors.

The doors swing open with a groan, a stale stench seeping out through them, revealing only darkness.

"Yessss!" the dokkaebi says.

The skeletons scuttle away, and I'm left alone with the dokkaebi breathing heavily next to me. A chill drenches my skin. This is the tomb. Not the gates, not the palace. This place of darkness.

A breeze swirls around my feet, scattering the dust and revealing a silver plate. I read the Chinese words:

ALL WHO ENTER WILL SURELY DIE.

Die? My Chinese is so poor, I could be totally wrong. I glance back at the wall, my heart aching for Marc. He would know.

"Hurry, hurry, pretty girl," the dokkaebi says. "Bring the treasure."

I step inside, where the air is still except for the padding of my bare feet against the marble floor and the pounding of my pulse against my temples. I hold my bow in place and creep in farther.

I squint into the deep darkness. "Komo," I say, my voice grating against the quiet. "Komo? Are you here?"

The doors slam shut behind me. I whirl around. "No!"

I stare blankly into complete darkness. I lower my bow. It's a trap. The dokkaebi tricked me. I've willingly entered my own tomb.

But Haechi said if I open the tomb, I could release the souls of our ancestors.

What if the immortals were wrong? My mouth dries up, and my arms ache from holding the bow. All I can think is that I've failed. All of this, only to fail!

I close my eyes and try to focus.

That's when I feel *them*, my ancestors, like a blanket covering me. It's as if I can hear them singing lullabies from another time.

The souls of my ancestors surround me. Reminding me that I stand here alive. The first of my line to escape marriage to that monster.

That's when I notice that my dress is glowing like purple embers from a fire. I strap my bow around my shoulder, reach into a tiny pocket inside my dress, and withdraw the amethyst that the Tiger of Shinshi gave me to guide my way. Its light glows in my hand, coloring my palm purple. A beam of light radiates from the gem, just like it had in the starry sky, and I realize I'm in some type of maze. The light leads me to the right, and I start following its path, weaving right and left and then up a series of marble steps.

I pause at the top to catch my breath. How can one series of stairs make me feel as if I just climbed a mountain?

The amethyst light beams out to the wall on my left. Shelves upon shelves have been built into them. Stacked on them in neat rows are jars of all sizes and designs. When I move closer, I see the jars are etched with names.

A chill drapes over me.

These are urns.

My fingers trace over the smooth pottery, and as I read each name written in Chinese, I remember them from Grandfather's scrolls and the walls of the pagoda. These are the names of all the girls Haemosu imprisoned here. These are my ancestors.

When I reach the end of the wall, my hand grazes over Sun's name. Though I've never met my other aunt, tears fill my eyes.

A glint on the floor reflects off the amethyst's light. A broken necklace. Even with the tarnish I can see it's a silver-linked chain with half a silver plate. The name LEE is written in Hangul. My heart jolts. This looks just like the necklace Dad carries around. Could it be the other half? I drop it into my pocket.

And then the last urn. Komo's name.

LEE EUN

I slip the amethyst back into my pocket and cup the urn with both hands, tears streaming down my cheeks. There isn't an opening; every side is smooth. I stare at the rows and rows of urns.

Too many.

There's no way I'm leaving Komo in this place. I have to take her with me, so I pull her jar off the shelf and nearly drop it. It feels as if it weighs a hundred pounds. I press it against my chest. Sun's urn screams at me to take it, too, but I can only manage one.

"I'm sorry," I tell Sun's jar.

It's then that I notice that the amethyst in my pocket is glowing brighter, until its light fills the entire hall. The room is empty except at the far end, where there's a pedestal holding a blue-tinted, egg-shaped object several times larger than a tennis ball.

No doors. No windows. Just stone walls.

But all I can think of is the dokkaebi's attempt at a deal. He had wanted some orb. Could this be it? And if he wanted me to give it to him, there must be a way out.

Or maybe this is one of the missing Orbs of Life that the Guardians of Shinshi are searching for. Hadn't Marc said that those orbs brought life or something?

I look down at the urn and back at the egg, wondering if it could bring Komo back.

Whatever it is, there's something about it that makes me wonder if the egg on top of the pedestal is the key to everything. As if its power is keeping my ancestors' souls here.

My whole body craves rest. I'm finding it difficult to think straight. Curling up on this stone floor feels pretty enticing right now.

"The orb," voices whisper.

Okay, so either my ancestors are trying to tell me something or I'm totally losing it.

I take a deep breath and slowly hobble to the pedestal. It's my only hope. My limbs ache and my knees pop. The urn in my arms is almost too heavy to carry. My breath comes out heavy and raspy, and by the time I reach the pedestal, I have to sit and set down the urn to catch my breath. I try to stand, but my back won't straighten.

"Take it," my ancestors' voices whisper.

I pull out the amethyst and set it next to the egg. It casts a glow on the pale-blue egg. I hesitate. Is this really such a good idea? What if this egg is something bad?

Then I notice in the glow how my bones press against my skin. How wrinkled my hands are. With shaking fingers I run my hands up my arm, terrified at how paper-thin my skin looks.

I feel older than Grandfather. I pull out Princess Yuhwa's hair-pin, allowing my hair to tumble down and fall over my face.

It's white.

My head whirls. I'm dying! My body will turn to dust, and my spirit will be captured within these halls, never to find peace.

I touch the egg. It pulsates between my palms, and a rush of energy flows through me as if I'm sucking in fresh air.

Odd.

I take my hands off it. The darkness of the tomb seeps back into my core, and I'm weak again.

Is this egg pouring life back into me?

Can it do the same for Komo?

I pick up Komo's urn and smash it over the egg. The urn shatters, and ashes pour over the egg. Like a sponge, the egg absorbs the dust. Wind rushes through the room, spiraling over me. The dust collects and gathers above the egg into the form of a human.

Komo.

Her body falls to my feet.

I pull Komo into my arms. Her body is warm against my skin, and when I touch her neck, I find a pulse. Her eyes remain closed, but she's alive!

Then a new fear hits me. How long will she last in this place where death is accelerated at an insane speed?

I manage to stand up, wondering if the egg has any life left in it. I pick it up, but it's now black and dull on every side. I'm about to set it back into place when I notice that under the groove is a lever with an antique oblong bronze lock fastened to it. Chinese characters are carved into the side. Could this be a way out?

But then I sag against the pedestal. It's locked. And I have no key.

So tired. So very tired.

I rest my cheek against the pedestal, letting the cold seep into my skin, barely able to stand.

In the pale light, I pick up Princess Yuhwa's pin and spin it through my fingers. Princess Yuhwa escaped with this same hairpin. I slide it into the lock's opening, my finger joints stiff, and wiggle it around. Nothing happens. And then—

Click.

The lock releases. I pull on the lever, and instantly two sections of the stone wall in front of me split in half and swing out. Light floods in, blinding me.

CHAPTER 44

The souls of my ancestors tickle my nose, my chin, my ears, like butterflies released from a cage, skimming past me with kisses and blessings.

"Tell your father to not worry. I am okay," one shadow whispers, and then they're all gone with the wind.

Sun.

I smile.

I've freed them.

I think of Mom. Soon they will be joining her.

Then I think of Michelle. She'd be proud of me if she was here. I think I finally understand what she meant about finding my purpose.

Half blind, I crawl out onto dead grass, dragging Komo's body with me. I'm back in Haemosu's world, and it feels like the most wonderful place ever. I laugh at the thought, but my laugh sounds more like a throaty cough.

"Jae Hwa! Jae Hwa!" It's Marc calling to me, and then his

face is hanging over mine. He pushes my white hair from my eyes. "Is that you?"

"Marc." I reach up and touch his face. "I did it, Marc. I found Komo."

"Jae. Oh, Jae." He touches my hair, my face. Then presses his lips to my forehead. "We heard the rumbling and ran over here. What happened to you?"

Grandfather leans in next to Marc. "The tomb. It must have accelerated her life."

I stare at them both, comparing the glow in their skin to my parched white hands. "You should go," I say. "Take Komo. It's too late for me."

"I am so proud of you, Jae Hwa," Grandfather says. "You saved Eun and broke the curse. You have brought our family such honor, I cannot possibly give up on you and lose you, too."

Marc moves to check on Komo, still motionless.

"Why won't she wake up?" I ask.

"It is not a good sign." Grandfather rubs his forehead.

Marc frowns and then holds up the black egg, scrutinizing it. It must have rolled out of the tomb with us.

"I used it." I'm breathless. "To bring Komo back."

Marc stares at me, his eyes wide. "It's one of the orbs."

Grandfather takes in a deep breath. "So he had it all along," he mutters. "That must have been his source of power to hold the girls' souls with. It has to be the Blue Dragon's orb. This heavenly artifact is supposed to have healing powers."

"This could be our way to save Jae." Marc stands and hands me the orb.

"All the orbs have different powers?" I ask, inspecting its surface.

"But of course," Grandfather says. "And this one will be an excellent bargaining chip."

"No." An image of the Blue Dragon slices through my mind. He's been my guardian angel through this entire journey. His artifact should never rest in enemy hands. I lick my dry lips. "We are *not* giving the orb to the dokkaebi."

"Grab Komo and follow me," Marc tells Grandfather, and then scoops me up into his arms and starts off down the path.

I lean against Marc's chest, too tired to argue. I must have passed out for some time, because when I open my eyes again I'm propped against a pile of hay in the stables.

Marc is moving about, sliding golden rods free from their locks and throwing open wooden doors. Out slither five dragons, tossing their heads as if experiencing freedom for the first time— the legendary dragons of the golden chariot, Oryonggeo.

If I had more energy, I'd have jumped up and bolted, seeing as those five dragons had hunted me down not so long ago. My arrows only temporarily injured these immortal beasts. And now I'm barely strong enough to lift my head.

Marc steps inside the chariot, but the closest dragon blows air from its nostrils. Marc holds his hands up in the air and backs away.

"Hey, Fighter Girl," Marc says. "Maybe you should give the orders."

"Palk." It's as if the orb is speaking to me and I know what must be done. "We need to return the orb to the Heavenly Chest, and Palk is the keeper. We should find him."

Grandfather nods in agreement. I study Marc for a moment, standing there so tall with his eyes on fire.

"Prepare the chariot," I command the dragons.

They cock their heads but surprisingly slither into their places, snapping their bodies into the harnesses.

"I'm impressed," Marc says. Then he picks me up again and carries me to the basket of the chariot.

"You're stronger than I thought, lugging me everywhere," I say as he sets me on the gold-plated bench next to Komo

He takes the reins. "Don't count your dragons yet." His brow furrows as he stares hard at the five dragons and says, "*Kaja!*"

They don't move. Marc glances over his shoulder. "Looks like you're the boss."

"*Kaja!*" I say, and the dragons leap to life.

We sweep out of the stable's double gate and glide toward the sky. I grab ahold of Grandfather to keep my balance. In moments, the pink-edged clouds slide between us like wisps of cotton candy.

"The legends say Oryonggeo can transport its rider anywhere with the speed of the wind," Marc says.

I lean back, savoring this moment and the rush of flying. We're finally leaving Haemosu's lands far below us. Soon the clouds fade and the air grows cooler, the sky darker. Stars sprinkle the skyline. We're entering the space between worlds.

The wingless dragons soar effortlessly through the air as if swimming through a pool of midnight. The gentle sway lulls me, and my eyelids begin to close. Then the chariot jerks to a halt in the middle of the starry sky.

"What is happening?" I ask, blinking.

Marc says, "It's *him.*"

CHAPTER 45

A figure hovers in midair before us, glowing. One glance and I know he's Palk, the god of light. He looks just like the picture in Mom's fairy-tale book, with a long beard and black hair that seems to have gold woven through it. He wears a traditional golden tunic and a crown with gems that radiate light. I duck my head because his glow is blinding.

"Daughter of Korea," Palk says in a booming voice. "What brings you to the Spirit World, riding in Haemosu's chariot?"

My bones rattle from the power of his words. I bow my head. "Haemosu kidnapped the souls of my ancestors. I killed him and then released their souls." Palk nods, but his face is impassive, and I wonder if he already knew all this. I add, "I believe we have something you may want."

"Indeed you do," Palk says, smiling.

The orb resting in my lap begins to change. The blackness fades, and it starts to glow a deep blue.

"Where did you find this, Daughter of Korea?" Palk says.

"In the tomb where Haemosu kept my ancestors' souls," I

say, and then rest my head against the seat, worn-out just from speaking. "Do you believe it really is one of the heavenly artifacts?"

"Indeed," Palk says. "It is one of the six Orbs of Life that sparked life into the Korean people. The Azure Dragon's artifact. But you know all this already, do you not?"

"So this is where Haemosu got his power," Grandfather says.

Palk rubs his beard. "I believe he used it to harness the power of the souls of your ancestors. But he would not have been able to do this alone. He must have been working with someone else. I will speak with the Others about this."

"Others?" I say.

"The other immortals," Grandfather whispers into my ear.

"This must go back to the Heavenly Chest, then, for safekeeping." I move to give him the orb, but my muscles shake from its weight, and I collapse on the golden bench.

"Here," Marc says, lifting the orb, "let me help."

Above us a star explodes, showering a cloud of crystal particles over us. They splatter across my weathered cheeks like aloe, and I savor the coolness as it coats my skin. It's so perfect and so magical that I almost wonder if I've already died and I'm on my way to the heavens.

A gold chest emerges from the cloud, suspended by a plum-colored cord, and descends along with the sparkling raindrops. It settles in the empty space at Palk's feet. Palk opens the chest to reveal two other orbs—one amber and the other a jade color—resting in silk, egg-shaped holders.

The orb floats out of Marc's hand and settles into the chest.

My heart dances just seeing it back with the others, as if somehow I've been a part of making things right.

"There are still three missing," Grandfather says.

"So there are," Palk says. With a flick of his wrist the lid closes and the cord lifts the chest into the darkness until another star sucks it inside. "The Others will continue to be vigilant in the quest to return all the artifacts." He nods toward Grandfather and Marc. "As will the Guardians of Shinshi."

I close my eyes. I'm tired of quests and monsters and darkness. All I can focus on is the need to rest. To sleep forever. To join my ancestors.

"A brave one, you are, Jae Hwa," Palk says. I start. He knows my name?

Palk smiles down at me. "I have been watching you, expecting you for many centuries. Haemosu's land needs a new ruler now to restore its beauty and grace. You seem worthy of the task."

My head reels. *He wants me to rule a land in the Spirit World.* Has he lost his mind and forgotten that I'm human? Or that I'm dying right before his eyes? "I don't belong there. Those lands hold nothing but nightmares for me."

"It is true," Palk says. "Haemosu's land has withered to waste. This will be your task. To right the wrong, just as you have done."

"You said you've been waiting for me, but all I've been waiting for is a normal life." I think about sleepovers and shopping with Michelle and Lily. Or finally going to the coffee shop or to the museum or on a real date with Marc. That is what I want.

"Besides, it's too late for that," I say, my breath coming out heavy. "I'm dying."

"Have we not been with you every step of the way, Jae Hwa? I empowered you as you fought the monster, helped you to draw in the strength of the land; and I sent Haechi to help you. You will never be the same, Jae Hwa. You and the Spirit World are forever connected. Intertwined."

As he speaks that word my whole body trembles. He's right. But I've been through so much suffering and pain, while he did nothing. "It wasn't easy," I say. "It was awful. How could you allow these horrible things to happen to my family? We've been suffering for centuries, and you've just let it happen! And look at Komo. She's here, but she hasn't even woken up yet. She may never wake up."

He glances at Komo. "She will return to us when she is ready." Then he focuses on me. "Would you wish for me always to interfere? Remove all suffering? Growth and strength come through suffering. Without suffering, humankind would be no better than children. Is this what you want?"

I press my lips together. He obviously knows me better than I thought, because I hate being told what to do.

"You are not a child anymore, are you?" Palk's face softens. "With choices come sorrows. Through your bravery, you defeated Haemosu and returned one of the orbs to Korea. Now you are dying."

I think back to all the times I had wanted to give up. I had felt so insignificant and small. I sure hadn't felt brave or special. I lay my head on the back of the chariot, feeling my eyelids droop.

"Jae!" Marc says, shaking my arms. "Stay with me. Don't you dare give up now!"

"I love you," I whisper.

"But bravery can only accomplish so much," Palk says, apparently oblivious to Marc's panic. "It was your sacrifice for the ones you loved that helped you succeed. That was the difference between you and the others before you. And because of this, I am giving you a gift."

Palk holds out his palm, and resting in it is what looks like a persimmon-colored tennis ball, the surface swirling with bands of cream. Palk blows against it, melting it into a liquid that streams out toward me and pours over my whole body, thick and honey scented. It seeps into my skin and rushes through my bloodstream. My heart quickens. My muscles stretch. My skin glows. My vision clears.

I'm alive.

CHAPTER 46

"Dad!" I yell, and race across the train station platform toward him, my dress billowing out around me.

Dad's head whips around at my voice, and he breaks into a sprint. We meet midway, hugging each other.

"I was so worried about you, Jae," he says, squeezing me tight. "If I had lost you, I'm not sure I could have kept going."

"I know," I say. "It's over now. It won't happen again."

Just having him here, safe, calms me, knowing I was able to keep Haemosu from hurting him. I hug him tighter.

"Hey, girl." Michelle steps out from behind him, biting her lips, forehead wrinkled. "You really need to answer your phone. You drove me insane with worry."

Then she wraps me in a hug, squeezing so tight I found it hard to breathe.

"Your dad told me about the police and the arrest and the terrorist attack," Michelle says. "I nearly died when I found out. I shouldn't have assumed."

"It's okay." I squeeze her hands, wishing I could tell her what really happened. "I should've explained it to you."

"But why are you wearing that dress?" Dad's brow furrows as he takes in my unusual attire.

"Yeah," Michelle laughs. "Didn't see that coming."

"It's my latest disguise," I say, grinning. It feels so good to smile. To see Dad and Michelle alive, safe.

Dad rubs his forehead. I want to tell him everything, but I know I can't. I wonder if there will ever be a day when he actually believes in the truth.

Grandfather and Marc join us, and Dad's eyes grow hard. When we arrived back in Korea early this morning, the first thing we did was carry Komo to the hospital in Kyongju. The diagnosis was vague. She's in a coma, but apparently nothing is wrong with her. Then we called Dad on our train ride back to Seoul to meet us at Seoul Station. I think Dad blames Grandfather for it. Like it's a replay of twenty-six years ago.

"And Eun?" Dad looks between Grandfather and me. "Any news?"

"The doctors do not have any answers yet." Grandfather's shoulders are hunched, and his face seems to have more wrinkles than I remember. "I am having her transferred to a hospital in Seoul when the doctors feel she's well enough to travel. She will return to us when she is ready."

Grandfather's repeating Palk's words, but there isn't any conviction in them. I want to reach out to him and give him the same motivational talk he gave me back on the beach, but the pain of our experience still burns fresh in my mind, as I'm sure it does in his.

Dad's eyes fall on Marc. "Thank you, young man, for what you've done. But I haven't changed my mind about Jae being with you."

"After everything?" I ask.

"Your parents called me, insane with worry," Dad says to Marc. "Did you know that? They had no idea what happened to you. They thought you were going to be gone for the night and be back the next day."

Marc's face turns about as red as my dress. "They know now." He holds up his phone. "I called them an hour ago."

All these words seem to slide right over Dad as he turns back to Grandfather. "I can't forgive you for what you've done. Getting these two kids involved in your schemes could have gotten them killed."

"You are right." Grandfather takes a deep breath. "I take full responsibility."

"Dad. Please," I say. "We're safe. And together. If it wasn't for Grandfather and Marc, I wouldn't be here." I pull out the other half of Sun's necklace. "Sun wanted you to have this."

Dad's eyes widen as I drop the necklace into his hand.

"*Eotteohke!* Where—where did you get this?"

"She wanted you to know that she's okay now," I say.

He withdraws the other half of the necklace from his pocket and matches the two broken pieces like a puzzle. Now I can read her full name in Hangul:

LEE SUN

Tears fill his eyes. He glances over at Grandfather, who nods once. "Sun has found peace," Grandfather says, "and Jae Hwa is safe."

Dad presses his lips together. I sense he wants to thank Grandfather, but maybe he's not ready yet. I can't blame him. After all, he's a fighter like me. Haemosu might be dead, but he's left his mark on all of us.

"I should go," Marc says. "My parents are waiting for me outside."

"Wait." I grab his elbow and look at Dad. "Can we have a moment? Please, Dad?"

Dad nods. "Say your good-byes." He and Grandfather and Michelle head over and wait by the taxi stand. I take Marc's hands in mine and press them against my heart.

"I'll never forget what you did for me." I bite back tears. What is up with me and crying lately? "You saved my life."

"Actually, I think it was you who started the whole saving-lives trend." His voice is teasing, but his eyes stare into mine. "Maybe we should start a new trend."

"Yeah," I say as he cups my face between his hands. "I'd like that."

Our lips meet, and for the first time I don't worry about Haemosu's jealousy or some monster's attack. It's just the two of us.

When we step back, I'm breathless. I could get lost in his kisses.

Behind him, I notice something odd about the bulletin on the wall. It seems to shimmer, and for a moment I think I see Haemosu's palace. Haechi stands at the gate, his fur blowing in the wind. He nods once.

Forget not, the wind whispers around me. *You are inter-twined with the Spirit World forever.*

"You okay?" Marc glances at where I'm staring.

I blink, and the wall is back to its normal self. Did that just happen? I bite my lip. I'd told Palk no, hadn't I? He'll find someone else to rule Haemosu's land; I'm sure of it. I just need to let my connection to the Spirit World slowly fade away.

"I'm fine." I force a smile. After all, if Marc didn't notice anything, I had to hope his sight had been cured. "You'll call me, right?"

"Absolutely. See you at school, Fighter Girl," Marc says. "That's if they let us back in."

Thinking about school makes my heart dance. I'm going to be normal again. Not some paranoid girl always looking over her shoulder.

Normal. A wonderful word.

I blow Marc a kiss and watch him saunter away, his hair all wild, hands in his pockets. I already miss him.

When I exit the station, I spot Michelle, Dad, and Grandfather at the curb. Seeing the three of them standing there safe and unharmed makes every agony I faced over the last two weeks worth it.

"I'm trying to convince your dad to un-ground you so we can finally do our movie date," Michelle says as I join them.

"I know I'm grounded for the next dynasty, Dad," I say. "But what if we do a movie date in our living room? I'm sure there's something we could rent online."

"You sure know how to get your way." Dad shakes his head, grinning. "How about we order in some *japchae*, too? You owe me a dinner date, remember?"

My skirts tangle around my legs, and I'm getting plenty of attention from pedestrians thanks to the wedding dress.

But I don't care. In this moment, the itchy, cumbersome dress doesn't bother me. I lift my face to the sky and let the sun caress my skin. I can taste the first hint of spring in the air.

The first taste of freedom. And home.

GLOSSARY

abeoji—father

ajumma—middle-aged woman

annyeong—Hello (informal)

annyeong haseyo—Hello (formal)

annyeong hashimnikka—Good morning

Blue Dragon—one of the four immortal guardians of Korea; guardian of the clouds

charyot—attention

chollima—winged horse

chumong—founder of the Koguryo kingdom and known for his archery skills

chuseok—Harvest Moon Festival

chunbee—get into the fighting stance

dobok—Tae Kwon Do uniform

dojang—training center for Tae Kwon Do

dokkaebi—gremlin, trickster

eotteohke—What can I do?

General Yu-Shin Kim—general of 7th century Korea who led the unification of Korea

ginseng—tuber plant credited with having medicinal properties

goong dae—quiver for arrows

Habaek—river god and father of Yuhwa

Haechi—legendary creature resembling a lion; a fire-eating dog; guardian against disaster and prejudice

Haemosu—demigod of the sun

hagwon—Korean night school

hana—one

hanbok—traditional Korean dress

hanji lantern—rice paper lantern

haraboji—grandfather

hotteok—brown sugar pancake

Hwarang warriors—an elite group of Silla male youth trained in the arts, culture, and combat

japchae—Korean dish made from sweet potatoes, noodles, and vegetables

kaja—go

kalbi—grilled beef or pork

kamsahamnida—Thank you

kim—edible seaweed

kimbap—Korean dish of steamed white rice and other ingredients rolled in sheets of dried seaweed and served in bite-sized slices

kimchi—spicy pickled cabbage; the national dish of Korea.

Koguryo kingdom—an ancient Korean kingdom located in the present-day northern and central parts of the Korean Peninsula

komo—aunt on the father's side

Kud—god of darkness

kumiho—fox-tailed female shape-shifter

Kyung ye—to bow

michutda—crazy

mwuh—What?

nae—yes

net—number four

ondol—underfloor heating system

oppa—father

Oryonggeo—Haemosu's chariot, drawn by five dragons

pagoda—temple or sacred building, typically a many-tiered tower

Palk—sun god and founder of the realm of light

poomsaes—forms; formal exercises in Tae Kwon Do

Princess Yuhwa—demigoddess of the willow trees

Samguk Yusa—collection of legends, folktales, and historical accounts relating to the Three Kingdoms of Korea

samjoko—three-legged crow; symbol of power and the sun

samulnori—music performed with four traditional Korean musical instruments: a small gong, a larger gong, an hourglass-shaped drum, and a barrel drum

Saranghae—I love you

Seijak—begin

set—number three

soju—Korean vodka distilled from rice or sweet potatoes

Tiger of Shinshi—protector of the Golden Thread that ties and binds the Korean people throughout time

tteok—Korean rice cake

tul—number two

waygookin—foreigner

won—the basic monetary unit of North Korea and South Korea

yo—Korean mattress that easily rolls up

ACKNOWLEDGMENTS

First and foremost, I am thankful to my Heavenly Father. Without you, I have no words.

I am indebted to the people of Korea for opening your hearts and letting me live in your land for nearly a decade. While there, I not only learned your culture, but came to love the Land of the Morning Calm.

I cannot forget all the students I have taught over the years, especially my students at Seoul Foreign School who are now spread over the four corners of the earth. In so many ways this is your story. To my *padawans* at Keene's Crossing Elementary: may the force be with you.

To my Tae Kwon Do instructor, Master Kim of Seoul, South Korea, for your expertise in Tae Kwon Do. I know it wasn't easy to train this dancer to throw a mean punch.

Thank you, Dad, for reading Tolkien and C. S. Lewis at my bedside each night as a child. You taught me the love and power of the written word. To Mom, for listening as I shared my hardships of this writing journey yet never doubting my abilities.

Thanks, David, for brainstorming crazy ideas with me and seeing them through the eye of a movie expert.

Every writer needs a muse to sneak through castles and get lost in Paris with. I couldn't have sent this book out into the world without mine, Julianne Vangelakos. When's our next inspirational trip?

A special shout-out to Lee Ellen Strawn for her expertise in Korean history and Jean Wood for answering my bizarre texts about Korean words. Any mistakes are completely mine. And to Larissa Hardesty and Tara Gallina for writerly lunches, last-minute reads, and get-togethers. A necessity for a writer's survival.

I owe a huge debt of gratitude to my black belt of an agent, Jeff Ourvan, who outwitted those secret agents in Vladivostok and secured a home for *Gilded* after "sailing solo across the Atlantic, swimming the English Channel, being taken captive by terrorists, and barely escaping with his life." Jeff, you rock.

Thanks to my editor, Miriam Juskowicz, for falling in love with Jae's story from the very beginning and becoming its champion. From your first e-mail, I knew you were the perfect editor for me, and after chatting over Starbucks coffee and sharing our love for books, I knew *Gilded* was in good hands.

I cannot forget to thank Timoney Korbar for all of her marketing efforts, to Katrina Damkoehler for developing the cover for my little book, and Deborah Bass for all her endeavors in public relations to make *Gilded* a success. To Andrea Curley, my genius of a copyeditor, and Natalie Mortensen, my proofreader, for spotting all those details. I'm also so honored to have Chanwoo Park, head of the English translation program for Literature Translation Institute of Korea, read for Korean inconsistencies.

I firmly believe that behind every good writer are brilliant critique partners. I'm a lucky, lucky girl to have worked with these Brilliant Ones. A million hugs to Beth Revis, for reading multiple drafts and tirelessly believing in *Gilded* when I wanted to give up. *Gilded* wouldn't be on the shelves if it wasn't for you. Someday we're going to watch Scooby Doo, eat ice cream, and laugh our heads off. To Casey McCormick for those weekly check-ins and complete honesty through each draft. I am eternally thankful to Ellen Oh for your insights (especially in all things Korean) and unwavering support. To the MiGs, who have a multitude of superpowers and are always an e-mail away: Debbie Ridpath Ohi, Andrea Mack, Kate Fall, Carmella VanVleet, and Susan Laidlaw.

How can I not thank my two Jedi knights, Caleb and Luke, for listening to me read scenes and guarding my plot secrets? I love you to the farthest star and back.

Finally, to the love of my life, Doug Farley. For believing and loving me no matter what. You make all my dreams come true.

Photo © Liga Photography

CHRISTINA FARLEY was born and raised in upstate New York. As a child, she loved to explore, which later inspired her to jump on a plane and travel the world. She taught at international schools in Asia for ten years, eight of which were in the mysterious and beautiful city of Seoul, Korea that became the setting of *Gilded*. Currently she lives in Clermont, Florida, with her husband and two sons—that is until the travel itch whisks her off to a new unknown. *Gilded* is her first novel.